Praise f

"There are no bad pe
and engrossing debu
intersections—an in
grant Russians, a mo

father unable to intervene, and friends too keen on growing up fast. Alyssa, Gelbwasser's heart-full narrator, stands at the center of it all—leaning toward adulthood, summoning her courage, determined to survive a world that cannot promise happy endings. *Inconvenient* is riveting and whole."

—Beth Kephart, author of *Undercover*

"Heartfelt, honest, and brave—Margie Gelbwasser isn't afraid to uncover painful truths."

—Sarah Darer Littman, author of *Purge*

INCONVENIENT

For my amazing little boy.
You were my good luck charm from day one.
I hope one day I can make you as proud as you make me.

INCONVENIENT

MARGIE GELBWASSER

Woodbury, Minnesota

First Edition
First Printing, 2010

Cover design by Adrienne Zimiga
Cover images: girl © Design Pics/PunchStock;
    rain © Enviroman/Alamy;
    butterfly © iStockphoto.com/ Janis Litavnieks

Flux, an imprint of Llewellyn Worldwide Ltd.

This is a work of fiction. Names, characters, places, and incidents are either the product of the author's imagination or are used fictitiously, and any resemblance to actual persons, living or dead, business establishments, events, or locales is entirely coincidental. Cover model used for illustrative purposes only and may not endorse or represent the book's subject.

Library of Congress Cataloging-in-Publication Data
Gelbwasser, Margie.
  Inconvenient / Margie Gelbwasser.—1st ed.
    p. cm.
  Summary: While fifteen-year-old Russian-Jewish immigrant Alyssa tries desperately to cope with her mother's increasingly out-of-control alcoholism by covering for her and pretending things are normal, her best friend Lana attempts to fit in with the popular crowd at their high school.
  ISBN 978-0-7387-2148-4
  [1. Alcoholism—Fiction. 2. Russian Americans—Fiction. 3. Jews—United States—Fiction. 4. Immigrants—Fiction. 5. Popularity—Fiction. 6. High schools—Fiction. 7. Schools—Fiction.] I. Title.
PZ7.G276In 2010
[Fic]—dc22
                                                                    2010025578

Flux
Llewellyn Worldwide Ltd.
2143 Wooddale Drive
Woodbury, MN 55125-2989
www.fluxnow.com

Printed in the United States of America

ONE

The cement beside the town pool is hot, the kind of hot where you can see steam rising off of it. The air is sticky, and the beads of sweat dripping off my arms and legs are forming a small puddle on my recliner.

"This is disgusting," says my best friend Lana, who is lying beside me on her own recliner. "How can I look good under these conditions?"

I pat her arm in mock sympathy and divert my attention to beyond the pool's fence. Five-year-old girls are running barefoot on the grass, their bikinis a little too big and a little too old for their bodies, trying to catch butterflies in their nets. When I met Lana five years ago, we were ten and only chased butterflies in our backyards because we were too old to be seen doing this in public. She always had a thing for butterflies—for all things pretty.

I glance at Lana out of the corner of my eye and see that she has taken a break from her momentary self-pity to observe the girls too. She winces when a preteen girl joins their game. Soon the preteen pounces too hard on a net, crushing a butterfly. She shrugs a half-hearted apology to the little ones and runs back to the pool. She jumps in, centimeters away from Lana and me, splashing water over the sides, mixing chlorine droplets with the suntan lotion on our legs, wetting Lana's new bikini that has a tiny butterfly clasp in the space between her breasts.

"*Suka*," Lana yells in the preteen's direction.

Suka means "bitch" in Russian, and Lana is right to assume the girl will understand her. Glenfair is New Jersey's *Malenkaya Moscva* or Little Moscow. It has two Russian stores, a Russian pharmacy, and a section devoted to Russian books and movies in the library. The fact that Lana and I are Russian should not be a big deal, but it is. Maybe because we're the only ones in our sophomore class. Maybe because everyone has to be picked on for something, and this is easy.

I think the preteen girl maybe really did feel sorry about the butterfly, that she just got caught up in the excitement of summer when she jumped into the pool, splashing us.

"Aw, she doesn't look older than eleven. I bet she didn't mean it," I say, at about the same time that the preteen smirks at us.

"*Kurva*," she yells at Lana. Whore.

"You think too well of people, Alyssa," Lana says, rolling over on her stomach to tan her back. "This town sucks."

And it sometimes does. Glenfair is a small town—with good pacing, you can walk from one end to the other in just under an hour. Here, everyone knows everything about everyone and CVS is the hot hangout spot. But at least here, unlike in Brooklyn where I lived until the fifth grade, Russians don't throw bricks through one another's windows.

"That's because Glenfair has the right kind of Russians," my parents always say. The Jewish kind. I can't blame them for feeling this way. They grew up in Russia, where my dad spent his childhood beating up everyone who called him a kike. The day their Russian neighbors found out about my parents' emigration to the United States, they cheered. One of them spat at my mom's feet and said, "That's one less dirty Jew to clean up after."

Lana's parents' experiences were similar, but they chose to not burden Lana with the details, only telling her that Glenfair "feels right." Anyway, Lana can't complain too much because she gets to spend every summer in the Catskills with her grandparents.

Lana looks at a small army of preteens doing handstands in the pool and groans. "The Catskills were so much better," she says.

"So I've heard." It always takes Lana two months after she gets back to stop bragging about it. Each year she returns with new sexual knowledge. This year it's how to give a good hand job.

"Can you put more lotion on my back?" She lazily hands me the bottle. I bet she's thinking about what a waste her new skills are if there's no one to practice them on.

"I think the lifeguard wishes he could do it." We came to the town pool two hours ago, and the lifeguard's eyes have not left Lana. But who can fault him? Summer has been good to her. While she was away, her blonde hair grew out of its choppy layers and now falls halfway down her back. She also grew five inches, giving her long legs and a small waist to go with her size-D breasts.

Lana yawns. "How do you know he doesn't want *you*?"

I laugh.

"No, stop. You have a body a lot of girls would kill for."

"Exactly. *Girls*. Small chest, thin legs." I frown.

"*Strong* legs. Plus, being able to eat what you want and not gain an ounce."

"I'd give it all up if I could gain some weight in the right places."

Lana rolls over again and stretches her arms above her head. She catches the lifeguard looking at her and makes a production of putting more sunscreen on her legs.

"I thought you weren't interested," I say, slapping sunscreen on my arms and legs in a less seductive manner. I'm more concerned with preventing sunburn.

"Doesn't hurt to practice," Lana says, pursing her lips, her mind focusing on what she feels is newsworthy. "Speaking of, isn't that Keith Michaels, your cross-country *friend*?"

I shield the sun from my eyes and look where Lana is pointing. Keith and three guys, all dressed in swimming shorts and flip-flops, towels slung over their arms, enter the pool area. They spread the towels over empty recliners and take out a deck of cards. He doesn't see me yet, doesn't see Lana still giggling at the word "friend" because she knows I want more than that with him. I steal glances at him for ten minutes, making sure he doesn't catch me looking at him. I watch how his hair, the color of caramel, falls across his right eyebrow, how you can see all his teeth—including the slight overlap of his two front teeth—when he laughs, how he pretends to fall off the recliner when a friend fake-punches him, how his mouth forms an "o" and his brow wrinkles when he's dealt a bad hand. His fingers, long and thin, are playing with his baseball cap while he tries to think of which card to put down next. I'm focusing on the area between his middle and ring finger on his right hand, where I know he has a small birthmark, when I feel Lana's eyes boring into my skin.

"What?"

"Why don't you walk over to them and say 'hey' or something? You know Keith." She sits up on her elbows.

"Because it's Keith. And he's not alone. I'm not walking over to a bunch of guys I don't know."

"Aw, come on. It'll be good for you." She squeezes my arm in what she thinks is a supportive way. I would think so too if I didn't know her true intentions.

"Nope. I'm good, thanks." I smile despite the annoyed look on her face.

"I dare you," she says, resorting to the game we have been playing since we were kids.

I shake my head no, aware that passing up on this dare will come back to haunt me later.

Lana frowns, but then perks up at some new idea apparently brewing in her head. "How about you ask them the time or something?"

"You mean ignoring the fact that there's a huge clock above the snack bar?"

"Why do you have to be so difficult, Alyssa?"

I sigh. It's the same conversation we've been having since last year, when Lana realized my cross-country running skills earned me nods in the hallway from the jocks and preps. She believes this is our pass into their hierarchy and doesn't understand why I'm not rushing to capitalize on it. Don't get me wrong, if a fairy sprinkled some magic "cool" dust on me, I wouldn't tell her to take it back, but until that happens, I'm not going to kiss butt for the same results.

Lana takes my silence as a willingness to listen to her tired speech and goes on. "You're cute, and in spite of what you think, guys look at you. All you have to do is step it up a little and say 'hey.' Why can't you do that?" She takes off her sunglasses so her eyes look directly into mine, as if they possess some kind of hypnotizing power.

"Why can't *they* say 'hey' to *me*?" I shoot back, looking away.

But we both know that's not how it works. The kings and queens don't make the effort; the peons do.

As though on cue, Jake Harrison, the much-sought-after king of our class, walks into the pool area. He looks in our direction, trying to be nonchalant, but I see his eyes pass over Lana's body. Lana blushes and looks away, enjoying every minute. She's had a crush on him since we were in middle school. For the most part, he barely knew she existed. But last year he chose her to be on his volleyball team in gym class, and ever since then, Lana's been convinced she has a chance. The truth is, Jake's choices were down to her and this girl who always smells like meat. Tough choice. But with Lana's new body, it may be her year after all.

Jake puts on his sunglasses, no doubt to give Lana a better once-over, and grabs a recliner on the opposite end of the pool. Two minutes later he's joined by Ryan Fishman, his personal court jester, and Trish Carney, Little Miss Popular herself, the powerful queen of our class. This summer—just by their presence—they've made the town pool the cool place to be, for our grade anyway. When Lana heard this on her return from the Catskills, she dumped her suitcase on her bedroom floor, grabbed a bikini, and barely waited until I put on my bathing suit before sprinting here.

"Yo, my man. Wassup?" Ryan's palm slaps Jake's, and he makes sure his voice is heard all around the pool.

Keith and his friends smirk. As seniors, they don't have to show off anymore to get attention.

Trish rolls her eyes at Ryan, glances at the lifeguard on duty, and slowly strips off her shorts and tank top to reveal a cleavage-enhancing bikini. The lifeguard's eyes now dart from Trish to Lana. Too bad he isn't cross-eyed. Then he could watch both of them at the same time.

Jake rubs lotion on his body, spending extra time on his muscular arms, puts a baseball cap over his dark, gelled hair, and lies down on his recliner. Ryan does the same, only the show isn't as good. It never is. Sports, looks, girls—Ryan always comes in behind Jake. And worse than that, you can actually *see* him trying.

Lana slips on her sunglasses so she can observe the

group she so wants to infiltrate. Her new sexy looks would, anywhere else, normally make her a shoo-in, but Glenfair has its own rules. Her transformation into a butterfly may have come too late for her to be popular. We're fifteen, and in Glenfair this means our roles are practically set in stone. It's kind of like if you're cute through seventh grade and everyone wants to be your friend, but then puberty does something ugly, you're still good to go because you've already carved out your place in the social circle. But if you start off unimpressive, you can change your looks and your name, but, like Prince, your original title will be the one everyone will always remember.

Too bad, because Lana has wanted to be Trish Carney since we were twelve. It was one of those dreams she'd ask her eight ball about or waste a birthday candle wish on. Our first year of junior high, Lana bought a bracelet that had charms that jingled as she walked—just like Trish wore. Last year, Lana wanted to have her hair cut in a layered style that framed her face. Just like Trish. If all the other girls weren't trying to copy her too, Trish might have wondered if Lana was stalking her.

Ryan whispers something in Trish's ear and she gives him a playful slap, letting loose her high-pitched giggle at the same time.

"You're out of control," she screeches, tossing her hair to the side.

Lana leans back in her recliner, moves her sunglasses to the top of her head, and again makes eye contact with the lifeguard. She then reaches into her bag, grabs a water bottle, and, her eyes not leaving the lifeguard's gaze, slowly takes a sip. He grins and winks. Lana finally looks away, cheeks flushed, but the butterfly on her bikini seems to flutter, wings beating wildly, winking back.

———————

"You think your mom is here already?" I ask Lana as I lead the way onto our deck, the chlorine pool smell still lingering in my nostrils.

"But of course. She wouldn't want to miss a minute of bonding with her fave and only daughter."

Two years ago, when our mothers watched a *20/20* episode about parents losing touch with their kids, they made a vow to devote the last Saturday in August to discussing the first completed week of the new school year and "reconnecting" with their growing teens. Lana finds these days corny, but I like them.

"Oh, they're in rare form today," Lana says, hearing our moms' screeching laughter. "My condolences."

"I'll survive." I roll my eyes, but I mentally thank Lana's mom Clara. My mom has been working too hard lately, and I'm glad someone can make her forget about that for a bit.

"Alyssa," says Clara Raikin when she sees Lana and me, "tell your mother peer pressure got old years ago." My mother is holding a pitcher and trying to refill Clara's glass.

"That's right, Mom. No means no," I say.

"Weekends are meant for unwinding," says my mother, managing to pour what looks like iced tea into Clara's glass.

"Yeah, lighten up, Mom. All the cool kids are doing it," says Lana.

She plops down on one of our cushioned chairs and grabs her mom's glass, taking a sip. Clara scowls, but doesn't make too much of an effort to take the glass back.

"Better she try it at home than on the streets, right?" Clara tucks a stray, perfectly curled tendril behind her ear.

Lana gags. "Damn, how much alcohol is in this?" She goes into the kitchen and returns with bottles of soda for the two of us.

"That's what I'm saying. I'm a two-drink girl, and one of those already has me feeling loopy. Any more and you'll be scraping me off the deck," Clara says.

I watch my mother refill her own glass and take a generous swallow. "Want to try?" she says to me.

She must be tipsy, because my parents don't let me drink except for a glass of champagne on New Year's or grape-flavored Manischewitz wine on Passover.

"No thanks. Lana's endorsement wasn't that glowing."

My mother shrugs. "Just as well. You girls can't hold your liquor like us old ladies can."

Lana smirks. "Oh, is doing the cancan defined as 'holding it' these days, Mrs. Bondar?"

"That's not fair, Lana," says Clara. "Julia and I were the most coordinated dancers at the Greenbergs' anniversary party." She laughs and pours herself another refill, past protests forgotten.

Lana and I give each other knowing looks. This is the Russian world. Drinking is what people do. Birthday, funeral, dinner, stress release—drinking accompanies all these things. The dinners start with a toast—a shot of vodka or gin "to our kids"—and then we eat. We have at least four more toasts—"to this great dinner," "to the parents," "to America," "to Alyssa's next A"—as the night goes on. It's actually when someone *doesn't* drink that everyone worries. Last Memorial Day, my dad was on antibiotics and couldn't drink.

"What happened?" my Uncle Vlad asked. "Has living in America all these years made you soft? Where's that European blood?"

So my dad ended up doing three shots of vodka and throwing up in the car on the way home—twice.

"What's new this year, girls?" my mother asks after refilling everyone's glasses again.

Lana's eyes light up. As much as she acts like she doesn't like these pow-wows, once the conversation gets started she shines as the center of attention. "Well, you know how some kids in our grade are stupid about us being Russian and all?"

Clara mistakenly assumes Lana wants a reply. "Julia and I were talking about that today. That's something we both will just never understand. I mean you two girls are no different—"

"*Anyway*," Lana interrupts, "I thought we might get a small break from the teasing, but it doesn't look like it. The first movie we're watching in our elective class is that James Bond flick, *From Russia with Love*."

Lana pouts and continues with her tirade, and I tune out by figuring square roots of numbers in my head. *Square root of 100 is 10.* I've heard all this before—yesterday, in fact. I hate that it's the way things are too, but this is Glenfair. Even though we went to Hebrew school with many of the kids at school—Jake and company included—we're just pegged as Russian. After we studied the Cold War in history class last year, some guys at school decided to go retro and call us "commies" for a few weeks.

When I told my dad, he laughed like it was the craziest thing he'd ever heard. "Why would they make fun of you? You're the same as them. Just explain that to them."

Sure, try telling a fourteen-year-old boy with the attention span of a gnat how you're the same as him. Once I actually did, and I got through a whole four-second speech before the dillhole said, "Hey, Brad, she says she's just like me. Do I look like a chick? Did I grow tits overnight?"

Eventually, the commie stuff got old and the guys decided it would be more fun to call us "hos." I thought this was because of *The Sopranos* or Russian Internet mail-order brides, but it could just be good ol' exploitation of women.

Lana has now moved on to a story about Trish and her group and is waving her arms animatedly to act out a scene. *Square root of 81 is 9*. My mother looks at me sympathetically and pulls me in for a hug. This is her way of telling me that we will talk later. She knows there is little conversation to be had once Lana gets going. *Square root of 64 is 8*. Lana finishes her story, and I laugh along with everyone else, like I was listening.

The pitcher is empty and Clara glances at her watch. "It's almost dinnertime. We should go."

"Would you mind going out the back way? I don't

want my nosy neighbors gossiping about those drunk Russians," says my mom with a laugh.

"I know how that is," says Clara, fumbling for her car keys. Lana doesn't ask if she's okay to drive. The answer would be yes. To say anything else would imply you've lost that European blood.

———

Once they're gone, I make a pitcher of lemonade and sit next to my mom on our deck swing.

"Lana sure looks different. How is she handling it?" she asks.

"You know Lana. Milking it for all it's worth. I wish I had her confidence."

"You look great too, you know."

"Not like Lana." I look down at my chest.

"Blame your genes. We Bondar women are not known for our boobage." She points at her own barely there breasts hidden beneath her flowery shirt, and laughs.

I laugh too and pour myself a glass of lemonade, setting it down on the table. Mom lifts my glass and slides a coaster beneath it. "I just Pledged that."

She must have sobered up if she's noticing rings on the old patio furniture again. She has this thing about cleanliness. You might say it's her obsession. When I was a kid I hated having friends over because Mom wouldn't just make them take off their shoes, she'd find reasons to pop into my room and dust-bust around us. And while most kids got to sleep in on weekend mornings, I'd be awakened by the vacuum cleaner, handed a rag, and told, "A clean house is a happy house." If someone were to ask me, I'd tell them my room seemed quite content with a few dust bunnies, my only pets. But no one asked me. In Russian homes, kids don't have much of a say on family routine.

I stretch out my legs, close my eyes, and take a sip of my lemonade. My mom does the same, and I can almost hear the relaxation music playing behind her lids.

"Anyone cute at the pool today?" Mom asks lazily, opening her eyes.

I haven't mentioned Keith to her yet, but I think she can tell I like someone. "Those boys at the pool are too young for you, Mom."

She pretends to swat at my legs, and I scoot away from her, laughing.

"I won't pry. You'll tell me when you're ready." She brushes the bangs from my eyes, and I put my head on her shoulder and inhale her lilac perfume, happy I don't have to think about anything but the fading sun in the sky.

"Tell me something about your week," I say. "Any new writing assignments?"

I feel my mother's body tense, and I'm immediately sorry I asked. Work has been hard on her lately, with the magazine she edited going under and a magazine she wrote for replacing her with a cheaper writer. She's been pitching articles to other magazines like crazy, and still has one steady gig she seems to like. But her expression lets me know it's draining her as well.

"You know that article I wrote back in April? The one about the best unique work-outs?" She runs her fingers through her hair.

I nod. I remember how excited she was about the assignment, interviewing everyone from personal trainers to wilderness experts and even scoring us a free rafting trip as part of the deal.

"Well, they finally decided to run it. Asked me to contact more experts and add details, which is fine—I'm used to that. But this new editor, Marian, Miss Super Efficient, wants me to get it done in the next three days. Like I'm not working on anything else."

I pat her arm. "You'll get it done. You always do."

She sighs. "I'll have to."

"You *will*." I kiss her cheek.

"You're my best supporter," she says, and I feel her breathing slow, her body relax.

We sit on the swing and watch the sunset, the colors of the sky highlighting the color in our glasses. Mom strokes my hair, absently splitting it into three sections and braiding it, just like she used to do when I was little.

I listen to our breaths, now even in rhythm.

"My best supporter," she says again.

I nuzzle my head deeper into her shoulder, glad to share her genes—boobs and all. She kisses the top of my hair, releasing an alcohol-stained breath that engulfs her lilac scent and the picture-perfect moment.

TWO

"*Bistreye, bistreye,*" says my father from the living room a week later. As he tells my mother to hurry up, I picture him pacing back and forth over the hard, wooden floor, glancing at his watch, comparing the time to the posted numbers on the evening news. If he had his way, he and my mom would arrive early to every gathering they were invited to. But my mother stalls as long as she can, knowing that by Russian standards, by Jewish standards, the time on the invitation is merely a suggestion. The real time everyone is expected to arrive is thirty minutes later. My father, the engineer, thinks this is ridiculous. He believes everything should have a proper order and refuses to accept this unwritten rule.

I hear the television volume get louder downstairs, a sign that Dad is losing patience. My mother is not rattled. She looks in the vanity mirror, turning her head to the left then the right, trying to determine if the bright lights around the mirror or her blush is making her cheeks look extra pink. I sit in the swivel chair beside her, and she smiles at me.

"You and Lana have a wild night planned?" She carefully applies her red lipstick, making sure it doesn't venture above her lip line. It never does.

"Mall and a movie, but you never know with Lana."

Mom finishes with the lipstick and passes it to me. She ignores my father's now-audible pacing, his new soles squeaking on the hardwood, and watches me paint my lips. I do the top lip first, moving the lipstick from one end, over the curvy middle, to the other end. I follow the same pattern on the bottom.

"*Babochkini krilya*," says my mother. "Butterfly wings."

This is how she taught me to do it years ago when I was five. Back then, we didn't have a big room with a fancy mirror, lights, and chairs. Back then, we didn't even have a counter that held lots of makeup. Our makeup room was the bathroom and our supplies were Walmart brand cosmetics—one red lipstick, small blue eye shadow, light rose blush, and black mascara stick. Once, when I watched my mother getting ready for an interview, she had surprised me with a sparkly, cherry-flavored lipstick she'd bought at the corner market for a dollar.

"Watch how I do it," she'd said, and then began to narrate the movements. "Smoothly, make it flow, gently over the curves. Look at your lips and think of a butterfly, the curve of its wings. That's how you put it on, like *babochkini krilya*."

Then she was ready to leave, and kissed me good-bye.

Her soft red lips left an imprint on my cheek. Like a butterfly's kiss.

"You've mastered the technique," she says now, placing her cheek on mine. I like our reflection in the mirror. Same wide-toothed smile with a slight overbite, same high cheekbones, same brown hair—that my father calls chestnut—skimming our shoulders. Same green eyes inside wide lids that give us a surprised, innocent look.

"Julia—*sevodnya*, today," my father calls.

Mom rolls her eyes and I can see laughter in them, and I smile at this gift we have of reading one another through eyes alone.

"Have fun," I say.

"Don't do anything Lana would do." She laughs and gives me a kiss good-bye, once again leaving an imprint of a butterfly's wings on my cheek.

———

"We made it through the second week of school! Now it's time to celebrate," Lana says when I get to her house.

"Won't your parents be home?" Lana's celebrations are rarely of the PG variety.

"Nope. They have another Russian party tonight, and you know how those go. They won't get in until three in the morning, and odds are they won't be sober." Lana laughs and wrinkles her nose. "Seeing your parents puke from drinking is right up there with catching them boffing. You know it happens, but it's not something you need to witness."

She starts rifling through my duffel bag as I lie down on her canopy bed. When we were in elementary school we called it her princess bed, and I loved sleeping over because it meant I could be royalty for the night. These days, Lana grumbles about having a "little girl bed," but sometimes when I'm over and she thinks I'm not looking, I see her finger the sparkly fringe of her bedcover while she stares dreamily at the star-covered canopy.

I close my eyes and imagine Keith beside me, waking me up with light kisses, using only the stars above us as a guide. His lips on mine feel so right and I ignore Lana calling my name, her voice getting progressively shriller.

She's standing over me now, and her garlicky breath ends my little daydream. "I said, you call this lingerie?" She dangles what I consider to be my cutest sleepwear—a pink cotton tank top and lace-trimmed pink boy shorts— in front of my eyes.

"If I didn't, I wouldn't have brought it." One of Lana's plans for tonight was to watch a DVD of the Victoria's Secret Fashion Show while modeling our own night clothes. She even designated an area of her living room for the catwalk and set up little night lights around it to act as spotlights. Of course, if she was a little less serious about this activity, it might be more fun.

"Fine. Did you at least bring decent heels?"

I close my eyes again, not to bring back my daydream

but to block out Lana's soon-to-come disapproval of my pumps.

"Alyssa," she whines, "these shoes are fine for synagogue but not for the show." She sighs and shakes her head. "I'll get you my mom's silver heels. You'll look hot in those."

I open my eyes and smile at the determination in her face. "Thanks."

"No worries. I know it's not your fault you have sensible parents," she says, already on her way to her mother's closet.

Unlike Lana's parents, who let her buy whatever she wants with her babysitting money, my parents do not understand the need for a dress or heels you'll only wear once.

"All right, girlie. We only have one hour to get ourselves ready for our debut." Lana pulls me into the bathroom and tells me to sit on the toilet while she disappears under a cloud of hair spray and hair clips. She splits my hair into three sections, wrapping each piece in ribbon and pulling on my bangs to spike them. "No, not yet," she says when I try to get a glimpse in the mirror. Her hand through my hair feels rough, not comforting like my mom's, but I oblige because a few minutes of discomfort are worth whatever Lana is creating.

"Use red lipstick," I say as she lays out makeup on a towel on the floor.

"Oooh, risqué. I like that." She instructs me to suck in my cheeks "like the anorexics do" and highlights my cheekbones and collarbone with glittery blush. Then she puts on the lipstick. Fast, quick strokes, not like my mother's butterfly wings. I smack my lips together as Lana instructs, and already feel myself being pulled into this new world of stiletto heels and sexy lingerie. A world where Lana and I will be models for imaginary passersby, where I can leave my sometimes clumsy, shy self.

"Done," Lana says, licking her lips. "Wait until we've both changed before looking in the mirror, 'K?" She runs to the bathroom in her parents' bedroom to get ready.

I pull on my tank and shorts, then slip into the heels and practice my walk on Lana's carpet. *I'm hot,* I think. *No, no photos please. Well, maybe just one. Trish? Yes, I've heard of her. No, can't say we're close. She's not part of the fashion circle. Keith? Yes, we're together, might as well admit it. Oh, hon, do get my good side, won't you?*

"Ready?" Lana calls from the hallway, strutting back into the bedroom. She's wearing a white lace teddy and thigh-high black vinyl boots, another find from her mother's shoe gallery. There's a white gauzy train attached to the teddy and her hair is loose and straight. She looks like she's floated in on a cloud. Magical.

Lana puts her hand over my eyes and leads me to the mirror in the living room. When she removes her hand, I touch my hair to make sure the reflection in the mirror is really me. The ends of the ribboned sections stand out around my head like a satellite, and I'm reminded of the exotic models in Lana's magazines. The ones whose made-up faces sparkle even in the darkness.

Lana puts in the DVD, then sets up her video camera and starts taking shots of me, of herself, of the two of us tossing our hair, smiling toward the lights on the walkway, blowing kisses to photographers.

"We own this runway," Lana shouts. Her voice echoes across the living room.

"You know it," I shout back, striking a pose with my hand on my hip.

The camera continues to record. We flash our toothy smiles as video after video is shot. Soon we're one big blur—Lana and me and the television models floating on their Victoria's Secret wings through a haze of smoke and glitter.

———

"I have one more thing for us to do," Lana says, a little past midnight.

We're lying on her canopy bed—on sheets that smell of ocean breezes—in T-shirts and sweatpants, our hair post-shower wet. Lana rolls over, opens a drawer in her night-stand, and takes out a small gold box. A spicy, cinnamon-like smell is released as Lana opens the box to reveal brown sticks. "Clove cigarettes. Everyone smoked them in the Catskills."

I take one in my fingers and sniff it. "At least they don't have that disgusting Marlboro Light smell." Last summer, that's what "everyone" was smoking in the Catskills, and Lana insisted I try a few with her. The coughing fit, and the stale smell that stayed on my fingers even after three soap scrubbings, took away any desire for repetition.

Outside on the deck, we prop our feet up on lawn chairs and Lana lights the cloves. She closes her eyes and inhales deeply from her cigarette. Then she exhales, and I can almost see all her thoughts in the smoke that now surrounds us. I look at the stars above and at the clove in my hands and take one quick puff, just to taste it. I don't cough this time, but the taste is too strong. I breathe out smoke too, and watch my small cloud connect with Lana's and trail high into the air. Lana, eyes still closed, takes another puff, but I just watch the small fire at the tip of mine. Little sparks fall on the ground and quickly turn to ash.

"I have something else." Lana pulls a bottle of champagne from behind the chairs.

I didn't even see her bring it down. "You're quite the magician."

"Oh, I'm full of surprises. Didn't you know that already?" She giggles, uncorks the bottle, takes a swig, and then hands it over to me.

I thought Lana only drank on holidays, like me, but maybe this was also part of her summer experience. My cigarette is almost done, the little fire barely burning, and I take a gulp of champagne. It's what models do, isn't it? I like how the bubbles fizz inside my mouth. Lana motions for the bottle and takes another huge swallow, and then another.

"Thirsty much?"

"You don't like it?" She lights another cigarette and this time makes smoke rings. "I love how light your head feels after drinking it. How you feel like you can fly."

"How we may have to have buckets near our beds?" I smile.

"Oh, Alyssa. Just relax."

She passes the bottle back to me and I take a few more sips, letting my head feel light and loose. I lean back in the lawn chair and close my eyes too, letting myself be carried away under the canopy of stars.

———

"Hey, girl." Lana runs up to me at my locker Monday morning and bumps my hip with hers. Then, seeing Ryan and Jake walk past our lockers, she adds loudly, "Were you like totally hung-over this weekend?"

Ryan and Jake exchange appreciative looks but keep walking, and I roll my eyes. "A little," I say, adding, once the guys are out of earshot, "Leave it to me to get tipsy from two glasses of champagne." I know Lana wants Jake and Ryan to have the illusion of us as party girls, out on the town, getting blitzed and stumbling around, not staring at the sky and drunkenly dreaming.

"Did you see their faces? They were mesmerized." Lana stretches out the word "mesmerized" so it hangs in the air like a piece of chewing taffy.

"Mesmerized by *you*, my dear." Which was the intent. Lana still looks like a model, wearing a top that skims her shoulders and low-rider jeans that show the tip of her thong when she bends over the water fountain to get a drink.

"By *us*," Lana insists. "But more importantly, you did have fun this weekend, right?"

I indulge her fantasy that having fun really is the most important thing to me. "I'd have to reevaluate our friendship if a weekend with you turned out boring."

"Well, that's why I'm here—to make sure your straight-laced ass doesn't follow you everywhere. Speaking of…" She takes the flyer announcing a cross-country retreat off the hallway bulletin board and shoves it in my face. "Why didn't you tell me about this? We need to get you prepped."

"It's just something Coach is trying this year to help us bond. A weekend of teamwork and crap. No biggie." I put the flyer back on the board.

"Of course it's a biggie. It's a whole weekend of Keith time. In the park, too, which you know screams picnics and romance."

I laugh. Dunkerhook Park *is* pretty and can be romantic, but not when you're running the trails, sweat pouring down your face and seeping through your clothes.

Lana reads my mind. "You may be in sweats and sneakers, but there's no reason you can't shake your groove thang." She moves her hips in a circle.

"It's not even all weekend, just the daytimes. And, anyway, it's not for a few weeks yet." I should know better than to think that this will be a roadblock for Lana.

"Then good thing I saw the flyer now, isn't it? Plenty of time to get you ready." Lana bounces on her heels, excited about teaching me the ins and outs of the love world.

"That's what you think." I get excited too, in spite of my desire to keep my cross-country life happy and drama-free.

Lana puts her arm around me and we bump hips again. "Don't worry. I got your back." And right now, I really believe she does.

THREE

My family has an evening routine. Dad comes home from his engineering job in Manhattan at 6:15, sometimes 6:30 depending on which bus he catches, then he kisses the top of my hair, pecks my mother on the cheek, and heads to my parents' bedroom to change out of his suit and prepare clothes for the next day. In the fifteen minutes it takes him to put his clean pants in a press machine—a necessity, I'm told, if you want them perfectly creased—and to steam a dress shirt, Mom has his beer ready and the first course on the table, a homemade Russian dish like deviled eggs with sardines. My job is to have a topic ready to discuss about my school day because I have limited time. The news starts at seven, and once it's on, we eat in silence, hanging on every word the anchor says. Correction: Dad hangs, and I think of ways to make the dinner go by faster—like guessing the smallest number of pieces I can cut chicken into while still being able to spear a bite-sized portion onto my fork, or determining the ratio of peas to carrots on my plate.

"They tell you the truth here," Dad says whenever I appear less than enthused to hear about robbery victims and the death toll in Iraq. "Not like in Russia, where the government decided what we were allowed to hear. You don't appreciate this enough."

To keep the peace and avoid a lecture of her own, Mom pretends to hang on every word too, and uses the commercial time to ask my father about points she "missed."

But today, she's not really trying. The first course is a basket of buttered black Latvian bread, and chicken and rice from one of the Russian stores. The beer is barely chilled and I have to put it in the freezer.

"Just had no time," she says when she sees me looking at her. "Too much work today." Her voice is drained and her eyes are tired. When I got home from school, she was lying on the couch, her eyes closed, crumpled-up papers around her.

"It happens." I give her a small smile and finish setting the table just as my father comes downstairs. It's 6:47. Thirteen minutes to catch up on our lives.

I sneak the beer out of the freezer and hand it to my dad. It's not as cold as he's used to, but not as bad as before. He looks at the chicken and rice and takes a sip of his beer, then frowns and sets it beside his plate. Mom leaves the room and returns with an orange-colored cocktail. She tenses and takes a large swallow of the drink, eyes closed.

"How was your day?" I ask my dad. I put a chicken wing and a heaping spoonful of rice on my plate.

"Busy as always. We just started another project—the plumbing structures of a new museum." He takes another sip of beer, just as my mother spills her drink on the table while reaching for the bread. Orange seeps onto my father's rice and my mother stares at his plate, perhaps to avoid looking into his unhappy face.

"I got it." I jump up for paper towels and wipe the table clean, but can't help the soggy rice. I see both my parents relax a bit, although my father's face still has a trace of annoyance as he moves the rice to the far corner of his plate.

Seven minutes until the TV takes over.

"So, this new project sounds exciting," I say once I'm back in my seat.

"Yes. It should be. But ... " Dad takes a sideways glance at Mom. "It will be more hours, later nights, weekends."

She doesn't say anything, just gets up and leaves the room. She returns with a beer.

"Let's make sure this one doesn't make it onto my plate, okay, Julia?" he says.

My mother forces a laugh and clinks her beer to his.

Five minutes of conversation left.

"Anything new at school, Alyssa?" Dad takes a bite of his chicken. "Not bad."

"We're doing proofs in math, and Coach Griffin says my running time is better than any sophomore girl he's seen in the last three years."

Dad nods. "Well, you're a Bondar." As if this explains everything.

I take a bite of my wing, which tastes dry. "Tell us about your day, Mom." *You have three minutes.*

"Oh, there's not that much to tell. Just finishing three different articles, figuring out comments on others. Marian is still criticizing everything I turn in." She takes another sip of beer.

"Well, you can handle it. Show her what you're made of," Dad says. All he needs is a whistle and he'd be transformed into my cross-country coach.

Thirty seconds. My mother turns on the television set. A blonde news anchor appears. "I'm Maggie Storm, and this is the nightly news," she says.

"Shhh. It's starting." My father leans over the table.

Mom closes her eyes again and finishes her beer.

I accidentally scrape my fork across my plate and Dad raises the volume on the television. I fill my mouth with rice to stifle any urge to speak. Mom gets another beer, and I marvel at Dad's concern over the trouble in other people's lives.

FOUR

There is a ringing in my sleep. In my ears. In my room. It gets louder, and I don't know why someone would trouble my dreams with this heinous sound. My eyes still closed, I reach for the phone, knowing it can only be Lana, and also knowing that if she's calling me at night, it's important. Or her version of important.

"You sick, girl?" she asks before I have a chance to say hello.

"No. You?" Only an ill person would invade my sleep time.

"Alyssa," Lana says slowly, finally realizing her intrusion and giving me time to wake up. "Why aren't you in school?"

My eyes are open now, and I see sunlight peeking in from behind my drawn shades. I also see my alarm clock, set to 6:30 … p.m.

"Crap, I overslept. I'll see you soon." I jump out of

bed, put the phone on speaker, and start getting ready, taking the phone with me.

"You're welcome, hon. I'm hiding in a bathroom stall with my cell, risking detention—" Lana, always the drama queen.

"I'm sorry. Thank you," I say through teeth brushing.

"Anything for you. You know, my mom would have poured cold water over me an hour ago. Where's yours?"

"Good question. I'll go find out. Later, and thanks again." I grab a ponytail holder and run to my mom's office, my sneakers half-on and my hair half-done, but almost fully awake.

I expect to see Mom hunched over her computer, heavily engrossed in an assignment for Marian or another editor, time having escaped from her. But she's not there, and there isn't even a crumpled-up piece of paper full of ideas on the floor begging to be rescued. The computer is off, and the only sound I hear is loud, deep breathing coming from my parents' bedroom next door.

I stand beside my parents' bed and breathe in the smell of stale liquor. Another party last night. That's become the new thing—celebrations on Sundays, since restaurants charge less than on Friday or Saturday nights. But this is the first time she's been too out of it to take me to school. Even if I start walking now, I'll barely make it to third period on time. A detention for being late is also inevitable, with the school's new zero tolerance on tardiness. My mother stirs, moans, and opens her eyes.

"Alyssa," she says in a whisper, "can you ask Lana's

mother to drive you to school today? I'm not feeling that good."

"I would, except that school started an hour ago. What happened to being able to hold your liquor?" I go into the bathroom and return with a wet washcloth to place on Mom's head.

"I know, I'm sorry. Your dad warned me they were making the drinks too strong." She closes her eyes and puts pressure on the washcloth in an effort to erase the pounding in her head.

It's difficult to feel sympathy for her, with a looming detention and then the extra laps I'll have to run for being late to cross-country. "I'll see you after practice. You'll be out of bed by then to pick me up, right?"

My mother nods and waves good-bye before rolling over on her side, too hung-over to lecture me on my tone.

———————

I get to school just before English and find Lana in the classroom. She's got her compact out and is touching up her mascara and bronzer—a regular ritual.

"Thank God you're finally here. What happened?" she asks, adding a copper-colored lipstick over her pink gloss. The pink gloss is the only makeup her dad lets her wear.

"Mom was working and lost track of time." I roll my eyes, and am not sure why I'm lying. Of all people, Lana would understand.

"That sucks." Her attention is already shifting away

from me toward the door, where Jake and Ryan are kicking a hackey-sack while a bored Trish looks on.

The bell rings, and the trio slowly make their way to their seats. Our teacher, Ms. Hoffman, is too giddy about the day's lecture on symbolism to worry about them. She begins by showing comics on the overheard—a "fun" way to cover an old topic—and asking why the writers used certain words and colors.

Then, her cheeks flushing with excitement, she brings the questions back to the literary world. *Why are all the tyrants in black? Where did white symbolizing purity originate? Why doesn't the little man really stand up to his ruler?* She's acting like she invented this, like we haven't heard this same spiel every year. She wants to know why we're not taking notes. Lana rolls her eyes and scribbles something in her notebook. She moves it to the edge of her desk and motions for me to scoot over as soon as Ms. Hoffman's back is turned.

This class blows. Check out Ms. H's outfit, Lana wrote in pink ink. She also dotted each "i" with a heart. Like Trish does.

I stifle a laugh. Ms. H has got to be pushing sixty, but she wears clubby clothes—V-necks that show off her sagging breasts, skirts that stop mid-thigh, and four inch heels. She's got a good body for an almost-sixty-year-old, and I bet she looked good when she started teaching here more than thirty years ago, but no high schooler is impressed. Especially not when she leans on our desks, her chest inches from our faces.

I write back, *Classic. Are you getting hot?*

Lana laughs and doesn't even bother toning it down. When she notices Trish, Ryan, and Jake looking in our direction, she laughs louder.

"Are you okay, Miss Raikin?" Ms. Hoffman asks in a clipped voice.

Lana gasps for air. "Yes, I'm sorry. My foot fell asleep." She smiles sweetly and I see Trish smirk. Lana's getting points by the minute.

"Well, I suggest you calm yourself down or you'll be waking it up in detention. Understood?"

Lana nods and stares at the board like she's fascinated by what water in a novel *really* means.

Out of the corner of my eye, I see Trish crumple up a piece of paper, stuff it into a pen cap, and drop it on the floor beside Ryan's feet. Since texting is banned in school, this is the cool way to pass notes. People like Trish and Ryan want everyone to know what they're doing. They want you to wish you could be like them and pass notes via pen cap. They want you to wish it but not actually do it. If you do it, you're a loser and a poser. Lana, calm now from her "hysterics," is playing with her pen cap, and I know she's wishing she could be them.

———

Lana is waiting for me when I get out of detention. She frowns when she sees I'm already in my cross-country gear. "What's with the change of clothes?"

"Uh, practice?" I heave my duffel bag and backpack over my shoulder and speed walk toward the field.

"But you're already late, and it's misting out. It's going to rain. What about your hair? How can you look cute with it matted to your head?" She's running out of breath trying to keep up with me.

I laugh, but her concern is sweet. "It's even ground. Everyone will be having a bad hair day." I don't bother to mention that everyone will also be focused on running. Lana would not get that.

She perks up. "Yes, that's true. And, anyhow, if it gets wet enough you guys can mud wrestle. Wink, wink."

Only Lana, I think, as I head to the practice field. But now, with Keith only centimeters away from me as we stretch our calves side-by-side, I think about my hair, about my clothes weighing me down, about my shirt clinging to me, accentuating how small my chest is. I bend further into the stretch, keeping my arms around me, trying to hide.

Keith bends down to stretch too, but I feel him watching me. "You cold?" he asks when I hug myself tighter. I look at him expectantly, thinking he's going to … what? Take off his shirt and give it to me as an extra layer? Wrap his arms around me? "You'll warm up once we get going," he says instead. There are raindrops on his lips, and I think of those cheesy movies where the couples share their first kiss in the rain, their arms around each other, their clothes meshing together, their wet fingers intertwined, kissing and kissing as it downpours.

I lick my lips, tasting the rain, and leave my tongue

out to catch the drops like I used to do as a kid, forgetting where I am for a second until I see Keith smiling at me. Then I'm just embarrassed.

He opens his mouth to say something, but Coach Griffin blows one sharp trill with his whistle, signaling it's time for partner stretches. When Coach first did this last year, Keith and I were standing right next to each other, so it was logical to be partners. After that, we just gravitated toward each other, saying we were too lazy to look for someone new. I don't know if that's how he really felt, but it wasn't true for me. I didn't want anyone else. Keith was mellow, funny, cute. The first time his fingers brushed mine I got goose bumps, and they've never gone away.

We shift positions so we're facing each other, toes touching, and pull on each other's hands to stretch our calves further. I see Keith wince and say, "Sorry."

"No, don't take it easy on me. I'll never keep up with you if I'm tense." We both know he'd have a hard time keeping up with me anyway, since he's a sprinter and only does cross-country to stay in shape until spring track season.

The rain comes down harder. I imagine Lana saying something about Keith making me wet, and I laugh.

"What's so funny? It's my hair, isn't it?" Keith says with mock sincerity, his hand flying up to his head. Normally it's gelled during practice, out of his face, but today it's plastered across his forehead. He looks cute anyway. He always does.

"Yes, that's it. You really look hideous." I'm not usually good with the banter, but maybe rain is my good-luck charm.

"Wiseass," he says appreciatively. Coach blows his whistle, meaning it's time to run.

It's getting close to pouring now, but unless there's lightning, practice is on. Some runners grumble and lag back, playing with their laces, pushing their hair out of their face, hoping for lightning, but I don't. And Keith doesn't. The rain pushes us forward, makes our legs push harder, and I don't even care anymore that I'll have to run extra laps. We set out for the streets and I hope for puddles.

We run past the CVS, past the pool, past the Russian stores we get dinner from, past Lana's street where kids are squealing under umbrellas. Cars zoom past us and I know the people inside are feeling sorry for us, wondering how our school can make us run in this weather. We run a mile, two, and I don't feel pain. I've pushed ahead of Keith, of the other runners, and feel the rain bouncing off my red mesh shorts. I picture all the other runners in their red mesh shorts, rain flying off them, rain hitting the cars in torrents, all the people under their protective hoods, umbrellas, and car roofs. I feel my feet flying through the puddles, my legs gaining strength with each leap, the events of this morning pounded away with every stride, and I feel sorry for everyone who's dry.

FIVE

The room is dark, except for the few rays of sun trapped in the blinds, and the television is muted static. Mr. Pinto is standing by the blinds, waiting for the moment everyone is seated and he can turn on yet another movie and call it teaching. Our Movies As Life elective is very popular. All we do is watch flicks and then debate each other on their cinematic and societal value. At least, that's how the class blurb describes it. Really, it's where we can pass notes without being seen and catch up on extra sleep while Mr. Pinto counts down the days to retirement. School legend is that last year's class couple got to third base during *The Way We Were.*

Mr. Pinto draws the shades and hits *play* on the VCR (our school is too cheap to kick in for DVD players) before plopping his feet on his desk. On cue, the sound of pens scribbling and pen caps flying across floor tile fills the air. Mr. Pinto moves his head toward the noise and warns,

"People ..." in a monotone. He doesn't really care, but this is still his job. For another 145 days, anyway.

The James Bond movie on the screen shows a Russian girl displaying marvelous agility by throwing her legs over her head to get out of an attacker's grasp. Lana pokes me. I'm sure she's rolling her eyes. A pen cap lands on our desk. She looks behind us, realizing it came from Jake or Ryan, and thinking they did not calculate the trajectory correctly, that the cap was meant for someone else. But then one of them kicks her chair twice, and even in the darkness I can see the nervous energy dripping from her body. She pulls out the note with shaking hands and squints to read it. I squint too, and when I'm done I'm ready to fight back.

DO ALL RUSSIAN GIRLS LIKE TO SPREAD 'EM? says neat, printed boy writing.

"That's disgusting," I whisper to Lana, but she's already writing back. She rubs her thumb over her fingernails and then shows me what she's written. *That's something you'll never find out about—from any girl.*

I laugh, and Mr. Pinto stirs in his chair but says nothing. Maybe I woke him. Lana leans back and drops the cap on the desk behind us.

A few seconds later, Jake lets out a low whistle and whispers, "Damn, man. She told you."

The five-minute warning bell rings, and Mr. Pinto jumps. He motions for someone near the door to turn on the lights so he can find the stop/eject button.

"Class, for tomorrow, I'd like you to come up with three ways women are stereotyped in this movie," says Mr. Pinto.

Ryan's hand shoots up. "What do you mean stereo-typed? You mean they're not that *friendly* in real life?" The class cracks up.

"Idiot," I mouth to Lana.

She shrugs and plays with her thumbnail again. I open my mouth to say something, to tell him off, and panic rushes into Lana's features. She squeezes my knee, and it's then that I realize she's not nervous about Ryan. She's nervous about me. She thinks I'll make a scene, end the vibe she's created with her note. That note wasn't an invitation to a fight, it was Lana flirting. How did I miss it?

Pinto frowns at Ryan and talks over the ringing of the bell. "Mr. Fishman, I suggest you rephrase your question when we resume this discussion tomorrow."

He turns his back to the class, and Ryan does a jerking-off motion with his hand.

As we pack up our things, I hear Ryan say to Jake, "Those Russian girls are tight, man. How can I get me some of that Russian lovin'?"

"Wouldn't you like to know?" Lana says, and it's like her lip-gloss sparkles extra, just for him—for this boy she doesn't even want but who's her gateway to the one she does.

"Sounds like she's offering to teach me," says Ryan. He's talking to Jake, but his eyes don't leave Lana's body.

"Sounds like," says Jake, running a hand through his gelled hair. It sounds like a drawl, if Jersey boys could drawl.

Lana takes strawberry-flavored gloss from her purse and rubs it across her lips, and Jake leans back in his chair, his muscled arms behind his head, like he's scoping out the pool scene once again. Nothing new here. He knows Lana's really flirting with him, not with Ryan. Does Ryan know?

Lana leans down and pretends to tighten the laces of her sneakers. Her scooped-neck shirt pulls away from her body, and I see Ryan and Jake glance at her cleavage.

"I don't think you could handle the lessons," Lana says when she straightens up. "They're pretty complicated."

I stand behind her and watch. Who is this? The only time Lana ever talked to guys like Ryan and Jake was when she bumped into them and said "sorry." Now she's not only talking to them but mocking them. And they're into it.

"Oooh. Look at her hatin', bro," says Ryan, and even Jake cringes at his lame attempt to sound ghetto.

Lana laughs and starts walking to the door. "Just tellin' it like it is, yo." Her voice wobbles. I know she's losing confidence.

We rush out of class as the bell rings again. In the hallway, Jake smiles and says to me, "You better keep your friend in line, Alyssa. She might get herself in trouble." I wonder when I became visible. This is the most he's said to me since I've known him, but he's not really talking to me. He's talking to Lana.

"That was hot," Lana says after Jake walks away.

"Yeah, awesome," I mumble.

I feel like we just finished filming a scene of some dumb Lifetime movie. The tag line would say, *How far will Lana go to fit in?* as some violin music played in the background.

We stop at our lockers and get our lunches. Lana opens her bag and frowns. "My mom packed me caviar," she says.

I packed my own lunch, since my mother was too busy sleeping off another hangover. "I have caviar too."

I smile, remembering how canned caviar and pumpernickel bread brought Lana and me together years ago. It was under our lunchroom's fluorescent lights, and I was hiding my Russian sandwich behind my lunchbox when Lana sat down next to me. She took out her own caviar-covered bread, pushed my lunchbox to the side, and smiled as Trish—not yet the popular queen she is now—walked up to us. "Eww. Is that caviar?" Trish said, a chicken nugget dangling from her greasy fingers. "My mom says those are fish eggs."

Lana took a large bite of her sandwich, squirting orange caviar juice on the table. "Yummy!" she said, laughing as Trish wrinkled her nose and stalked off.

Now she asks, "You don't want to eat that shit today, do you?"

"Why not?" I know she really means, "You don't want to eat that Russian shit here—in front of everyone. Especially Jake."

"I'm just not in the mood, 'K?" she says really slowly, like we're speaking a different language—not just from everyone else, but from each other.

Then she sticks out her tongue and crosses her eyes, and for a second I see the girl with the caviar juice around her mouth, the orange beads on her lips glistening under the fake lighting like sunshine.

"Fine, dorky girl." I cross my eyes back.

She tosses her lunch bag and mine in the trash, and I say nothing.

SIX

"Haven't you heard, darling?" says my mother. "The four p.m. cocktail is so the thing right now." She bats her eyelashes, sits up straight, and takes a sip of her drink, pinky out, playing the socialite.

"Fancy, but is 'the thing' magical too?" I nod at the blank computer screen and the wastebasket overflowing with notebook paper.

"All my writer friends swear by it. They say it's what gets those writing juices flowing again." She closes her eyes and takes another sip of her screwdriver, hoping that ideas will fill her head.

"Just write anything," I say. "Even if it sucks. It will get you one step closer to something good."

My mother smiles and opens her eyes. "When did you get so smart?"

"It's what you used to tell me whenever I had an English paper due." A piece of paper totters at the top of the trash and falls out. I unfold it and smooth it out.

Mom shakes her head. "That's old. I already handed in a version of that, but it obviously isn't what Marian is looking for." She hands me a manila envelope, and I look at the women's health article inside. There are pages of carefully researched work, interviews with experts, quotes, charts, all covered with Marian's oozing green pen. *Needs more flare* and *Make it sexy* are written in all caps.

"Sexy? You're writing about dental habits."

Mom shrugs. "The article wasn't even my idea. She assigned it to me, and now she wants a completely different angle, maybe a different topic. Who knows?" She finishes her drink, sets the empty glass on a coaster, and mixes another.

"Maybe I can get you coffee instead?" I offer, thinking of her hangover of Monday. "I just have math homework, which is easy. I can help you brainstorm." I put the envelope aside and grab her notebook and a pen.

"Don't you remember? Recent events aside, this old lady can hold her liquor." She takes another sip.

"Oh, I know, I just wanted to help," I lie, and start jotting notes based on what Marian wrote.

Mom puts her hand firmly on mine, stopping its movement. "I'm fine, Alyssa." Her face looks stern, then it softens. "But you know how you can help me, *dochenka*? I bought pickled cabbage, beef kabobs, and *borscht* at the Russian store. If you can get everything on the table and heated by the time your dad gets home, that would be great."

"Sure, not a problem." I put her notebook and pen back on her desk and move the manila envelope and its offensive green marks away from her view.

"And, Alyssa?" she says as I'm almost out of the room. "Put all the food in our own Tupperware and throw out the containers from the store. No need for your dad to see I didn't slave all day. Let's just keep it between us girls."

She's smiling, but her eyes look sad, tired. She taps her foot on the floor, waiting for my answer.

My dad has been working more lately, taking on extra projects to make up for my mom's lost ones. Greeting us with grunts and blaring news on the television, shushing us more in between commercials. I decide to keep the peace. "No problem," I say again, and my mom reaches for the manila folder. She scans the contents and then replaces the papers. Again she closes her eyes and picks up her glass. When she puts the drink back down, there is an imprint of her lipstick on the glass's rim, a broken butterfly wing.

SEVEN

"Your mom is so cool," Lana says, breaking off a piece of cinnamon bun, a special treat just for us that we discovered when we got home from school. It's my mother's secret way of apologizing for the lie she made me tell my father.

I snort and point to the newspaper spread out over my bedroom carpet. Mom is out meeting with sources for a new article, but if she were home, she'd be able to sense food out of its rightful place in the kitchen and she'd come up here dust-busting away. The newspaper is my compromise.

"Everybody has their quirks." Lana licks her fingers. "At least she cooks. Contrary to the Russian way, my mom has decided to liberate herself from household duties. I'm all for women's rights, but my dad's cooking tastes like ass."

Other than the mean omelets my dad likes to make on Sunday mornings—something left over from his time in the Russian army—he makes no other cooking effort. My mother never complains.

"Mmm. So good." Lana licks her fingers again.

She closes her eyes and sucks hard on one finger, finishing by seductively licking the tip with the end of her tongue. I throw a pillow at her when she opens her eyes.

"Any step closer to actually using these skills you're trying to perfect?" I ask.

"Give me time, Al. Give me time." She winks at me and starts sucking on another finger.

I groan. "Why do you want him, Lana? It's not like he's even nice to you." I give her a wet wipe for her hands and remove the newspaper.

"You have to read between the lines, Al. You saw how he talked to us in Movies As Life. There's obvious potential."

Lana opens *Cosmopolitan*, or The Love Bible as she calls it, and flips to the section about pleasing your man.

I want to be a supportive friend. "You're right. You never know."

"Speaking of potential, what's up with you and Runner Boy?" She plants little kisses down the side of her index finger.

"Nothing good. When we line up for practice runs, he started doing this thing where he'll push me and say, 'You all right there? Good thing I'm here to catch you or you'd have fallen right over.' Or he'll pull my ponytail. Stupid stuff."

"Oh, sweet, Alyssa," Lana says in her I'm-so-wise voice. "He's obviously flirting."

"Really? But it's so older-brother-like. Anyway, I have no idea what to do back."

Lana starts reading, "To show a man you're interested, ask him about his wants and desires and touch him lightly on the arm. A man's arms have hidden erogenous zones and soon he'll be thinking about you without even knowing why."

She folds her arms and looks at me expectantly. "See? It's just what I've been telling you. What proof do you need besides the bible itself?"

I roll my eyes. "Remember the last time I tried asking him about his interests? I said, 'So, do you like running?' And he said, 'Uh, no, I just do it because I'm a masochist.' Thank God Coach Griffin blew his whistle and put me out of my misery."

But Lana looks determined. "That's all in the past. We still have to get you ready for the retreat. Kiss your hand," she says, pushing *Cosmo* aside. *Cosmo* women already know how to do this.

"I told you there will be no time for that there." My index finger traces geometric shapes in my carpet. My kissing experience consists of a Spin the Bottle game at age twelve. The guy I had to kiss tried to slip his tongue in my mouth, but he reminded me of a toad and I pushed him away.

"If not there, then soon. I know what I'm talking about, and you're going to need the practice. Now kiss your hand." Her lips are already pressed against her hand, and she waits for me to do the same.

I sigh and kiss my hand. Lana wants to study education in college so she practices her teaching skills by modeling the right ways to hook up. One day she'll list me as a reference on a job application and I'll say that she has superb oral skills.

She parts her lips and moves her tongue slowly across her hand, and I follow. She ends the demonstration by lightly biting what she says is the upper lip. When I do the same, she gives me a thumbs-up. My hand seems to enjoy it, but all these lessons do is remind me of the real boy lips I'm missing.

I hear the front door open and scan my room for crumbs while Lana pushes the crumbled-up newspaper deep into my trash. We're no match for my mother's radar. Two minutes later she's at my door, vacuum in hand. I guess cinnamon buns require the big guns.

Lana and I move to the doorway to give her room. "How did the article interviews go?" I ask.

"One was passable, two canceled, and Marian called my cell on the way home to let me know that she's thought of yet another way to present this story. But it's all typical, right?" She gives us a small laugh and turns on the vacuum, sucking up dirt both real and imaginary. The creases around her eyes and mouth seem to disappear as her face becomes peaceful. She moves the vacuum to the carpet area under my desk and fixates on the spot. We weren't even near there, but the Hoover is combing it, back and forth, back and forth, like all the dirt in the world is in that one space. She turns off the vacuum and leaves, and when she returns she's holding two cans—cinnamon-scented Glade spray and a foamy cleanser. She gets down on her knees and sprays the carpet with the foam, then takes a rag out of her pocket and vigorously rubs the area. I can no longer see her face, but the slump of her shoulders tells me she's no longer content. She shakes her head, and I hear her breath come out jagged, the way mine does when I'm trying not to cry, and I know today was worse than she let on. In my head, I am already emptying the trash to make room for contraband containers of store-bought food.

Lana shifts her feet and moves her eyes to the poster on the wall next to my bed. Under the words *Chase Your Dreams* is a runner. Her hair is flying behind her, the crowd is a blur, and somewhere, far, far away, is her goal. Her face is focused, her fists clenched like she's already holding part of that dream. This is the poster I picture when I run. My mother bought it for me when I made the middle school track team four years ago, the same year her magazine was named "Most Promising New Rag" at a journalism convention.

"One day you'll be able to stop chasing because everything will finally be within your reach," she had said.

I didn't know what she'd meant. But now, as I watch her shoulders shudder, her hands absently fingering a spot of dust no longer there (maybe never there in the first place), I wonder if she's thinking about how the dreams she had in her clenched fists have started to disappear.

EIGHT

A lyssa, get up or I'm going to miss the bus," says my father as he nudges me awake.

I roll toward the scent of his cologne, fresh and musky, and open my eyes.

"I'm sorry, honey. Your mom isn't feeling well today so you're going to have to walk to school." The impatience is gone from his voice, but his face has a trace of annoyance. I am thinking that it's directed at my mother.

"Geez. Again? Can you please tell your friends to stop throwing parties on Sundays?"

"I'll make a note." He kisses me good-bye, then adds, "Maybe Lana can take you." He looks intently at me when he says this, his eyes giving away what his mouth does not, that I don't have to explain to Lana why I need a ride. That I *shouldn't* explain to Lana why my mother can't take me. That my mother made a mistake, a few mistakes, but the business is only ours. No need for anyone to get the wrong idea. Just like with Lana and her mom using the back door to leave our house a few weeks ago.

"Asking Lana is a good idea," I say aloud, and then let my eyes speak with his before adding, "Have a good day. I'll keep your dinner warm." These words too are an understanding. It's me knowing he will be home late, a given. Like Mom's Monday hangovers.

He thanks me and goes to catch his bus away from here, leaving me to check on my mother.

My parents' room smells rancid. My mother's breathing is deep and she doesn't hear me come in. The cool washcloth has fallen off her forehead and her face is buried in her blanket, a little too far from the thankfully empty bucket by the side of the bed. I move her head closer to the bucket, replace the washcloth, and call Lana. So much for holding her liquor.

———

"I wouldn't be so hard on your mom. It's not like she's ever done this before, right?" Lana puts her arm around me as we walk to our lockers.

"No, not really." I keep some of my unvoiced promise to my dad.

"Those parties just get out of hand sometimes, you know? Remember when you slept over last year and my parents woke us up with their off-key singing? Only difference is that this is a school day and it sucks for you. I bet it won't happen again."

Except that it did, twice already. "I'm sure you're right." I give her a one-handed hug.

"Oooh," says Lana, excitement in her voice, "I know what will cheer you up. I elect this a Dare moment."

I groan. This game could make me laugh or ruin my day further. "Be gentle."

Lana rubs her palms together. "Got it. Ask the next guy who rounds the corner if he wears boxers or briefs."

Her last dare required me to ask my health teacher to review the proper way to put on a condom using a larger banana. I didn't do it. I breathe a sigh of relief at this tame dare. Until the next guy rounds the corner. He's wearing denim shorts that stop mid-shin and a blue Mets shirt with a long-sleeved ribbed shirt underneath. A lock of caramel hair brushes his eyebrow. Keith. "Sorry, not doing it. Give me something else."

Lana shakes her head and gives me a wide smile. "You know the rules. You said no to the last two dares, so no freebies. I even let that pool dare go."

I take my time removing my backpack and slowly examine each book as I place it in my locker, hoping the bell will ring before I have to do the dare. Lana looks at the clock above our lockers and clucks her tongue. "Uh uh. Ain't gonna work. The dare will just get stretched to homeroom, and I think you'd rather take your chances with Keith than asking one of those a-holes."

"Fine, you just wait until I give you my dare," I mutter as Keith gets closer.

"Bring it on." She giggles, already thinking about what

I'll make her do and loving it. Lana has never said no to a dare.

"Hey, Al," says Keith, giving my ponytail a tug.

"Hey, how's it going?" I look at Lana, who is tapping the nonexistent watch on her hand.

"I guess she really likes homeroom," Keith says. "I won't keep you. See you at practice."

I'm ready to let him leave, to see him escape into the mob of students ahead. I take a deep breath and launch into a speech, not giving myself a chance to back out. "Wait. I have to ask you something. See, I'm doing this project for math. Graphs. And my group came up with a question."

"Yeah?" He looks amused, sensing my discomfort and that something good may be coming at the end of my monologue.

"Yeah, and ... so ... we're asking the guys if they wear boxers or briefs." I feel hot, feel sweat collecting under my clothes. I'm afraid to look up at him.

"Well." He glances at Lana, who now looks like she'll burst from holding laughter in. "I wouldn't want you to fail your project." He puts his hand on my shoulder and leans in close to my ear, so close that his hair brushes against my lobe and I can smell the peppermint on his breath.

"Today, Al," he whispers, "I'm going commando."

NINE

You're just doing team activities at this retreat, right?"
My mother walks into the powder room to witness me trying out the sixth hairstyle and third lip color of the morning. It's her first morning up early in three weeks.

"Well, you should always try to look your best. Something about respecting authority and stuff. Isn't that what dad always says?" I scan the perfumes on the counter, opting for a vanilla body spray. I pull my hair into a half pony-tail and check out my profile in the mirror. So like hers.

My mother laughs. "Oh, it's about your father, is it? Not about any members of the opposite sex maybe?" She moves behind me and brushes my hair with her fingers, smoothing back loose pieces.

"I'll let you know if there's something to tell, okay?" I fix my tank top and let my mother fasten a stray hair with a bobby pin. The bobby pin somehow makes all the difference.

"Sure, *solnushka*, sunshine. Have a good time. I'll be

sending good thoughts your way while I'm working on my projects." She kisses my forehead.

"Do you have a lot of them?" I ask her reflection. The reflection that looks more like the normal mom and not the Sunday partier. After this past Monday's "inconvenience"—that's how my parents keep referring to these incidents—Mom swore she'd keep the weekend drinking to a glass or two of champagne, the midday cocktails to one.

Mom makes a face. "Too many and not enough. Let's not ruin your good mood and my temporary good one with a lengthy work discussion."

"That annoying editor again?"

"What persistence. You really *are* my daughter. How about I tell you more when there's something new to tell, okay?" She brushes my bangs from my eyes and smiles.

For a moment her eyes look heavy, but she turns her head when she notices me staring. "Don't worry about your old mom. Just have fun." She hugs me and turns to leave.

"Wait." I hug her back, and when I move to pull away she holds me tighter.

————

Our first activity at the retreat involves Coach calling out names, and one by one we take turns standing in the middle of a circle with our hands crossed in a V on our chests and our eyes closed, the sun warming our eyelids. When he says "fall," we lean back and hope someone catches us.

To me, it's not about *someone* catching me, it's about Keith catching me.

"Bondar, you're up," says Coach.

I stand in the center of the circle, making sure my back faces Keith. Almost everyone has had a turn already, and the activity is getting old. It's time to crack jokes. I close my eyes and someone yells, "Tiff, put that cell away. Do you want Alyssa hitting her head?"

Tiffany calls back, "Funny, Gary. How about you get your hands out of your pockets? I don't think any of us want to know what you're really holding."

"Shut up, all of you, or you'll be doing laps." Coach, of course. I wait for his command to fall.

In spite of the sun, I'm getting chills on my arms. I shut my eyes tighter and picture Keith's arms around me, thinking if I visualize what I want hard enough it will happen.

"Fall, Bondar."

I lean back and feel my toes leave the ground. I'm falling, falling, lower and lower, my heels feeling like they'll come out from under me. And just when I think I'll be the first one who hits the ground, strong arms catch me at the elbows. I open my eyes and before I turn around, I know it's Keith who's holding me. His long fingers with the hidden birthmark give him away.

"Good catch, Keith. Next!" I don't even have the chance to look at him, to see if he wishes, like I do, even a little, for me to fall again, for his arms to brush mine again and again and again. But as I move away from his touch, I think I feel his hands squeeze my elbows.

Coach pairs us with our stretching teammate and tells us to do partner runs through the park. He calls it "free time," meaning we can take any route we want as long as we complete five miles. I think he just wants *real* free time for himself, but time alone with Keith is not something I'm going to complain about.

I spend extra time in the bathroom, hoping that if I stall long enough there won't be anyone left but Keith and me. When I finally get back outside, I see only Coach—lounging on the bleachers by the baseball diamond, a magazine over his face—and Keith. He's leaning against a tree, his face away from me, stretching. I watch him for a moment before joining him.

"I thought you were standing me up," he says when I walk up to him.

"Nah, just things to do, people to see. You know how it is."

I lean on my calf to ease the stiffness and tell myself to be cool. Lana's mantra for hooking potential boyfriends—*it's good to leave them curious; don't make yourself so available; be mysterious*—plays in my head, and I hope I have the chance to use her moves after all.

He cocks an eyebrow and shakes his head. He thinks I'm funny, confident. He likes this side of me.

We start jogging side by side, light and easy strides. I let my mind absorb the trees, the sound of a waterfall nearby—the main reason I like this park—the changing colors of the leaves. Beside me, Keith is breathing hard.

I like the sound my feet make on the pavement, like they're beating out a rhythm of their own. Some new chant they created. The orange marker in the grass says we've run two and a half miles, but my legs aren't tired and I'm still breathing easily. My lungs won't feel the sharp pain that comes with needing air for another two miles.

The clean, earthy smell of a nearby creek fills my nostrils, and I breathe deeply. The marker in front of us says three miles, and Keith's running becomes a slow jog. He motions for us to stop at the waterfall ahead.

I slow down, and we sit on the dirt hill overlooking the falls. A light breeze blows and a spray of water sprinkles over our skin. Keith squints against the sun and stares into the distance, catching his breath.

"It's nice out here," I say, feeling miles away from the girl I am at home.

"Yeah, my dad and I used to come here." His voice trails off and he runs his fingers through his hair. I wait for him to give more details, but he doesn't.

"My mom and I did too," I say to fill the silence. "There was this time last year when we forgot which path we took and ended up two towns over. We had to ring some random person's doorbell to get directions, and the guy offered to drive us back to our car."

I laugh at the memory and our poor sense of direction, and how we said we didn't want to ever be that lost again.

Keith lets out a low whistle. "Now I know why they

put those maps on the back of our high school schedule. Glad to know the secretaries aren't wasting their time."

I don't mind that he mocks me, because that's our thing. And he no longer has that distant look in his eyes.

"You're lucky you're bigger than me," I say, and playfully kick him.

He hooks my leg with his and crosses them together so we're connected. We touch for stretching, but not like this. Here our legs fit together, and it reminds me of the three-legged races we had to run in fifth grade gym, only now I'm paired with someone who makes my stomach flip. I look down at my hands, afraid if I glance up he'll see I'm blushing.

"Hey," he says. It comes out soft, almost overpowered by the sound of rushing water.

I look up and smile.

"You have a nice smile," he says, taking my hand.

I know it's clammy, and for a second I'm afraid he's going to let go. He doesn't, and I think of his lips on mine.

"Thanks. You too." I glance around, but see no one from our group. I wonder if he scoped out the trails while I was in the bathroom, checking who was running where, choosing this one for its privacy.

I see him leaning in, and I want to tell him that I've never really kissed anyone before because I don't want him to pull back and say, "Why didn't you tell me you didn't know what you were doing?" He's centimeters away and I open my mouth to warn him, but he takes this as a cue to kiss me. He kisses without tongue, just soft, open-mouthed kisses, lips meeting lips. He tastes like peppermint, and I know I will never again eat anything peppermint without thinking of Keith. His eyes are closed, but I keep mine open for a few seconds to make sure I'm moving my mouth correctly. He squeezes my knee, and I close my eyes and follow his lead like Lana told me to. His teeth gently bite my upper lip and he slowly pulls away. I keep my eyes closed three extra seconds to remember the moment in my mind.

"That was great," he says when I open my eyes, and I wonder if he's just saying that. Can he tell how inexperienced I am?

"Yeah, you must be a pro." I mean it to come out flirty, but it just sounds like he gets around.

He laughs. "I have trophies and everything. You'll have to see them sometime." Then he pulls me to him and kisses me again, and I'm afraid my legs are too rubbery to ever run again.

I feel the warmth of his breath in my hair. "You smell like vanilla," he says.

I think of saying thank you, but that doesn't seem right, so I say nothing and just smile. I wonder if he'll always associate that scent with me.

We look out on the water and he plays with my hair, tracing circles on the back of my neck with his fingers like we have all the time in the world. Then he's kissing me again and already I'm imagining us hanging out in school, him casually leaning against my locker waiting for me, him calling out "Hey, Al" and running over to me, his friends knowing that's how it is and giving him that *go be with your girl* look, and people walking around us as we create hallway traffic because we're too busy kissing to notice anyone else. I want him to want to know everything about me even though there are things I can't tell him.

I wonder what he's thinking and accidentally ask him this out loud, breaking the moment.

He pulls away and gives me that *you're such a girl* look, the one that's accompanied by an eye roll, and smiles his toothy smile. Other than the two front ones, his teeth are perfectly straight.

"I'm thinking," he says, moving really close to me so his mouth is almost on mine again. My heart beats quick, quick, quick. "I'm thinking," he says again, lips so close that I breathe out my breath but inhale his, "that I really like vanilla ice cream." Then he lies down on the grass with his hands behind his head and gives me a sly smile.

My heart is still thumping away, and I can tell he knows. He likes teasing me. And just when I think he's not going to kiss me again, he pulls me onto the grass with him and puts his mouth on mine, literally taking my breath away.

"You're trouble. I can tell," he murmurs into my neck.

"Funny, I was just thinking the same about you." This boy who doesn't care when we get back to the group, who's not bothered at all about making out when we should be running, who came up with this plan too easily, like he's done it many times before. I start to wonder how many other girls were trouble, but then his lips are again on mine and I am pulled under, drowning in his touch, my worries pushed into the water below.

We're late getting back and are greeted by whistling and snickers. I've used up all my store of suave, and my face is flushed. Keith doesn't have this problem. I'm sure he's already decided what he'll say.

"How nice of you two to join us," Coach barks.

"So sorry," Keith says before I can open my mouth. "Totally my fault. I was slowing Alyssa down." His face is surprisingly contrite.

I don't know if Coach believes him, but he was obviously in the middle of a rehearsed speech when we interrupted him and is eager to get back to his notes. He jerks his head toward the bleachers, clears his throat, and scans his cards for his next line. I glance at Coach and try to focus, silencing the breath-altering images of Keith and me in my head.

"I've been talking with other coaches," he announces, "and they believe that a close-knit team brings better results." He reaches into his bag and pulls out markers and construction paper. "So, if our rivals swear by pansy exercises, then we will too. Thirty minutes, team," he says as he hands out the art supplies. "Write an anonymous note for each teammate and your favorite coach. Say something nice. No idiotic comments." He glares at Tiffany and Gary.

I can't work on this with Keith so close, so I move to an overhang on the other side of the bleachers. Keith winks at me, and I feel happy and sick at the same time. I get through everyone's note pretty quickly, saving Keith for last. *Good sense of humor* for Tiffany and Gary and *considerate* for Jeff, who always brings snacks to eat after meets, *great sense of commitment* for Coach. I flip through some of my other comments and stare at my last piece of paper. With Coach reading these, I can't write *gorgeous* or *amazing kisser*, and a one-word generic phrase like *nice* is lame and doesn't capture that unbelievable experience by the falls.

"Five minutes," says Coach, scribbling away on his own papers and maybe even enjoying it.

Still no closer to writing something for Keith, I doodle pictures of a string of running shoes.

"Two minutes."

I look over at Keith. He's done and lying on his back, a smile on his face, iPod on, hands behind his head. I stare, trying to get inside his head, and now there's a shadow on the ground around me.

"Ready, Bondar?"

"Can you come back to me in one minute?" Coach moves on to collect everyone else's words of kindness. I look at Keith one more time and think of his long fingers around my elbows, his hands gently squeezing. I write, *nice hands*.

———

My mother's hand is white, like the glass of wine in her hand, and she motions at the stack of notes on my floor. "Can I look at these with you?" she asks from my doorway.

"The two glasses at dinner didn't cut it?" I ask.

"Don't be a wiseass, Alyssa. Your dad will drive you to the retreat tomorrow. Give me a break." She takes a sip. A drop falls on my carpet, but white wine doesn't stain.

"I'm sorry," I mumble, looking through the papers, searching for Keith's.

"This is a nice idea," she says, eager to change the subject. "What did everyone say about my girl?"

"I got a bunch of 'really good runner,' some 'nice.'" *A dedicated and talented young woman who will go far.* That one was definitely from Coach, and surprisingly eloquent. "One person wrote 'thanks for helping me with my time.' I think it's this girl Coach teamed me with last fall. Really nice of her to remember."

"You never know how you touch others," says my mother the Hallmark card. "And that boy. Is there anything to know yet?" Her eyes smile teasingly, not at all sad.

I think of telling her, but the moment doesn't feel right. Instead, I push the papers toward her. "Maybe. I've been trying to figure out which one is his. I doubt he'd just write 'nice.'"

Mom takes the papers in her hands and examines each one, tracing her fingers over the letters. "I think it's this one," she says after a few minutes. "The writing is definitely a boy's."

I read the paper and laugh, and my mother feigns concern. "Interesting," she says. "Should I be worried that some boy thinks my daughter has 'great elbows'?"

TEN

On Monday morning I'm floating. Sunlight peeks in through my shades and I imagine it's a trail of Keith's kisses, carrying me to school. I feel weightless and untouchable, like I'm about to sail through the day on the sunbeam. I keep my eyes closed and become part of the sun's morning dance routine. It pirouettes to its own music, but a strangled sound interrupts the choreography.

In the back of my mind I know what the sound is, but I follow it to my parents' room anyway. Outside, car doors slam as our neighbors leave for work, oblivious (just as my parents like it) to what is happening only windows away. The noise has turned into groaning and gets louder when I enter my parents' bedroom. The door to the bathroom is wide open, and Mom is on her hands and knees on the bathroom floor hunched over the toilet.

Her face is pale and there are beads of sweat across her forehead. She's moaning and swaying back and forth—the hair on my arms stands on end. *Five squared is 25.* She looks at me and I see no emotion, only the red veins in her eyes. The liquid in the toilet is shades of red, green, and yellow. *Six squared is 36.*

"Are you okay?" I ask, moving closer to her. The sour smells of bile mingle with sweat and sickly sweet juice, and they stick to me in layers, totally killing my sun buzz. *Seven squared is 49.*

"Does it look like I'm okay?" she snaps, but I only want to help her.

"What can I do?" I find a rubber band in the medicine cabinet and put it around her hair so it doesn't get more vomit on it. It already looks stringy and dirty.

She heaves into the toilet as her reply, then curls into a ball on the tile floor and clutches her stomach. *Eight squared is 64.*

"Should I call someone?" I know this is not really an option, but I've never seen anyone throw up this much.

"Don't be stupid. This will go away."

"Fine," I say, my voice breaking. "Stay there." I back out of the bathroom but I don't leave. I stand in the bedroom doorway and watch her crawl to her bed, remembering the promise she made me after last week's "inconvenience." I'm glad I never told her about kissing Keith.

She rolls over onto her side with her back to me, and groans some more. This time I don't ask how she is.

———

that would be missed if I wasn't watching him so intently. I bet he's wondering how the prize pupil he was promised (he said to me the first day, "I've heard great things, Miss Bondar, great things") was replaced with this tardy girl who doesn't even apologize for being late. But it's not like I'm a disappointment. We've had three quizzes—I got As; twenty homework assignments—of which I missed only one because my mother accidentally threw it out while on a cleaning mission; and we have a test this Friday. I plan on acing it, and then he'll see he has me pegged all wrong.

I hear light snoring behind me, and Mr. Schmidt walks over and slams a binder on Ryan's desk. Everyone is awake now. Ryan makes an exaggerated production of jumping out of his seat and there are stifled snickers around the room.

"Detention, Mr. Fishman," says Mr. Schmidt, and the class is quiet once again.

"What? What did I do? C'mon," Ryan whines, but he's enjoying every minute of the attention. It will be something to talk about next period with Jake and Trish.

I look at the problems on the overhead. Mr. Schmidt puts up a new example. He's trying to get us to participate and says he'll give a prize to whoever can solve the equation first. I bet the prize is some dopey eraser or stick of gum—even though we're not allowed to chew gum in school—but as soon as Mr. Schmidt turns on the lights, the pencils move furiously. Even Ryan puts on his studious face. Hey, we all like to be winners.

Mr. Schmidt's eyes sparkle as he walks around the room. That *wow, I'm making a difference* sparkle. It's working—at least on me. I want to solve it first. I want to show him those notes teachers give each other about past students were right. I finish the equation with two minutes left and raise my hand. Mr. Schmidt breaks into a wide smile after reading my answer.

"Nice job, Miss Bondar, nice job." He gives me a stick of Juicy Fruit. Some students groan; the cooler ones act like they don't care. For the benefit of the powers that be, who may have this room bugged, Mr. Schmidt reminds me loudly not to chew it on school time.

The bell rings, and Mr. Schmidt says, "Everything all right, Miss Bondar?"

"Just one of those days," I say, glancing at the clock and hoping he'll get the hint.

"I know you're bright," he says, obviously not caring that I might be late for my third class of the day too. "But full attendance is very important. You can't expect to understand everything if you keep coming in late."

I stiffen. "I know. It won't happen again."

I don't really know if it will or not, but this is what he wants to hear.

He smiles, looking like he wants to say more, but then changes his mind. "Good. See you tomorrow, Miss Bondar."

Maybe he realizes you can only be so chummy when you don't even call your students by their first names. Maybe he knows everyone has issues, but it's easier to stick with problems that have clear solutions. Or maybe, like my mom and dad, he sees my tardiness as just one of life's inconveniences.

ELEVEN

Did I not call this? You have to tell me *everything*," Lana squeals by our lockers at lunch.

Moments in the park flash through my mind—Keith's face centimeters from mine, his lips soft and wet, the way his fingers performed figure eights on the back of my neck, our bodies rolling on the grass. Then Sunday, with drills instead of partner runs, Keith pulling me behind the bleachers for quick kisses, his fingers tickling me behind my kneecap during stretches. My legs feel like they're going to give, and I lean against my locker and give a low moan.

"It must have been some kiss," Lana says with a grin. "Spill."

"Oh, God. It was so perfect." I tell her everything, from how he said I have a nice smile to the way I got little shivers when he twirled his fingers in my hair. "I just hope I did everything right. What if he could tell I never kissed anyone before?" I slump down on the tiles. Nothing like anxiety to bring a good moment to its knees.

"Stop it. I'm sure you were great. And he kissed you more than once—that means he thought you were awesome. I bet he went to bed hugging his pillow last night going, 'Oh, Alyssa. Yeah, you're so good. Oh, yeah.'" Lana pretends her book is Keith's pillow and kisses it all over.

We both crack up and I kick her ankle. "Shut up."

"Will you be getting all badass on me now, what with sneaking out during your retreat and everything? Do you need me to show you moves on a soda bottle after all?" She forms an O with her mouth and moves her fist in an up-and-down motion beside it.

The halls are full and I push her hands down. "Seriously, Lana, cut it out." She laughs, and I appreciate how this would be funny if it weren't happening to me. But since it is, I'm just embarrassed.

"Relax, I'm only playing," she says. Then she nudges me and nods her head toward the figures heading in our direction.

I notice Keith first. He's wearing a green flannel shirt tied around the waist of his low-hung baggy jeans, and a green T-shirt with a faded tree logo. His hair flops on his forehead, and just as I think of my fingers combing it, a girl's nails—fire hydrant red—brush the strands away from his eyes.

Her hair—big auburn curls, with bangs streaked blonde—is loud too, just like her laugh, which seems to brush Keith's cheek before wafting over to me. Her fingernails now grasp Keith's arm, and he laughs too.

"He's friends with *her*?" Lana says, noticing Redhead at the same moment I do.

I swallow, trying to find words. "I guess. Do you know who she is?" My voice is hoarse.

Redhead's hanging on him, shiny, pouty crimson lips opened wide, laughing like what Keith is saying is the most hilarious thing in the world.

"The Bitch," Lana says. "Her real name is Holly Bichner, but no one calls her that. She was the reason Trish dumped Matt Leonard, that hot senior, last year. Holly went down on him in the parking lot during the spring dance while Trish was home sick."

I groan. I'm glad I'm already sitting on the floor, because a wave of nausea hits me and I would have fallen down if I'd been standing. I put my chin on my knees.

"Hey, Al," Keith calls. It sounds like his voice is far away, but when I look up he's standing over me. Alone.

I raise my head and see his mouth, chewing away. The smell of peppermint burns my nose.

"Hey." I grab hold of his extended hand and pull myself up.

Lana moves away from us to give us privacy, feigning great interest in her lunch bag.

"You feeling okay? You don't look too good," he says.

I listen to his tone and think I hear concern. "Didn't have a chance to get breakfast this morning, so I felt light-headed. I'm fine now."

"Good," he says. "I was worried I'd have to take it easy on you on the practice field."

"Keith, we're going to be late," the Bitch calls from the gym doors before I can respond.

He raises one finger in the air and I wonder if that's new to her—a guy telling her to wait.

"You should go," I say, shifting my weight from one foot to the other. I look into his eyes but can't read them. Does Holly always brush his hair from his eyes? Have her lips ever touched his? I can't ask him this. We only had a few kisses. I don't own him. I lick my lips and my pulse races. My mouth aches.

"Is that what you want?" he says into my ear, teasing.

I shake my head no. I hate that my spunky retreat-self is gone, that my brain has gone to mush. Like melted vanilla ice cream.

"Come here," he says and pulls me to him, kissing me hard.

I imagine the irritated look on Holly's face and the kiss feels that much better.

"See you later," he says, smiling as he saunters off.

"Holly be damned," Lana says in awe, walking up to me. "Wow."

"Yeah, wow," I echo as we make our way to the cafeteria, my feet barely touching the ground.

TWELVE

According to the administration, the current footballs used in gym class are a hazard. Soft Nerf balls are the safer option, and cross-country practice is cancelled so staff can discuss this critical issue. For once I don't mind the change of plans, and Keith finds me after school anyway.

The temps are in the low sixties, perfect fall weather, and I take my time walking home. The sun shines on my face, and I pretend Lana and I are at the pool checking out boys and butterflies. An ice cream truck passes by playing "Pop Goes the Weasel," but he's wasting his time on these streets. There are no little kids in my part of town. I use mental telepathy to direct him to Lana's neighborhood, where there are a ton of rich, sticky-fingered brats who she babysits for major cash.

A police car drives by, sirens blaring. I watch the lights—red and blue, spinning away. Images of this morning flash in my mind. Swirling reds and yellows. My stomach clenches in resistance to whatever waits for me at home. I hope to smell Lemon Pledge, which would mean my mom was sober enough to clean.

I walk into the house and am greeted by the smell of citrus and *pilmeni*. I don't see my mother, but in the kitchen there are two pots on the stove—one with simmering meat-filled ravioli, the other with *compote*, homemade fruit punch my father loves. Not counting the cinnamon buns, this is the first homemade meal in weeks.

Mom walks to the kitchen door and waits there, like she's not sure if she should come in. I see her grimace as her eyes take in my sneakers. Even when she's apologizing, she can't stomach the possibly dirty shoes on my feet. I replace them with the pair of slippers set out for me in the hall, grateful for something to do besides think of things to say to her.

I go to the stove and wait for her to make a move, although maybe she feels she already has, with the food and her appearance. She's wearing a brown velour jogging suit with a white tank top, and her hair is pulled back in a brown clip. She's even wearing lipstick. Quite an improvement over her morning look.

She bites her lip and her chin wobbles. I know if she starts crying, so will I.

"The house smells great," I say, walking toward her.

She beams and almost runs to me. Her arms pull me close, and even as I tell myself not to forgive so easily, my cheek is already resting on the soft velour.

"I'm so sorry." Her voice catches. "What happened this morning won't happen again."

The Lemon Pledge, ravioli, and her shiny red lipstick make me believe her, even though this isn't the first time I have heard her "sorries." She hugs me tighter, strokes my hair, and then whispers something in my ear that makes me stiffen. But she's asking, and her voice is pleading, and the *compote* and *pilmeni* are bubbling, and I tell her, like I have done before, that this will stay between us. But this is the last time.

"Thank you," she says. She pulls away, cheeks wet.

My face feels wet too, and I feel our tears binding us together.

———

"I got a writing assignment for a new health and wellness magazine this afternoon," my mother says at dinner, during a commercial. "I called them on a whim and pitched them an idea called 'Conquer Ills Without the Pills,' about natural cures for sickness." She waves her hand in the air like she's writing the title on the ceiling.

"That's amazing, Julia. I knew you had it in you," says my dad between mouthfuls. My mom's new appearance and dinner must have put him in a good mood because he's shushed us only once since the news started.

"I'm really proud of you," I say. She smiles, but it's a tired smile, not our smile.

"This calls for a celebration," says Dad, one eye on the television.

He has a minute and a half before the commercials

end, and he heads into the dining room and returns with a bottle of wine. He's going to celebrate my mom's new job and bad hangover with alcohol. *I understand irony now, Ms. Hoffman. The key is real-life examples.*

I glare at him.

"Don't give me that look," he says. "You know you can't drink yet."

He doesn't understand, and I can't tell him anything else. I made a tear-sealed promise.

They clink glasses—*na zdorovje*, to health—again, and again, and again. By the end of the meal, the news completed, they're laughing and holding hands. My father helps my mother clear the table, and she washes the dishes. When I go to kiss them good night at ten o'clock, I find them both reading on the couch, CNN put on hold. Their arms are around each other, their cheeks almost touching, wine thicker than tears.

THIRTEEN

It's been less than a week since that first kiss with Keith, but my days are spent waiting and craving the ritual we've developed. Deep, urgent morning kisses, my body pushed against my locker; relaxed pre-lunch smooches, Keith's hand casually wrapped around my waist; lingering touches at practice, our hands carefully walking the lines of what's appropriate, subtly crossing into the gray too often; and more kisses in his car, his hands roaming but not venturing beneath my clothes.

"Impressive," says Lana at lunch. "That boy has self-control."

"We haven't even had a real date. Besides, I'm not going to flash my boobs to the whole student body. That's not exactly a Dear Diary moment."

Lana shrugs and absently spoons yogurt into her mouth. I'm guessing that if she and Jake were making out, she wouldn't care where they were. I must look annoyed because she sighs and says, "I wish I was kissing someone right now."

"You will be soon enough. The gods just feel I'm long overdue, you know?"

She puts her arm around my shoulders and smiles. "I was being a pain, wasn't I? A crappy BFF? Sorry. Support-ive Lana is back now."

Jake passes our lunch table and I'm feeling generous. "Yo yo," I say. "What up?"

Lana stares at me open-mouthed as Jake slows down. "Hey, girls, what's going on?"

I make small talk—dissing on Mr. Pinto and Ms. H— especially since Jake is doing his best to look at me when he talks. Then I excuse myself to go to the bathroom, giv-ing Lana and Jake their alone-time.

Lana's eyes shoot me a thank-you, and I give her a toothy smile. It's nice to help others' love lives rather than worry about my own.

———

"That was so cool of you," Lana says for the tenth time since lunch.

I roll my eyes. You'd think I'd physically pushed them together for a kiss. "Just stop. Please. If you want to know the truth, you were getting a little too mopey for me."

She gives me a light punch and laughs. "Now, how can I be of service in these crucial minutes before practice?"

I feel my anxiety returning. "Put something in his water that makes him ask me out on a real date." I'm trying to be funny but Lana grimaces. She bites her lip, and I know she's debating whether she should say something.

"What? Just tell me." I pull my hair into a ponytail and gather my books as I wait.

"It's obvious he likes you, but this whole dating thing is a game. No one is exclusive in the beginning. It's not the fifties, where the guy gives you his ring and you go steady and it's all sweet and innocent." She looks sorry, like she's giving a life-is-tough speech to one of her babysitting charges.

"That's just stupid." Now I *sound* like one of her little kids.

She continues to look sympathetic, and this annoys me.

"Fine. What do I do?" I slam my locker shut.

She looks at me like the answer is obvious. "Play the game."

I don't like games with ambiguous rules, which is why I chose cross-country. There are no rules. You win by running fast, you lose by running slow. Don't start before the whistle is blown and you're golden. But, as I walk to the practice field, I am playing sample, flirty conversations in my head and telling myself to let things unfold easily and naturally. Contradictions, really, because making our relationship exclusive is what would really feel natural.

Keith sees me and nods. I raise my hand to wave, but the figure beside him dulls my brain function. Her laugh, like it's some kind of hypnotic charm, pulls Keith in just like it did the first time I saw her, and her fingernails—now with jewels on the tips that sparkle in the sun—are squeezing his shoulder. He's nodding and laughing too. Then he raises his hand as well, and for a second I'm relieved because I think he's going to motion for me to come over, but instead he brushes his hair from his eyes. At least Holly isn't assisting him this time.

Lana would tell me to go over there anyway, to show Holly she's got competition, but I'm a newbie to this crazy game and Holly's already playing at expert level. I pick a sunny patch in the grass and focus on my solitaire stretching. I try to keep my head straight or low to the ground to avoid looking at my least favorite duo, but I get a glimpse of Holly hugging Keith good-bye, her breasts leaving no breathing space between the two of them.

"You started without me," Keith says, running up to me.

My legs are wide open in Russian-split style, my elbows on the ground. "You were busy," I say, not looking up at him, trying to keep my jealousy in check.

He kneels behind me and puts pressure on my back to make me go down farther for a deeper stretch. "Never too busy for this," he says, fingers dancing on my spine, his peppermint breath warm against my cheek, thawing me out.

Coach blows his whistle and we switch positions. Now I'm leaning on Keith's back. If Lana were here she'd say something like, "It's got to be even, girl. You both need to be on the receiving end of things, you know what I mean?" Of course I would know what she meant. You can't watch her suck her fingers and learn nothing. I wonder how much Keith knows about these things. I've seen him talk to girls before, before he and I were anything, and his confidence makes me think he's done plenty.

Another whistle, another position change. This time we're facing each other, legs open—a variation on the rainy day calf stretch—and taking turns pulling our partners by their hands. My heart is beating fast. His hands holding mine and our faces inches apart is making me too excited. I keep my head down so he doesn't notice the blush in my cheeks.

We switch, and I'm pulling his hands now. I let my fingers graze his arm, in case *Cosmo* is right about it being an erogenous zone.

"Why so quiet today?" he asks, and I wonder if he really can't tell I'm worried about Holly or if he's playing the game too, if this is some script I'm not aware of.

"Just a lot on my mind."

Keith nods and says, "If you want to talk about it, let me know." But he doesn't ask any more questions, and I'm thinking that Lana may be wrong. Maybe not everyone does things her way, maybe she's the one who's clueless.

Two quick whistle blows. Stretching is over and we walk to line up on the track. "Ready to eat my dust?" asks Keith.

I relax and call on my inner wiseass, but she must be busy because "Ready to eat me?" comes out of my mouth.

Keith cracks up, and I want to die. Right here, right now, on the soft grass.

"Are we at that stage already? Sweet! Catch up to me when practice is over," Keith says, and Coach shoots his pistol.

Runners race ahead, dirt from their sneakers and Keith's laughter marking the route I will follow. I stare after them, longing for a playbook, my face burning.

FOURTEEN

As I make my way home, I push the "eat me" comment out of my head and focus instead on the crimson border the setting sun left around the sky and the leaves under my feet. I make a production of kicking the leaves just so I can hear their crunch under my sneakers.

I'm halfway home when a blue Honda Accord pulls up beside me, a crackle of leaves rumbling beneath its tires.

"Get in," says a chipper voice, a woman's voice that sounds very much like my mother's, only I'm sure it can't be because my mother would not have taken a break from her work to meet me.

I bend down and pretend to fix my shoelace, waiting for a sign as to who this person really is. The sun buys me time, acting as a shield through which I can get a glimpse of the lady behind the steering wheel. She looks like the mom I once knew—not the irritated, beer-goggled mom, or the sad clean-freak with slumped shoulders, or the perfectly quaffed mother who looks like she's auditioning for a new Gap ad. This mom is wearing old, fitted jeans and a poet shirt that she found at a street-fair market in Manhattan. Her hair is loose and neat but windblown, a piece resting over her eye that she tries to move by blowing air out of the corner of her mouth. The only makeup on her face is pink lipstick, perfectly drawn, and her skin looks smooth, like she just got out of the shower and put moisturizer on it. The sun is working on her too, making that loose piece of hair stick to her forehead. I think she's happy about this, because now it's not in her eyes and she can see me better.

She taps her fingers on the steering wheel, to the music playing in the car it seems, and smiles at me. A relaxed smile, not cajoling, not apologetic, just there. The kind of smile that once came naturally and would highlight the creases by her eyes, eyes that are now missing that lost look they had when she dust-busted my room. Eyes that stare back at me when I look in the mirror. I haven't seen this woman in a long time. I get in the car.

"How was practice?" she asks, her tone light and easy like she picks me up from school every day.

I want to tell her about Keith, have her tell me how silly Lana's rules are, to swap the best and worst parts of our days—the good canceling out the bad—like we used to do when I was younger.

Instead I say, "Fine. Hard, you know."

She nods, but she doesn't know. Not really. Not how the practices are this year. She must figure they're just like last year—same high school, same coach. This year, though, I'm better, quicker, more is expected. This year, there's

Keith and that makes it all new. This year, there's more to run through, more thoughts to get out of my head, more I need to get away from, more of me left behind in the dust trails under my feet.

I think of what to say to keep this conversation going. I remember how it used to be easy, how my mouth just opened and words flowed, not pausing, not getting sucked back because they were the wrong ones. I think back to that girl on the porch swing, lemonade in her hand, head on her mother's shoulder, and close my eyes willing her to appear. I feel parts of her coming through, and that's enough to latch on to for now. She's warm, happy, light in my heavy skin, and I let her make a home in this weighty person who's unfamiliar to her.

I feel her attach herself to me, like Peter Pan's shadow, and pretend we are the same person. "How was your day?" I ask. As Old Alyssa, this question does not worry me.

My mother shrugs, still smiling. "Just a regular day. A deadline and rejection here, a new assignment there. Nothing crazy."

And, yet, here we are in a car after school like this is normal. *But of course it's normal*, says Old Alyssa. *Didn't we used to do this a lot?*

I push my questioning thoughts to the pit of my stomach. Old Alyssa would not worry that her mother was neither drunk nor Stepford happy.

"Where are we headed?" I ask as she gets on the highway, opens the window, and blasts music. A gust of cold air, a slap to the deceptive sun, stings my cheeks.

The wind reddens my mom's face and she laughs, open-mouthed, like she's trying to get as much of this new air inside her as possible. I open my mouth too and suck in the air, forcing the cold into my stomach, hoping it will eliminate the worry I stashed there minutes before.

"I think the mall is a good idea," says my mother, barely checking her rearview mirror as she pulls into the exit lane.

We used to do a lot of mall trips. Neither of us are big shoppers, but we liked to sit on the benches around the carousel and people-watch. Everything happened at the carousel. It was where moms and dads rode with their kids on the multicolored ponies or carriages; where the woman who gave out samples of the pretzel du jour stood, making sure no one got more than one piece; where teenage boys, with low-slung pants and heavy-metal shirts, looked around them before ducking into Bath & Body Works to buy their moms or girlfriends presents; and where my mom and I sat and decided what all these people were *really* doing there and what their thoughts *really* were.

I feel the weightiness of my skin evaporate as Old Alyssa does a twirl and swings her legs. People-watching with her mom was one of her favorite activities, and she gets giddy remembering how they would collapse with laughter as they tried to outdo each other's crazy stories about passersby. Old Alyssa's excitement is contagious and I feel the worry inside me disappearing.

The mall is packed, as usual, but since it's a weekday, finding a parking spot doesn't take long.

"10B Red," I say, glancing at the marker by the car, and my mom takes out a notepad from her purse and writes it down. The organized mom I remember.

We pass a Häagen-Dazs stand on the way in, and my mother buys us chocolate-chip-mint fro-yo in waffle cones before we each get a sample of cinnamon-sugar pretzel with white frosting dip. The weekend sampler lady always smiles, reminding me of someone's Jewish grandma—the kind that says, "Eat, eat. You're too skinny." I always think it pains her that she can only give out one piece per person. Today's sampler worker is a sour-faced teen who acts like giving you samples is a gift from God. I imagine that if Peter's Pretzels didn't require uniforms, she'd be wearing a goth get-up. As it is, her eyes are outlined in thick, black eyeliner, only letting you see tiny slits.

"I bet she has a warm heart," my mother says when we park ourselves on a bench near the carousel.

"The question is, whose?" I say, licking the tip of my cone.

My mother laughs. "A little harsh, no?"

"It's a cruel world out there." I smile the smile I used to wish would create wrinkles by my eyes too.

Mom nods and loses some of her smile, and I wonder if she's thinking of the world she's inflicted upon me. I feel Old Alyssa getting nervous, unsure about these weird vibes that are ruining her high. I want her to stay happy. I want the me in this borrowed skin to stay happy.

I move my tongue along the top of my ice cream slowly and sensually, like I've seen Lana do.

The Hall Nazi du Jour glances up from her grade book and assumes her Gestapo voice. "Miss, can I see your pass please?" She taps a pen on her mini desk.

"I was just heading to the office to get one," I say, but she's still staring at me, tapping. "I'm late."

"Fine, keep moving." She sounds annoyed, but I don't know if it's because she can't write me up for wandering the halls passless or because she thinks I'm some delinquent who doesn't care enough to show up to school on time. I'm guessing it's a little of both.

In the office, the secretary doesn't even look up as she writes me a late pass. If she did, she'd recognize me as the girl who's been late three times since school started more than a month ago. And if she then went to check my records, she'd see that that's three times more than all of last year. But she's eager to get back to her paperwork and makes a *hurry along* motion with her hand. Before I can leave, she turns around and walks to her cubicle. For the second time today, I am left staring at someone's back as she chooses to do something more important than talk to me.

———

I hand my pass to Mr. Schmidt, my geometry teacher, and slide into my chair. The room is dark because he's showing proof examples on the overhead, so I don't know who in the class is paying attention, sleeping, or staring at me. Mr. Schmidt watches as I take out my homework, notebook, and pencil. He shakes his head slightly, an action

My mother raises one eyebrow. "Something you want to tell me?"

I grin and shake my head. "Just something Lana taught me."

"I'll bet. That Lana is quite a teacher."

I shrug and Old Alyssa floats. Tension averted.

My mother looks like she wants to say more, and I help her. "Relax. My love life is nowhere near as exciting as that."

She searches my face, checking to see if there is something I'm not saying.

"Does that mean there is a *little* excitement, then?" She strokes my hair, a gleam in her eyes like she can read my mind.

And that's all Old Alyssa needs to spill her guts. She forces my mouth open and tells my mom everything—from the math "survey" to Holly to the stretching to the "eat me." She saves the kisses by the waterfall for last, and just hearing the words leave my mouth scares me. It has been so long since my mother has been this connected to my life.

"Oh *kookalka*," she says, calling me her little doll, something she hasn't done in years. "Your first kiss." Her voice breaks. "I'm sorry you couldn't tell me sooner."

I bury my face in that familiar spot on her shoulder. "I'm telling you now."

"Thank you," she says and gives my shoulder a squeeze. "I wouldn't worry about today's practice either. You'd be surprised at what men find adorable."

I want to talk more about Holly, but that's hard to do

without giving revealing details of the make-out sessions with Keith, something I don't want to discuss.

Mom kisses the top of my forehead and, her mom-radar kicking in, changes the subject to the carousel again.

"What do you think of them?" she asks, pointing to an elderly couple in a blue and gold carriage.

The woman's hair is white and wavy and looks like it's recently been styled. She's wearing a pink blouse and gray skirt. Her husband (I think) is wearing a brown cap that matches his brown jacket. I don't think they're going to or coming from anywhere fancy. It's just this classy way older people have of dressing up wherever they go.

"Oh, their story is a good one," I say. "They've been married since the 1940s, and he actually proposed right before he went to war. Only she said no. She's younger than him, and she just wasn't ready. No one understood it—a girl of nineteen not wanting to get married. But he got it. That's what drew him to her. This independence she had, not wishing to conform to what others wanted. She wrote him while he was in the service, even went on a few dates, but what she didn't let anyone know was that she wanted her army man to come home and ask again. And when he did return a year later, he was happy to see her but he didn't ask. Not right away. See, he wanted to show her his independence too, to show her he could tango with her."

My mother watches me, amused.

"And one day, while they were having a picnic in a field full of lilac trees," I continue, "he got down on one knee. They were married two weeks later. And every year on the anniversary of the proposal, they go on the carousel because that's what they did on their first date."

"You're quite the dreamer, Alyssa," my mom says affectionately. "Reminds me of how I was at your age." She's wistful now and has that look adults get when thinking back to the "good old days." I wonder whether she's thinking about when she was in school or more recent times, when we both chased our dreams.

I'm hungry and glance toward the pretzel samples. Same girl. Same sour look. An office type is waiting in line for a sample. Her hair is pulled back in a tight bun and her lips are pursed. Her pencil skirt leaves little room for the stick that is obviously up her butt. I bet sample girl is hoping for a quick death if she ever ends up like stick-in-ass professional.

"Check her out," I say, jutting my chin in the pretzel direction. "Uptight much?"

My mother inhales sharply and goes pale.

I put my hand on her arm. "What's wrong? You know her?"

"That's Marian, the editor who hates everything I write." She attempts to compose herself and brings her hand to her hair trying to smooth it out, probably wishing she had it in a bun too.

"I think I see a stick you can put in your jeans so she won't outdo you," I say, trying to make Mom smile.

Her mouth quivers, but she can't manage to move her lips up to complete the movement.

I squeeze her hand just as Miss Super Efficient notices my mother.

"Julia," she calls in a high falsetto, like my mom is some long-lost friend.

My mother gets up from the bench and leans against its back, I think as much to look casual as to support herself. "Marian, what a surprise!" She attempts to smile again, and it comes out tight-lipped, creating no creases by her eye.

"Decided I've been working too hard and need to treat myself," says Marian. She licks sugary frosting off her finger and then wipes it on her Saks Fifth Avenue shopping bag.

"Yes, we all need a break now and then."

"You always work too hard, Julia. I have frequently said some time off would generate new ideas and foster creativity. So glad you're finally heeding my advice."

I want to slap her, but the best I can do is envision the rod that is already in her butt wedging itself deeper.

My mother blinks a few times and then tries to smile again. I hate that she has to play nice with this bitch who wields too much power. Maybe I need get used to games, as they don't seem to stop no matter how old you are.

"Shouldn't we be going? You have assignments due and that interview with the head of that drug company," I say.

Marian suddenly looks interested. "Oh, is that right? So things are going well for you?" She sounds disappointed.

"Yes, I'm hanging in." My mother's voice is meek, all traces of the woman who picked me up from school gone. Old Alyssa creeps down into my belly, unsure about what is happening.

"Well, you keep at it. Sounds like your work is improving." She licks another finger. "I anticipate your next assignment for me will need less of my green pen. I swear, I thought I'd run out of ink." She laughs a disgustingly strident laugh.

I grit my teeth and am about to tell Marian that my mother's work was never the issue, just her wench of a boss, but my mother squeezes my hand hard.

"Have fun the rest of your day. Nice seeing you again," she says. She moves her hand to her head again, like perfect hair will fix everything.

"Yes, same to you. All the best." Marian walks away, her Saks bag gently hitting her leg, the click-click of her heels echoing with each step.

"Don't listen to her," I say. "She's just jealous."

My mother smiles, not the tight-lipped one but not the one that reaches her eyes either. It's worn, defeated. "Oh, honey, she's editor-in-chief of one of the biggest magazines in our area. There's no reason for her to be jealous."

"Well, she's wrong, you know. You're a great writer. If you weren't, you wouldn't be getting all your assignments."

But my mother is no longer listening. She's walking toward the doors, her shoulders slumped, the familiar pre-drink posture I'd hoped I wouldn't see again.

I jog to her side and rub her arm. She smiles stiffly and rummages in her purse for the paper with 10B Red, getting frustrated when she can't find it. I want to save her the trouble and tell her I remember the number, but I see a tear fall on her purse and know it's not about the paper at all.

FIFTEEN

Glenfair's new *Can the Candy* campaign has forced all schools to go healthy. The high school's answer is to stock up the vending machines with dried fruit and bottled water and revamp the lunch menu. Today's highlight is tofurkey pot pie. Lana spends the lunch period griping about how there is nothing good to eat, and she ignores me when I tell her that she brought this on herself by throwing our food in the trash again—this time, Russian salami sandwiches. Ironically, Ryan, Jake, and Trish are not even in the cafeteria today, so we're eating crap for nothing.

In cross-country, Keith smiles at me, and I give him a (hopefully) blush-free smile back. Then I focus on keeping the imitation turkey down and thinking about what may be waiting on the stove at home. Maybe blintzes with caviar or sour cream. Or maybe my mother made *plov*, spicy rice with bits of meat. I promise my growling stomach that something good awaits, and it stops flipping and rumbling long enough to let me focus on running.

But when I walk into our house the only smell I'm greeted by is stale beer. There's a half-empty bottle in the sink, traces of beer spilled on the floor. Newspaper cut-outs with highlighted paragraphs cover the kitchen table and crumpled-up computer paper forms a trail to the stairs. I think how much better the trail would be if it was made out of food, but I know that after the mall trip it was just a matter of time before we were back to this. My stomach spasms—its response to my broken promise.

Upstairs, I hear my mother at the computer and peek into her office. Her eyes are fixed on the screen, her fingers tapping away. She must have gotten a second wind. There are no bottles here, but when I lean over to kiss her hello, her breath—warm and sour with a hint of coffee—coats my senses.

"Hi," I begin, but she cuts me off by holding a finger in the air.

It hangs there until she finishes her paragraph.

"Sorry about that. I was on a roll," she says, spinning around in her chair. "I just got an assignment to do a write-up about a new vegetarian restaurant, the Veggie Vixen. I've been researching their recipes and you'd be surprised at how tasty they sound. There's even a turkey substitute called tofurkey that customers claim tastes just like the real thing."

I make a mental note to avoid the Veggie Vixen at all costs. "Sounds like a good day," I say.

"Oh, it was. It was." She nods excitedly. "And I'm sorry about the mess downstairs. I'll clean it up as soon as I'm done."

"You're practicing holding your liquor again?" I wish Old Alyssa had never told her anything about my life.

My mother waves her hand dismissively. When she speaks, her voice is soft but firm, like she's speaking to a small child. "I had a beer or two, no big deal. But I was working at the same time and it spilled over my notes. That's why I came back up here. Teaches me to drink and type." She chuckles at her lame joke and her breath hits me again.

"Whatever," I mumble.

Her voice is calm, but her eyes are hard now. "I'm the adult, Alyssa. You just have to trust me and stop questioning everything I do."

"Fine. Do you want me to make dinner?" By this I mean warm up the already prepared food and "accidentally" leave a container or two on the table, ending her ruse.

She glances at her watch, surprised. "After five already? Time flies when you're working hard, huh? Yes, that would be great. How 'bout you make cutlets?"

"Are you forgetting that my culinary skills stop at pasta?"

She takes a deep breath and shakes her head. "I had no time to go to the store today, Alyssa. When I was your age, I had dinner on the table when my mother came home from work. You need to learn to help out around here. There's a green cookbook beside the sink. Open it. I need to finish this article and then have to send ideas in to some editors. Now that I'm busy, I'm counting on you."

I stand behind her, thinking of how I've helped her already, of the kitchen mess she had no intention of cleaning up until she was sober, of the empty food containers I've hidden from my father, of what his face would look like if he came home to no dinner. And then there's my mother's face—the lost, fragile woman from the mall, the one who needs protecting—clouding all the other images.

She doesn't wait for me to respond, just turns back around and continues typing about fake food. How it looks like the real thing on the outside, but inside it's filled with imitation ingredients, mixed and blended and hidden until no one can tell the difference anymore.

SIXTEEN

"Any exciting weekend plans?" asks Keith at practice, stretching my arms behind my back for me.

I wonder if he's just making conversation or if he's finally going to ask me out. But the truth works, either way. "Not much, just sleeping over at my friend Lana's."

"Oh yeah? When's that?" He pulls my arms over my head, letting his finger run down the insides.

My heart jumps. "Tomorrow night."

"Then you two should meet me at the barn."

"The barn?"

"Yeah, you know. Glenfair High's big fall happening? First weekend in October? Upperclassmen only?"

Riiight. The abandoned barn in the woods, ownership unknown, where Glenfair's teens bring a stereo, food, and illegal substances to smoke and imbibe all night. No froshes allowed, but we're sophomores now. I don't know how it could have slipped my mind. Lana's been talking about it for weeks.

"Maybe we'll see you there." I try to sound flirty, pretending like his touch doesn't make it doubly hard to concentrate on what he's saying.

"It's like that, is it? I'll see you if I'm lucky?" We're sitting on the grass now, palm to palm, heel to heel, and I picture his arms around me as we sway on the barn's dance floor.

"If you play your cards right." I'm so cool, cool, cool.

Keith takes his hand off my palm to let it brush the inside of my knee. "Will this help my chances?" he whispers, and I get goose bumps.

Coach blows his whistle and motions for us to line up for practice runs, saving me from saying something mortifying or incoherent.

We run to the track, visions of Keith and me at the barn dancing in my head.

———

"Pick one," Lana says, holding up two shirts, both slutty.

She's already dressed, in a gold, long-sleeved V-neck that hugs her breasts, a denim skirt that stops two inches above her knee, and black platform shoes that lace up at the ankle like ballet slippers. She's waiting for me to do the same.

"They're risqué," she says, growing impatient as I stare at the shirts. "And they make a statement."

"Yeah, and along with the thong you made me wear, the 'statement' is that I'm easy."

Lana rolls her eyes and tosses what she decides is the

less offensive shirt in my direction. It's pink, tight, and buttons down the front. She insists I leave the first three buttons open. The right bra, which Lana also gives me, is supposed to "enhance cleavage," although the word *enhance* implies that there's something to work with. But the snugness of the shirt and the miracle bra, even without the cleavage, showcase my boobs more than normal, and this is good enough for me. Lana frowns. I can see her brain working, trying to figure out what else can be done to make me hotter.

"This is as good as it gets. It's tight and barely covers my belly button." I turn sideways and look in the mirror. Not bad. This Alyssa doesn't look that sweet and innocent. She's more of a catwalk strutter, the spunky girl Keith likes. Her life is more fun than mine.

"Just pull your jeans down a little lower so they rest on your hipbones, and wear these," she says, retrieving a pair of platforms from the back depths of her closet.

The platforms seem to have the effect Lana wants, and she lets out a low whistle. "Seeexy," she says, grabbing my hand. "Keith won't know what hit him."

She twirls us both in front of the mirror and laughs. I laugh too as we dance under each other's arms and cross our hands to spin each other. Soon the room is spinning too, and I'm reminded of how, when we were kids, we'd twirl, twirl, twirl until we collapsed on the floor. Eyes closed, we would see the whole world spinning behind our eyelids and imagine traveling to a magical place. Lana spins me hard, and we fall on the floor as we did years ago.

———————

The barn, twice the size of our high school's gym, has lanterns looped across the walls, the little red and white lights casting a soft glow over the dirt floor. There are CDs playing, a mix of rap and dance music with some pop thrown in. Some people are dancing, grinding against each other, the same moves regardless of the song. Lana squeezes my hand hard as we enter. There are two kegs of cheap beer and a vat of puce-colored punch, and someone is passing out Jell-O jigglers in the shape of pumpkins. Cute. Lana pulls me to the keg and we wait in line for someone to fill our clear plastic cups with beer.

"Designated driver," I say to the shaggy-haired guy behind the keg when he goes to fill my cup.

"Sucks to be you," he says, tossing me a soda. He then tips Lana's cup so it gathers less foam.

"What was that about?" Lana asks as we move away from the keg, stepping over spilled punch.

"I don't feel like drinking," I say, like this is something we do all the time and I'm taking a break for the day.

"Why not? My parents are out, you're staying over. This is perfect." She stretches out the *per* syllable like she's a cat.

"Just not in the mood. Besides, I have enough trouble thinking of clever things to say to Keith when I'm sober. I don't need anything else messing with my brain." I sip my soda, and Lana downs half her beer in one gulp.

"But maybe it will make you more relaxed," she says,

scoping out the barn, already losing interest in convincing me.

I look around too, hoping to see Keith. No such luck. "There's Trish," I say, nudging Lana.

Lana perks up and finishes the rest of her beer. "Time for another." She makes a beeline for the keg, thrusting out her chest and giggling so that the keg boy serves her before the others. She returns with two beers and hands me one. "You don't have to drink, just hold it so we don't look like dorks, okay?"

I take the beer and hold it loosely in my hand, like holding it too tight will burn me.

Lana stares at me, getting annoyed. "Geez, Alyssa. Lighten up."

The thong cuts into my butt, reminding me what I'm wearing. I grip the beer tighter. It seems to go with my new outfit.

"Let's go say hi," Lana says, nodding toward Trish and her usual posse of two. She chugs half of her second beer and pulls me through the sweaty crowd, causing my beer to "fall" on the floor and leave behind a trail of yellow foam.

Trish, Ryan, and Jake, clear cups in hands, are sitting on bales of hay. They scoot over and motion for us to sit down. "Dry night tonight, Alyssa?" Trish asks, eyeing my empty hand.

My designated driver line won't work here, since they know neither of us can drive yet. "Just pacing myself," I say.

"Well, you better catch up, yo," says Ryan, handing

me a pumpkin Jell-O shot. It appears like he's caught up for me three times over.

I stare at the little Jell-O pumpkin.

"Just eat it," says Jake. "You wouldn't be true to your Russian blood if you didn't."

"Here, here," says Lana, grabbing a Jell-O pumpkin. She holds her pumpkin to mine and clinks it, like our families do at all occasions.

"To Russian blood," she says and giggles, swallowing the pumpkin.

I look for Keith, hoping I can find a way out with him, but he's not here. Four pairs of eyes stare at me. Maybe I *am* the freak and everyone else is normal. Maybe I've been making a big deal out of nothing. Isn't this what I've seen many times already, what's part of my mom and Lana's lives, of my dad's life? Maybe I'm the crazy one for trying to escape it. I down the shot and they cheer. And soon there's another in my hands. In their hands too. We do the shots together. More cheering. To Russian blood. To Bondar blood.

It's almost three in the morning and I'm sandwiched between Trish and Ryan, our bodies moving in sync to the pulsating music. Ryan pulls at my hair and then moves his hand down my neck, and Trish pushes harder against me. Beside us, Lana smiles approvingly as she grinds on Jake, her body slithering up and down his. She and Jake move closer to us, connecting their bodies with ours. The red lanterns light up their faces, all smiles and vacantness—like they're all in the same happy place that isn't this barn. Lana and Trish throw their heads from side to side as the musical beats quicken, sweat dripping from their clothes and faces. Do I look like I belong with them, in this world I've never wanted but somehow entered? Does my face look empty too? Ryan's hand moves to my waist, his fingers pressing the small of my back under my shirt. I push his hand away and stumble back, my head feeling fuzzy. Ryan continues dancing, either not noticing or not caring that I'm no longer there. I feel the room rushing toward me and begin to fall, and a hand catches my arm and leads me to a bale of hay.

I'm hoping for Keith, but it's only Keg Boy. "So much for being the DD, huh?" he tsk tsks.

In my head, I'm explaining how we don't live far so driving is not an issue, but all that comes out is, "Walk."

He nods, an expert in understanding drunk talk.

I close my eyes as he sits me down, red spots moving with the music in the room—spinning, spinning, spinning. I think about my fantasy of dancing with Keith, but he must have changed his mind about coming. Then his voice is beside me.

"You're trashed," he says, irritated. He sits down next to me, making the hay move and increasing the queasiness in my stomach.

"I was looking for you. Where have you been?" I rest my head on his shoulder. It helps steady the rest of the room.

"Around. Seemed like you were having plenty of fun dancing without me." He leans away from me but lets my head stay where it is.

Does he really think I came here to dance with *Ryan*— with *anyone* who wasn't him? I want to explain and try to focus despite the throbbing in my head, the feeling of nausea that's getting worse by the second. "No, I was looking for you," I say again, hoping these words alone are enough for him, enough to erase whatever he thinks he saw.

"It doesn't matter. I only came by to check if you had a ride home." He slowly moves my head away from his shoulder and gets up. "Do you?"

I nod, afraid if I open my mouth again it will be to throw up.

"Later," he says, barely looking at me as he crosses the dance floor. To Holly.

She puts her arm around his shoulders and he puts his around her waist. She looks like she's wasted too, but this doesn't seem to bother him. I hear her laugh and Keith smiles, pulling her outside. The music gets louder and Lana and Trish run for the bushes outside, hands over their mouths. The room spins faster and I feel vomit rising in my throat. I can barely move, but I make myself run to the bushes too. It's more dignified than sitting in your own vomit on a bale of hay, watching the boy you like leave with someone who can hold her liquor.

Lana and Trish see me and Trish squeals, "Vomit sisters," and then pukes again. I don't know how long we stay there, all of us on our knees, no one holding back our hair, but when we're done, and my hair reeks of bad mornings with my mother, I put my finger down my throat and try to throw up some more, anything to get rid of this thing that's supposed to be part of my blood.

SEVENTEEN

I finish my laps to applause and look up to see my dad by the fence, fingers in his mouth, ready to let out an ear-piercing whistle. I shake my head vigorously so he won't do it, and he grins.

"You have quite a cheering section," says Keith, coming up behind me and smiling, his first nondetached gesture of the day.

I nod, but I still don't understand what happened at the barn. Did he think I cared more about drinking than finding him? Did he think I wanted Ryan? It seemed like he wasted no time finding a new place for his arms, wrapping them around Holly's waist instead of mine. But if he's not going to explain, then I'm not either.

"Looks like you do too," I say, nodding toward Holly. Her red hair blows around her face as she beckons Keith from the bleachers.

There is ice in my voice, and his expression tells me he notices. "Alyssa," he begins, his voice soft.

We've had all day to talk, but he chose to act busy, hurrying through the hallway barely waving, joining me late for stretches because chatting with Holly was obviously more important. Now I'm the one who's busy. "Later," I say, echoing his words from Saturday night.

"Later," he says, and I'm more interested in seeing my father—who has never seen me run—than wondering if Keith is sad to see me go.

Back when my mother came to my meets and practices, she came alone. My dad's job wasn't flexible like hers was, and I accepted this. After a while, I didn't even hope to see him. That wasn't his role. My mom was my cheerleader, my dad the stereotypical European provider-dad. We would all go on vacations together and he would be there for me, but the little things like school plays, band concerts, and track meets were left to my mom.

"You're good," he says, impressed.

"You had your doubts?" I tease him, trying to make things light, not wanting to say what's hanging between us—that this is new to us, that even though I'd accepted everyone's roles, it didn't mean that I didn't miss him being there. That he, now seeing me as my mother has, is now missing the years gone by that he can't get back.

"Nah, you've got Bondar genes. I would expect nothing less."

You're a Bondar. His standard reply. But there's something more around these words, something familiar. Bondar genes. Expect nothing less. And there's a memory that starts to creep up.

"Of course." I laugh and hand him my gym bag and backpack. "How did you get out of work?"

"The building is going through some electrical issues and the power went out. All the computers and phones are down, so they let us go early."

We head to our car, but I see him glance in Keith's direction and then back at me. His eyes linger a little too long on both of us. He looks as if he's debating the topic. To give fatherly advice or not. He settles on something in the middle.

"Who is that boy you were talking to? Is he Jewish?" he teases.

"Yes, but it's only Keith Michaels. Just another runner." I push away the pang I feel at the truthfulness of these words.

He mulls this over. I can tell that he knows there's more to the story, but he decides to let it go, maybe file it away as a building block for future conversations.

"What about school?" he asks, adopting the no-non-sense persona that rears its head whenever academics and discipline are involved.

"What about it? It's there." I kick a pebble with the toe of my sneaker. Academics aren't what interest me these days. School is just Lana using each class as an opportunity to move up the social ladder and me analyzing the meaning behind Keith's actions while trying to show teachers I'm not a slacker despite my tardiness. That's what school has been about.

My father rolls his eyes. "Such an American response."

"What can I say? I'm an American girl." Inside, I laugh.

"That's not a good thing, in this case. The one thing Russia did right was education. There was always homework, everyone was expected to work hard, there were no choices in classes like they have here. Art elective, ha!" And he's off on his rant.

I tell myself not to get roped into this discussion. Just tell him what he wants to hear. It will be easier this way. "You're right," I say as I open the car door. "It seems like I'm the only one in my class who cares about math."

This appeases him and he nods, smiling. "None of you kids realize the opportunities you have here. You need to take advantage of them."

I think about how much easier it would be to take advantage of things if I got to school on time.

"You're a strong girl, Alyssa."

Bondars are strong, says the memory.

"You shouldn't let, um, other things stand in your way." Like he's reading my mind. His way of saying to suck everything else up. Bondars stay focused.

I say nothing, and the words pull me back to our first home here in America, to an incident I had long forgotten or maybe convinced myself never happened. In this waking dream, I am five. The hallway of our one-bedroom, mouse-infested apartment—the only one we could afford— is dark, but there is a light coming from the kitchen. Or what you would call a kitchen—a small stove and sink, a chipped wooden table with uneven legs we found on the curb, and supermarket crates, covered with blankets, which serve as our chairs. I creep in the dark, my hands feeling the walls for guidance, and stand behind the kitchen entrance, watching and listening. My dad is doing his usual midnight routine of emptying used mousetraps and setting up new ones. There is a vodka bottle on the table. My mother sits at the table, focusing on the drink in her hand, hoping it can erase this new world she stumbled into. This world that my father promised would bring freedom and opportunities but instead taught her which cheese catches rodents best. My father sets up the last mouse trap and sits beside my mother. He pours himself a shot and clinks his glass with my mom's. She pours herself more vodka and stares, not lifting it to meet my dad's raised glass.

"You need to be strong, Jules," he says. "Bondars can handle anything."

My mother laughs bitterly. "I guess that's the problem. I'm only a Bondar by name. I don't have those Bondar genes."

"I thought mine would have rubbed off on you by now." Dad pours himself another shot.

"Not everyone can be strong all the time," she mumbles. "I'm going to bed."

She gets up, stumbling, her leg catching on the chair. She grabs at the table to stop herself from falling and knocks her shot glass off in the process. Sharp glass now coats a section of the floor, and my mother starts to cry but makes no move to pick up the pieces.

"Just go to bed," says my dad quietly. He does another shot and begins to clean up the floor as my mother shuffles out of the kitchen.

I remain in the shadows watching him, looking to see if he's crying too, wanting to tell my mom, "It's okay, you didn't mean to break it. Don't cry." My father's face looks sad, disappointed. At the time, I thought he was sad because my mom was sad. Now I know I misunderstood. He was disappointed because she couldn't deal with our circumstances like he could, because she wasn't strong and focused like Bondars are supposed to be.

My father turns on the radio and I'm back at the car, the air seeming to close in around me. I play with the radio, trying to find a music station, something light to ease the suffocation, the weight I'm expected to carry.

"What are you doing? The news is about to start."

"Sorry. I forgot." I switch the dial back.

The radio launches into its familiar theme music, and my dad's face takes on a serene expression. There will be no more talking about school or anything else going on in my life. I tune out. That's what American girls do.

EIGHTEEN

Another Sunday night. Another party. Another reason to drink.

This time it's for Lana's parents' twentieth anniversary celebration. The room is burgundy, with walls that look like they're made of soft velvet. A champagne waterfall lights up the entrance, where a waiter hands out glasses of the bubbly. At the other end of the room is the band and dance floor, which is where Lana and I are.

A pattern of lights moves in a circle around the floor, courtesy of the disco ball overhead. The music is loud and I feel it pulsing through my body. Beside me, Lana is waving her arms and kicking her legs like the music has really taken over her. Here, it feels like we're both part of the music, rather than escaping in it like in the barn.

The band takes a break and Lana and I make our way to our table, where dish upon dish of steaming food await. It's like a food carousel with a new course coming every fifteen minutes. When we first got here, the table was filled with eight different kinds of salad and cold dishes—marinated mushrooms, deviled eggs, red and black caviar, seafood, and a gelled chicken dish that tastes a lot better than it looks.

While we were dancing, the waiters brought out meat- and veggie-filled pastries, blintzes that you top with caviar, and roasted vegetables. Now they're replacing these with rice dishes, chicken, and lamb. Lana and I quickly fill our plates with the old courses so that we can try those before the eager wait staff removes them. I notice Lana has caviar piled high on her plate.

I look at my parents, sitting two tables away. It's actually their glasses I'm looking at. My father's is filled with vodka, and my mother's looks like it has seltzer water. Maybe this will be all she'll drink today. Lana's parents are at the head table, not watching as Lana pours herself a glass of beer. That's the beauty of Russian restaurants—free-flowing alcohol (vodka, cognac, beer, wine) on all the tables. Any teenager's—or drunk's—dream.

"You know, you'd get major points with Trish's group if you brought them to a place like this," I say, gesturing to Lana's drink.

Lana's eyes light up at the idea, but then she frowns. "Can you imagine what they'll think with all that Russian music playing? Free drinks wouldn't make up for it."

"It'd just add to their Russian-lush image." I glance at my mom again. Now her glass is filled with cognac. "But if you want to hang out with them, they'll have to deal eventually, won't they?"

Lana sighs. "Alyssa, you really don't know what you're talking about."

My father is drinking a beer and my mother does a shot of vodka. It seems I don't understand anything these days.

The music starts up again and everyone goes back on the dance floor. I grab Lana's hand and we make our way toward the disco lights. Here Lana can be the Lana I like best, the one closest to the *real* Lana of the many people she's trying to be.

The band gets into a rendition of "Hava Nagila," the classic Jewish tune played at weddings, bar and bat mitzvahs, and now anniversary parties. We all link hands and dance the hora in a circle, moving our feet in a criss-cross pattern across the floor. Then I feel Lana's and my hands separate and a firm grip clasp my fingers. My father is beside me now, one hand holding mine, the other holding my mother's—she's a bit unsteady but doing her best to keep up with the moving bodies around her. I move my feet quickly, matching the cadence. It's a Russian-Jewish *Lord of the Dance*.

Lana's parents are lifted on chairs and given a napkin to hold between them, which represents their bond. Everyone cheers, claps, and stomps their feet. It reminds me of my bat mitzvah, where my parents and I were lifted on chairs. I remember my father and mother tearing up about how all this is possible in America, about how no one has to mask his identity. I remember some kids from school saying after they got their invites, "Wait, you're Jewish too?

I thought you were Russian." I remember trying to explain and them just waving me off. "Whatever. We don't need a life story. It's a party."

Lana looks my way and smiles, and in this moment I feel she gets me. I also know she'll go back to hiding our lunches and who we are once we're in school, and I wonder why it has to be like that.

Beside me, my mother is leaning on my dad, and other tipsy husbands and wives are leaning on whatever will hold their weight. No one thinks this is weird. A part of me thinks that maybe it isn't. I remember the barn night, me barely holding myself up, Lana and Trish giving in to the sickness, finding it all funny, a bonding moment. When is it not normal? Does it just depend on whether you can hold your liquor? Are my mother and I simply broken?

The music finally stops and people stumble back to the tables for more hot dishes, toasts, and vodka. I wonder if any other kids will be cleaning up their mother's vomit tonight.

"Your parents look like they're having a great time," Lana says, winded.

"Yeah, everyone is," I say, catching my breath too.

Someone gets up to the mic to make a toast to the happy couple. When they finish, everyone drinks, taps on their glasses, and yells "*Gorko!*"—bitter—so that Lana's parents will kiss. To replace the bitterness with the love and sweetness of a kiss.

Lana clinks her glass, now filled with water, with mine

and makes her own toast. "To getting the guys we want, and, um…"

"And to friends," I say.

Lana giggles and doesn't let me drink until she adds, "And to Russian parties."

My mother's head is now resting on the table. So is Lana's mom's and other guests' as well. Lana looks at our mothers, then around the restaurant, and laughs again. "And to good times."

I raise my glass and clink it with hers, making a mental note to ask her for a ride to school before the night is over. To Russian parties, to Monday hangovers. "To good times."

NINETEEN

One Day in the Life of Ivan Denisovich—the story of a man's imprisonment in the Gulag—is Ms. H's version of a good time. She looks excited, but I know nothing good will come of today's class. Ms. H focuses on the historical background first. She wants to make the Russian world come alive for us—show us photographs of the Kremlin and Red Square, teach us about Russian culture. I wonder if she forgot that the book highlights prison life. Her face lights up as she passes around shiny, hardcover books and photocopied pictures of Russian events and people. I slouch down in my seat and think myself invisible. Eventually she'll turn to Lana and me. They always do this. Go to their resident Russian experts. Too bad my dad wasn't told about today's class. He would have loved to tell everyone how grateful they should feel to be living here.

She starts a PowerPoint slide show. A woman in a kerchief appears on the white screen. Then two men in those furry hats that go over the ears—hats my parents still have, tucked away in a bag of mothballs, but no longer wear. The men are playing chess in a park. A slide of a long line of people waiting for bread.

"It is not like this anymore," says Ms. H. "But it's important to understand the climate of the world we will read about."

Nobody cares if it isn't like this now. It's just more ammunition for them to use. I feel Ms. H's eyes on Lana and me. Lana is not riding low in her seat, but her face is stone. Just daring Ms. H to ask her something. Beside her chair, away from anyone's view but mine, she rubs her thumb across her fingernails and takes a deep breath. She disguises the breath in a yawn. Her binder "accidentally" crashes to the floor and Ms. H jumps at the sound. She will not ask Lana anything and her eyes move to me. My invisibility spell obviously didn't work.

"Ms. Bondar, can you tell us more about these pictures?" she asks, her face eager.

"I don't remember anything," I mumble.

"Oh, come now. Something must stand out," she says, still smiling.

"I came here when I was four. I don't know." I look down at my desk.

Her voice tenses. The class is not going according to plan. How perfect it would be if she had a speaker to spice up the lesson. I picture her plan book—*show slides, begin discussion about people of former Soviet Union, have Lana or Alyssa give speech while I put my feet up and pat myself on the back for such a creative lesson.*

"Well," she says, trying to make her voice sound light. Instead, it comes out almost squeaky. "Maybe your parents spoke to you about these things. Did they talk to you about waiting in line for food? Or maybe the Kremlin? Even at four that would have been memorable."

I would feel sorry for her if I didn't hate her so much at this moment. Everyone is looking at me. They're no longer bored, because my fidgeting is amusing to them. "Were your parents part of the Communist Party, Alyssa?" someone calls out, and the class snickers. "Did they dress you in red?" I'll have to thank the history department for the recent lessons on McCarthyism—they obviously got the point across.

Ms. H doesn't even tell anyone to be quiet. She thinks their taunts are enthusiasm. I look over at Lana, and her face is still stone. She doesn't turn to me, but I see her clench her fist. I think of these last few days—Keith and I exchanging polite waves as he and Holly walk past my locker; our silent stretching routines, hands always behaving; the messy kitchen probably awaiting me; my mother's liquored breath near my face; my father leaving my passed-out mother on our couch after Lana's parents' party, me eventually walking her to bed, putting on her nightgown, tucking her in while my father snores. I really don't need this right now. I think about what Lana would do.

"There *is* something my parents told me. I remember now," I say sweetly.

Ms. H beams. "Yes?"

"Yeah. The toilet paper was rough, like sandpaper. Did a number on your ass."

————

Lana is still talking about English class when lunchtime rolls around. "That was just awesome," she says. "Totally worth that detention."

The high of being a bad seed has worn off and I'm thinking about the extra laps I'll have to run for being late to cross-country practice.

"Yeah, I guess," I say, taking a bite of my peanut butter and jelly sandwich. How much more American can you get?

Lana looks around, dips her whole-wheat soft pretzel into organic honey mustard sauce, and takes a small bite. She chews carefully, her lips forming a little bow as she bites.

"They're not even here," I say. "Just eat."

She scowls at me but doesn't bother to deny that all her actions revolve around Jake, Trish, and Ryan.

"You know," she says, after swallowing and making sure there's nothing in her teeth, "you should do stuff like that more often. Ms. H is a stupid bitch and needs to lay off."

For a moment, Lana forgets to be cute and viciously bites her pretzel. I bet she's pretending it's Ms. H's head. I say nothing and focus on my sandwich.

"I even heard Ryan and Jake talking about what you said," she says, perking up.

I snort. "Oh really? Ryan *and* Jake? Will they be my friends now?"

"Shut up," she hisses, tilting her chin slightly like it's a pointer. Ryan is walking toward us, and the peanut butter in my mouth feels stickier than usual.

Lana quickly looks over at my lunch, no doubt to make sure there's nothing Russian there. I can't help but think about our full plates at Lana's parents' anniversary party and how she was so free and happy there.

"Yo, wassup?" says Ryan, grabbing a multigrain chocolate chip cookie from Lana's lunch tray.

"Not much, *homeboy*," Lana says, making a half-hearted effort to get the cookie back. Not like she would eat it in front of him anyway.

"You making fun of me, girl?" he says, mid-chew, getting crumbs all over his shirt.

"Oh no. That would be too easy." Lana bats her eyelashes and lightly touches Ryan's arm.

"Snap," he says. "You're harsh. Jake told me to watch out for you."

Lana scans the cafeteria and tries to sound casual when she speaks again. "He did, huh? Where is Jake anyway?"

Ryan's eyes dim for a second, but he quickly recovers. "Loser had to make up a math test. But he wanted me to give you guys something."

I look at him at this acknowledgement. Suddenly I'm being spoken to, I'm part of "you guys." I know Lana expects me to say something back, but I wouldn't exactly call his words an invitation. At least Jake has enough social skills to look at both Lana and me when he talks. I give Ryan a nod—just like he does when he sees me in the halls.

"Oh yeah? What's that?" Lana wipes her hands, now sweaty, on her jeans while Ryan turns around to rummage through his binder for our "gift."

"Something to make you feel at home," he says, one hand behind his back.

"All right already, give it," says Lana.

"Shop teacher says it's the good kind." He places a piece of sandpaper in Lana's hand.

"You're such an ass," Lana says, laughing.

"No, that's what you use it for." Ryan laughs too.

The bell rings and Lana clutches the sandpaper like it's a prize.

"Be sure to share with Alyssa," says Ryan as he walks away.

"What a jerk," I say as we gather our books.

Lana just smiles and puts the sandpaper in her folder.

TWENTY

It's ten o'clock, the news is on, and it's only a matter of minutes before my dad tries to "educate" Mom and me about the state of world affairs.

But my mother has already escaped. I see her on the porch, an almost empty wine bottle at her feet. She looks at the stars and takes a swig. A finger rises to the sky and she traces a pattern, like I do in my room. What shapes calm her? What answers lie in the twinkling darkness? As if in reply, her finger moves to the left corner of the sky, and she traces back and forth, thinning the blackness.

Bombs go off on the TV set in the living room and I start to wash the pile of dishes in the kitchen sink. There is no dishwasher to help me with the bits of now hardened and crusty food because my parents feel that old-fashioned scrubbing builds character.

"You gotta listen to this, Julia," my father shouts from the living room.

"It's just me, Dad."

A pause, then, "Well, you can benefit from this too, Alyssa. See what's happening outside our country. Animals, that's what they are. Pure animals."

I've seen it before. We get the paper. Children killed in Israeli cafés, people killed on buses. Whatever I miss, my father tells us about at dinner—a topic that doesn't need to be shushed.

"I have to clean the kitchen." The water runs hot now and pushes the bits of food aside. Soon they're swimming in white, soapy suds.

"Where's your mother?"

"Outside," I say as the water turns my hands red. I like how the color contrasts with the soap.

He mumbles something—maybe "animals" again—and turns up the volume. Now neither my mother nor I can avoid the explosions. I watch her through the kitchen window. Her body is limp, her head resting on the porch chair. The wine bottle is now empty, and she's safe from the noise.

The news anchor gives the daily death toll and there is screaming in the background. As the news team fades out and the anchors move on to sports coverage, my father lowers the volume. I scrub the floor, the sounds of bombs still in my head.

———

In bed, I breathe in the silence. Above me, the stars and shapes twinkle, but I can't unwind. I close my eyes and pretend I'm at cross-country practice, running through the streets of Glenfair, my dad cheering me on instead of yelling at the television. I take deep breaths and soon my body is separated from my feet. They move on their own—under tunnels, past moving trains, over puddles. I pick up speed and there's no one else around me. The light wind blows through my hair and over my cheeks and it's as if my shoes have wings, like Hermes. I feel my body relax and breathe deeper. And then the air changes. The wind carries with it the smell of wine, a Kryptonite to my wings. I crash.

"Are you awake, *kookalka*?" my mother whispers.

From downstairs, I hear news anchors discussing Israel again, which means my father has switched the channel. Most likely to Fox News. I say nothing and focus on my breathing.

"Remember when we used to exchange good and bad thoughts?" she slurs, getting into bed beside me. "It's been so long, hasn't it?"

The smell of booze clings to my pajamas and I can't make it go away.

"I'll start," she says. "The editor didn't like the tone of my restaurant review. She said it was too 'conversational.' What does that even mean? That's how they're supposed to be written. It's all such bullshit."

"Maybe she can give you ideas on how to change it," I say.

But this—offering suggestions—was never part of the game. Just say your worries, then say something good so the bad doesn't linger, then move on.

She moans. "Noooo. It's not easy like that. How do I fix it?"

"You used to do it all the time, remember?" I turn to her and she lays her head on my arm, like I used to do to her when I had trouble falling asleep.

"You say something," she mumbles.

How will you apologize tomorrow? With cinnamon rolls or pilmeni?

"I had a rough day at school today." But she's already passed out.

I gently pull my arm from under her head and move to the far end of the bed, as close to the wall as possible. I close my eyes again and try to imagine myself running, flying through the air, but the thoughts don't come. My mother snores beside me and I remember how I used to love her lilac scent, now gone. I feel myself drifting off.

Then I remember that we never finished the game. There are now two bad things floating around, with nothing good to counteract them.

TWENTY-ONE

Yom Kippur makes good Jews out of all of us. This day of repentance allows you to screw up all year, go to synagogue for a day, fast until nightfall, and then breathe easy as all is forgiven.

This year I decide that I'm going to really focus on the prayers and food deprivation. Maybe if I suffer some, God will decide to fix the mess that is my family.

According to the rabbi's morning sermon, if God can pardon us, we should be able to extend that same olive branch to our fellow man. I look at my parents, slumped in their cushioned seats. My father's jaw is set in a firm line and it doesn't look like he's ready to offer any branches. Is he thinking about my mom? About his job? I know he gets frustrated whenever he has to take a day off because he says there's double the work when he returns. You would think he would be thankful for this opportunity to pray, since Jewish worship wasn't allowed in Russia, but his gratitude must only extend to news networks. Or maybe he's just bothered he has to spend a whole day away from the office, which makes it harder to pretend everything in his house is normal. Makes it harder not to "let other things stand in the way."

My mother is bouncing her knees up and down, kind of like she did when I was little and sat on her lap. She'd sing this song about a bunny hopping through the forest—the bunny always found some hole he'd fall into. At that point, my mom would open her legs so I could fall down too. We'd both laugh. I loved that game.

Now she's bouncing her knees and wringing her hands because she hasn't had a drink yet today. I'm actually surprised she's even able to do this, but she's a stickler for holiday rules. I wonder why she can do it for God and not for us. She closes her eyes and rocks back and forth like some people do when they're praying. Is she asking for forgiveness for our thought exchange, for forcing me to be the mom?

I take her shaking hand and squeeze it. She jumps, like she's forgotten I am here.

"Are you okay?" I whisper.

It doesn't really matter if I whisper because we've been sitting here for three hours and everyone is getting restless. In front of me, two sisters are tickling each other and their parents are too tired to stop them. The rabbi clears his throat and gives them a stern look; they ignore him.

"Just very tired, and I'm nauseous and have a headache," she says.

I want to say, "How about some vodka? That'll clear

those symptoms right up." But I don't. Instead, I let her lean her head on my shoulder.

My stomach growls and I try not to think about what we're having for dinner. My mom's head feels heavy on my shoulder, and maybe it's the lack of food, but I need air. When we were kids, Lana and I would take our breaks together and play hopscotch in the temple playground outside. But then her grandparents got older and it was hard for them to make the trip to Jersey from Brooklyn. So Lana and her parents started going to services in New York to be with them, leaving me alone.

"I have to go to the bathroom," I say to my dad, and make my escape.

In the lobby, I hear a familiar voice behind me. "Hey," says Keith. "You couldn't take it anymore either, huh?"

With my thoughts focused on praying and making pacts with God, I'd pushed the possibility of seeing Keith out of my head. He loosens his tie and rolls up the sleeves of his jacket.

"Man, it's hot in here. You wanna head out?" he asks eagerly, and I wonder if it's the prospect of us finally talking about things that he's excited about or just getting out of the stuffy synagogue.

They're about to start the Yitzkor—the prayer service for the dead—and I don't have to be inside because both my parents are alive. Works out well.

"Sure." My voice sounds a little too willing.

Outside, I try to walk in front of Keith so I can organize my thoughts rather than wonder if his touches are accidental.

"Slow down. We're not racing." He gently pulls me back.

"Sorry." Already I feel tingles, his touch affecting me even though I wish it wouldn't.

He sits on a bus stop bench and leans his head against the ad behind us—a guy and girl wet from the beach, hugging each other and laughing. *Purchase Your Daydreams* it says, in fancy writing across the two of them. I like it until I see it's an advertisement for tequila. Keith glances at it and snorts.

"Bullshit," he mumbles.

I don't know if he's thinking what I am—that alcohol is not something that makes your fantasies come true—or if he means that the ad is stupidly sappy. Either way, the scene makes me think of the barn, and I get tense.

It's warm for mid-October, but in my short-sleeved dress I start to shiver. He drapes his jacket around my shoulders without me asking, and the gesture helps erase some of the awkwardness of the last few weeks.

"Thanks," I say. I put my hands through the sleeves, and the warmth he left there strokes my bare arms.

"No problem." He moves closer to me.

"We should talk, right?" It's easy to be brave when there's nothing to lose.

He fidgets with his tie. "I was an ass. I'm sorry."

I wasn't expecting that. Nice. "Me too. I really did look for you, you know."

"I'll take your word for it, but really, you don't owe me an explanation. We weren't even exclusive or anything."

This bothers me, him not being possessive at all, like he's okay with us doing whatever. With whoever. But I stay calm. It's better to just talk this through, get an answer, be done with the games. "And you don't want to be?"

He answers quickly, which lets me know he's thought about this too. "I don't know what I want." Obviously, he hasn't thought about it enough.

"Holly?" I offer, my voice too saccharine.

He waves his hand dismissively. "She's not my type. I'm not into the party girl." He looks apologetic. "No offense."

I stare at him like he's crazy. "You think I'm a party girl?"

"I get it, you're only a sophomore. I can see why that scene would be fun. I'm just not into that."

Now he's being annoying. "It. Was. One. Night," I say slowly. "And anyway, if you're 'not into that,' why were you all over Holly?"

"I was helping her to my car," he says. But there's something else in his face, something that makes me think he's not being completely honest. He must have done or said *something* that made Holly think she was wanted at our practices.

I look at my watch. We should be getting back. I return his jacket and get up. "I'll see you at practice," I say. Our stretching exercises—endless and torturous movements— loom before me.

"Alyssa, wait." He doesn't look at me, and I can tell

he's struggling. "This isn't really about you," he finally says, letting his eyes meet mine.

I roll my eyes. "Seriously? The it's-not-you-it's-me speech?" Isn't it bad enough I'll have to feel his touch every day? Why is he dragging this out?

He shakes his head. "I've been in relationships like that before and watching you that night gave me flashbacks. I freaked. Sorry."

That's what this has been about? His exes? I sit down next to him again. "I'm sorry about whatever those other girls did, but that's not me."

He searches my face, like he's still deciding whether to believe me. He nods, like he's finally figured something out. "So can you dress like that again for me sometime?" There's his familiar teasing smile.

Damn Lana and her skanky clothes. "Nah, I usually like my underwear to stay *inside* my clothes."

"Terrible," he says with a fake grimace.

"Yep. You should have had your way with me when you had the chance." I offer him my hand and we pull each other up.

I look at the happy couple on the billboard and I'm drawn into my own happy place of Keith and me, the perfect couple.

Keith gives me back the jacket, playing perfectly into my fantasies. "Just wear it until we get inside."

We walk back in silence, letting our minds wander. The fact of Holly still nags at my thoughts, and I know there's more we should still talk about, but I hope it will be easy to fall back to our old routine. I liked the consistency of our locker kisses, of our flirting fingers during stretches, of our grinding in his car. It feels good to know that I'll have things to measure my days by again, something constant besides my mother's drunkenness. In the back of my mind I still hear his words about not knowing what he wants, but I leave them there to collect dust.

We stop a few feet in front of the synagogue and Keith pulls me in for a kiss. His peppermint breath is like smelling salts and our lips fit together just like they used to. My stomach does its familiar flip. I ignore my promise to focus only on fasting this year as we kiss and kiss, lost in our own daydreams.

———

Past Yom Kippur fasts have always ended with pizza, but today my father opts for a microwave dinner. My mother rewards herself with a mixed drink—a glass of vodka with just enough cranberry juice to make the liquid a light pink.

I know the answer to my question, but I ask anyway. "No pizza tonight?"

"Why don't you fix yourself a sandwich, and you and I will go out for pizza some other night?" says my dad. He looks tired. Again.

"You want to watch a movie?" I ask.

We have so many recorded, and I remember when we had weekend movie nights. I'd make the popcorn with extra salt and butter for my dad, extra salt and no butter for my mom and me. We'd dim the lights, turn on the sur-round sound, and get extra pillows so the seats would be soft, just like in a real theater. If it was a movie we'd seen dozens of times, we'd take turns shouting lines at the screen. We haven't done that since summer.

"Sure. I'll pick one we haven't seen yet." My father must remember too.

"Do you want to watch with us?" I ask my mom. "I'm making popcorn just the way we like it."

The "we" makes me sad.

In the living room, my father lowers the television vol-ume in anticipation of her answer.

"Not tonight," she says, pouring herself another vodka-cranberry mix.

The television blares, louder than before. This is how I know my dad disapproves. Retreat to another world, and this one will fix itself or go away.

Standing in the kitchen doorway, my mother closes her eyes and sways back and forth just like she did in tem-ple. Is she making her own pacts with God? Is she hoping for His forgiveness? For ours?

TWENTY-TWO

On Sunday I wake up to the smell of *blinchiki*, Russian pancakes, instead of my dad's usual omelets. This is my mom's way of apologizing to both of us for last night. She must have gotten up early to have them ready before my dad left for work. His new project has him working Saturdays again, and he has to make up for yesterday's lost hours. Not that he minds.

"Good morning, *kookalka*," she says, wiping batter from her eyebrow with one arm and pulling me in for a hug with the other. I cringe at the greeting, remembering the last time she used it, but allow her arm to warm my shoulders and comfort *me* for a change.

"Making *blinchiki* from scratch," I say, pointing at the messy mixing bowls and flour-covered floor. "I'm impressed."

She smiles and sets a plate of hot pancakes beside the container of sour cream on the kitchen table. "We have a lot to talk about." It seems lately I have been a magnet for uncomfortable conversations.

We sit down and I spear a pancake onto my plate. I smother the thin dough with sour cream. Mom looks at me expectantly, and I pop a piece of the pastry into my mouth so I won't have to talk first. I know what's coming.

"These are great," I say, my mouth full.

"This will be just one of the changes around here." She looks into my eyes.

I look at my pancakes and dip another piece in the sour cream and sugar mixture I created.

"Things have not been right here. You should not be the one cleaning and taking care of things, of me."

Out of the corner of my eye, I see her try to gaze into my eyes like she can control my thoughts. I know everything she's telling me. I don't need to be convinced that my family is all wrong.

"Alyssa, please." She gently lifts my chin so I'll look into her moist eyes. Batter is splattered in her hair and sticking to her cheeks.

I put down my fork and stare, as if by staring hard enough my energy will become a part of her in the same way she wants hers to infect me.

"What's different this time?"

Her eyes light up, like she's been waiting for this question. "Well, there I was yesterday asking God for forgiveness, telling him I will change. And then I get home and tell myself it will only be one drink, the last one. But there I was passed out again. And when your dad told me this morning you did the movie night, I just—"

Her voice cracks and more tears fall, making the batter

on her cheeks pasty. I reach over and take her hand. She squeezes mine and shuts her eyes. Thirty seconds later her eyes snap open, and she lets go of my hand and stands with such force and decisiveness that I think my strength may have really shifted into her body.

"Enough of this feeling sorry for myself. It's all in my head. I was in control of the drinking before, and I can be again."

Our first apartment flashes in my head again. My mother crying. Drops of spilled alcohol on the floor. That's the worst I remember. How did she snap back and regain that infamous Bondar strength? I don't bring this up. They must think I don't remember. And, maybe, I'm remembering it all wrong. Maybe it never happened like that. Maybe my mind is just playing tricks on me, trying to help make sense of my life today.

She moves over to the sink and begins washing the dishes, like this is the first step. She isn't looking to me for reassurance anymore. And when she whispers, "Things are going to change," I know it's not me she's trying to convince.

TWENTY-THREE

It rains on Monday. Drizzle first, little droplets into puddles, enough to make Lana worry about her hair. By practice time the drops double in speed, falling on me like firm fingers kneading my legs and back, alternating with Keith's hands. When our run ends, he offers me a ride home but I refuse, choosing the rain, enjoying the weightless feeling that comes with splashing in puddles. Despite my mother's promises, I'm never certain what I'm coming home to.

"Poor girl!" my mother says when I walk into the kitchen, the floor already covered with towels in anticipation of my soaked sneakers. "I have tea waiting for you and dry clothes warming on the radiator for when you get out of the shower."

"Thanks," I say, a lump forming in my throat.

Back when we did the thought exchange, we also did the radiator thing. Before bed, my mom would warm my pajamas so they would feel all cozy. Sometimes I'd surprise her by putting her nightclothes on the radiator too. My dad refused to warm his clothes. Real men tough it out, he had said. He did a stint in Siberia while serving in the Russian army; he surely could survive untoasted pajamas.

———————

After my shower, my mother and I sit across from each other at the kitchen table. She's wearing a red velour sweat-suit, her hair tied back with a red ribbon. Her lipstick, a shade of reddish brown, makes her appear even more put-together. She pours tea into our cups and we add milk and sugar like proper British women. She's waiting for me to talk, but somehow the scene feels all wrong, like someone decided to stage a play with horribly miscast actors.

I search for the comfort zone. "How did work go today?"

Her face brightens. "Fantastic," she gushes. "I rewrote the Veggie Vixen article and the editor just loved it. Loved it! They want me to review three more new businesses. There's also a new women's magazine that contacted me about guest editing and being a regular health columnist. And the stick-in-the-ass editor only put two green marks on my last piece."

"That's wonderful, Mom. Really great!" I say, gathering all my enthusiasm.

"Oh, and I meant to ask you—do you mind staying home alone tonight? Your father and I have a date." She blushes.

I laugh. "I'm fifteen. I think I can manage a few hours on my own."

"I knew I could count on you." Her eyes get dreamy and she fingers the fringe on our place mats. "It's been so long since the two of us did something romantic together."

Our own little version of the perfect family. "I'm sure it will be great." The beginning of hope starts in my stomach, but I'm afraid to let it grow.

"I can understand if you're worried, but you'll see." The dreamy look is still in her eyes, and I want to believe, for her, in her. "Things will be different. I can get the drinking under control, like I told you."

"You're doing this yourself, though? You don't want to join AA or something?" I split a piece of fringe on my place mat.

"Your father and I talked about that. We both agreed I can do this on my own. Why get the whole community involved? Anyway, AA is for people with a real drinking problem—the ones stumbling around for all to see. This is just between us."

I wonder how long she practiced this speech.

"You know what confirmed it for me? This morning, before the recyclables pick-up, nosy Mrs. Stein came across the street and actually pretended like she had something to ask me. But you know what? That was just an excuse to look at our garbage can and see what was in it. I could tell from the way she kept peering around our lawn. Lost dog—yeah right. So imagine if she had confirmation that something was going on. We didn't move here to stand out like that, to have people say, 'Oh, those drunk Russians.'"

I push my tea away and fold my hands in front of me. "So you're not going to AA because of Mrs. Stein?"

My mother waves her hand in the air like I'm talking nonsense. "No, Alyssa. I think you know exactly what I'm saying. It's not Mrs. Stein per se. She's just an example. Do you need people talking about what's going on in our house?"

The image of our street holding a block party to discuss what's in our recycling bin is laughable, but this is how my parents think. When I was eleven, I wanted a breakfast cereal which was never on sale but I'd noticed my mom had a coupon for it. I was pretty excited and said, kind of loudly, "Mom, can we get it? You have a coupon and everything!" She put the cereal in our cart but quickly walked me to another aisle. Then she leaned over and hissed, "What's wrong with you? You want people to think we don't have enough money to buy you the cereal you want?"

I think of Lana trying to fit in with Trish, Jake, and Ryan, how I tried too but ended up in the bushes. "It shouldn't be about what other people think," I say. Unless those people are me and my father.

"You'll understand when you're older, Alyssa." She waves her hand again. "Enough of this 'me' talk. Tell me about your boy—Keith, right? Anything new?" Her voice becomes low, like we're kids at a slumber party about to swap secrets.

I stir more sugar into my tea and watch it sink to the bottom, grain by grain.

I feel Old Alyssa push at me, but she's not getting her

way this time. I'm not ready yet to let my mother in again. The phone rings, ending what little was left of the spell the tea and warm clothes had created. My mother looks at me and waits, and the phone rings again.

"You can get it. I have homework to do anyway."

"We'll talk more later?" Her hand is already on the receiver.

I nod yes, then wave good-bye and head upstairs.

In my room, I look out the window at Mrs. Stein's house. She's roaming the streets with an empty collar, calling her dog's name. No doubt a conspiracy to spy on us.

TWENTY-FOUR

"What do you think of this?" Lana asks, holding up leopard-print material.

It's a week before Halloween—one week of my mom's sobriety—and we're at the mall looking for costumes and accessories. This is the first year our school is letting underclassmen dress up. A sure way to increase school spirit, or so say the class presidents.

"What is it?" The outfit looks pretty skimpy, some version of a leotard with a deep V-neck.

Lana rolls her eyes. "It's for my cat costume. All I have to do is sew a tail to the back and buy one of those headbands with ears, and *voilà*!"

"And you think your parents will let you leave the house with your boobs hanging out?"

"I'll just put a shawl on until I'm out the door," she says, crossing her arms across her chest as an example.

I resist the urge to tell Lana that her "costume" borders on a call girl's outfit. That's probably the point.

She turns to check herself out in the mirror, then looks at me, giving me the once-over.

"You have good legs," she says. "We need to make sure your costume shows them off. Bring that Victoria's Secret Alyssa back."

I sigh. The night at the barn showed me that the wild Alyssa who Lana wants, who I sometimes want, is not really me. What's the point of being someone else if everything is worse when the mask comes off?

"I'm thinking of going as Dorothy," I say. If only I could find real ruby slippers to take me away from here permanently. With Keith, of course.

Lana looks horrified. "You're kidding, right? Our outfits have to be hot, sexy. Dorothy screams lots of things, but *smokin'* is not one of them."

This from the girl who, just two years ago, started crying because the costume shop ran out of Shrek outfits.

"How about a flapper?" That would fit with Glenfair's strict social rules, while its length—short enough to show off my legs—would work with Lana's rules.

"Yeah, that could work. I bet Keith would like it." Lana winks at me. "Assuming you stay sober."

I make a face at her. "I explained that to you."

"Whatever. He acted like a douche. Boohoo, he got hurt. Shit happens. You don't see Trish swearing off seniors just because Matt screwed her over."

She models her costume in front of the mirror, leaning over to check out her butt and boobs. She then licks her lips and blows a kiss to her mirror self.

"If only everyone had your self-esteem," I say, smiling.

"The world would be a much better place." Lana laughs.

We pay for our costumes and head for the food court, Lana still excited about her cat costume.

"So you think I looked hot, right?" she asks, an extra bounce in her step.

"If I weren't so into Keith, I'd do you."

Lana laughs again and it sounds so real, like how I always remember it, not this new giggly one she's been working on. It makes me feel as if things between us are like they used to be. So, of course, this is when Ryan appears beside us.

"Hey, Al. Wassup?" He looks at me for a full second before switching his gaze to Lana. Jake must have given him a few tips on social etiquette.

"Not much, just shoppin'," I say.

"Oh, yeah? What'd you ladies buy?" He glances at our bags.

Lana pulls hers closed. "You'll see on Halloween," she says, and winks.

"Will you dress up as Russian Bond girls?" Ryan asks, hopeful.

He's such an idiot, but I try to smile at him for Lana's benefit. It comes out as a sneer. "In your dreams."

"Why the nasty tone, yo? Jeez, Lana, is she always this uptight?" Ryan asks, running his hand through his hair—a move I'm sure he thinks is cool.

"She just wants to show you that you got us Russkie girls pegged all wrong," Lana says in a throaty voice.

"Is that so?" he says. "Does that mean you girls won't teach me how to get Russian booty?" He leans closer to her, his mouth almost touching her ear, and Lana clenches a fist and runs her thumb over her fingernails at her side where he can't see.

"I don't think you're ready yet," she says, and giggles in a way that sounds like a cross between a girly laugh and a ho laugh.

I am grateful when my food is ready. "I'll see you both later." I pick up my tray and scope out a table.

I glance back at Lana to indicate where I'll be, but she's too busy laughing and playing with her hair to notice. She seems to have already escaped who she is, no costume necessary.

———————

It is already dark when I get home, the only light coming from the living room television. My father is in the room alone, and for once the television is not blaring. I watch him from the doorway. His elbows are on his knees and his head is in his hands. The television is there for the comfort of its familiar buzz, nothing more. He lifts his head but still doesn't see me, and scribbles something on a paper before him. I wonder if it's a Sudoku puzzle. We both love these and compete to see who can finish them the fastest. He appears more relaxed as he scribbles more, so when the television's light shines on his face, I'm surprised to see the worry there. He would not want me to see it, to see him this way.

I knock gently on the living room wall. "Hey. How was your night?"

He quickly sits up and looks around, like the contents of the room might give something away.

"Good, good. Lots of work. You know how it is." He smiles a tired, defeated smile.

I smile back and nod, helping him play his game of pretend. "Where's Mom?"

As his body tenses, my hands get cold. "She had a long day. Went to bed early. That new women's magazine she was excited about looks like it's going to fold. Apparently, no one bothered to tell her."

"At least she still has the reviews she's been working on," I say.

"One was accepted, the other probably not. The magazine wants to go a different way, whatever that means," he says.

His eyes tell me what his mouth does not, and he looks away. Maybe he's trying to protect me the best he can or maybe my eyes hold the same answers and he doesn't want confirmation.

He picks up the papers in front of him and gives me one. In the television's dim light, we race to complete the puzzles, as if by finishing them we can find the answers we seek.

TWENTY-FIVE

I pace. I sit. I sweat through the black cashmere sweater Lana has given me for tonight's date with Keith.

"Look who's finally decided to step it up," she'd said. "Good to see he got over that whatever-it-was." Lana's new theory—*and don't be mad at me, Alyssa*—is that Keith only used the barn night misunderstanding as an excuse to keep things from getting too serious.

"Be nice, please. I'm nervous enough as it is."

"You'll be fine. It's just like your car make-out sessions, only you get free food and a movie out of it. And more clothes off."

"That's supposed to make me feel better?"

Lana had shrugged and winked. "It always works for me."

Ten minutes to go, and I rub my sweaty palms over my denim skirt and push those thoughts out of my head. *Think of running. Think of math. Think of more things you can say to shock Ms. H.* I smile and listen to my mother's drunken typing in the kitchen, my father's loud silence in his downstairs office. If they stay there until I'm out the door, my life will be much easier.

I go over conversation topics in my head. *Cosmo* and Lana suggest I *keep it light, ask him about his favorite things.* Not terrible advice, as we really don't know too much about each other. After Yom Kippur, I looked forward to going back to our routine, but I also hoped things would move forward, that our conversations would evolve from innuendo. But a date is a step in that direction, isn't it?

Five minutes to go, and my mother leans in the doorway, scotch in her hand. Her oily hair is matted to her forehead and she's wearing a housecoat with large yellow and black flowers that looks like something from the seventies—and not in a good retro way.

"When's that boy of yours coming?" she slurs, then stumbles, falling on the recliner chair. "We need to meet him."

I clasp my hands together to stop them from trembling and search for my voice, which has disappeared somewhere in the booze vortex. I shake my head "no."

"It's not a choice, Alyssa. Are you embarrassed by us? After everything we've done for you?"

She slips off the chair and bangs her leg on the hardwood floor. This doesn't stop her from recounting the to-be-thankful list: coming to America, big house, clothes. She forgets to mention the opportunity to be her maid and caretaker.

She picks herself up off the floor, and I see a black-and-blue mark developing on her shin. "Marty!" she calls.

"Marty!" But my father is already in the doorway, a look of pain and disgust on his face.

"Tell her we have to meet this boy of hers. We can't have her running off with whoever doing whatever."

She grabs my father's arm, but he untangles himself and moves her back to the couch, pushing her down.

Is this where he will spout his fatherly advice, thoughts tucked away from when he saw Keith at practice?

"Ungrateful, spoiled girl," my mother mutters.

"Dad," I whimper, tears falling down my cheeks.

I see him struggling with what to say. Is he going to tell me this isn't a big deal, that I need to be stronger? "She's not going out there, okay?" he says, hugging me to him, about to take on the role my mother should have. "But *I* need to meet him." His voice is soft.

I don't protest; this alternative is better than what could have been. I nod and look to see my mother's reaction, but she's passed out on the couch. A car pulls up and the door slams. I cover my mother with a blanket and smooth out her dress—mentally thanking her for blacking out—before heading outside.

———

After my father and Keith do the usual handshake and good-to-meet-you bit, we head to Keith's car where he opens the passenger-side door for me. This must set my dad's mind at ease, because he waves to us and heads back inside the house. I flip down Keith's visor mirror to check out my eyes.

"These allergies," I mutter when I see the puffiness.

The exceptionally low pollen count and the decrease in allergies were the highlight of yesterday's weather forecast, but Keith doesn't question my brilliant statement.

Instead he hands me a tissue and tilts my head up to kiss me. "You look nice," he says.

I swallow twice before speaking to make sure my voice doesn't quiver. "Thanks. You too."

I put my hand on his arm and he squeezes my knee.

"Your dad seems like a good guy," he says. He doesn't turn to look at me when he says this so I figure he's just making conversation.

"He has his moments." I smile.

I think my voice sounds heavy, but he just says, "Don't all parents?"

He seems relaxed, like he didn't worry about what he would say at all. I turn on the radio and try to find something peppy, but all the stations have apparently held a secret meeting and decided to play commercials at the same time. I slump back in my seat.

"Do you like The Cure?" he asks. He takes a CD out of a case that says The Smiths, a band I've never heard of. "I'm one case short, so nine out of ten times the CD won't be in the right case," he explains.

"The Cure's great." The only song I know by them is "Friday I'm in Love," and that's because Lana always plays it when she's depressed. "Even if you're not in love," she says, "it makes you feel like you can be, and that's just awesome." What kind of guy still has CDs? What kind of guy listens to The Cure? I never hear their songs on the radio, and if I had to choose a band that screamed Keith, I'd have picked something more mainstream—to match his striped dress shirt and faded black Tommy Hilfiger jeans.

"What kind of music do you like?" he asks me. He takes his eyes off the road and looks at me.

I don't really know anything about music, so I name a band Lana and I once danced around to. "The Killers."

"Okay, so you're into lyrics. The Cure has some cool wordplay shit going on too. Like this song right here," he says, raising the volume.

The guy sings about the girl's smile, "vanilla smile" he calls it. I think of her melting into him, with him, maybe because of him. I want to make Keith melt.

"That's cool, huh? I mean if you hear the whole song it's better because it tells a story. All their lyrics do," he says, and his voice is excited.

I laugh, and he blushes. "I guess I get into these things," he says and squeezes my knee again as the traffic light in front of us turns red.

"No, that's not why I laughed," I say. "We've just never talked about stuff like this before."

"Really? I think we've talked about some things," he says, slowly moving his hand up my thigh, ignoring the green traffic light.

I turn up the volume on the radio and curse myself for ruining the moment we just had, and Keith makes a left into the movie theater parking lot.

We go to a romantic comedy. One of those flicks where Boy wants Girl but his job, her father, and a hurricane all keep them apart.

Keith and I kiss during previews but stop when the movie comes on. He puts his arm around me when the lights go down and his hand starts at my collarbone. It's resting on my breast by the time the movie ends. It's dark so I don't make him move it. And as Boy and Girl finally get hot and heavy during the last thirty minutes of the movie, all I can think about is kissing Keith again.

"Where to now?" he asks, back in his car.

My house seems far away, and I love the feel of his fingers pressed against my thigh. Would I seem slutty if I asked him to go to his house?

"Wherever you want," I say.

He steps on the gas and goes through a yellow light. "I have more CDs in my room we can listen to, you know, next to my kissing trophies."

He gives me a teasing smile, making his intentions obvious. How easy it is to be a boy.

"Is anyone home?" I'd feel more comfortable if his parents weren't two rooms down listening through their walls.

"Nope," he says and brakes, just in time to avoid running a red light. "Is that okay?"

"Sure." I will the light to change faster.

Keith's room is part typical boy, part indie guy. He has a signed poster of Mike Piazza on one wall and a Giants calendar on another. Beside his bed hang signed album covers of old bands I don't know and a movie poster with a hot actress I don't recognize. Her feathered hair tells me she's from the '80s. And there's the street sign—*Michaels Place*—that the local paper listed as missing a few months back.

His bed is not made and his desk is a mess, and if my mom or dad ever saw this room, they'd think Keith is a bad influence.

Keith puts on music that's so calming I'm afraid I'll fall asleep if I close my eyes. "Bob Marley," he says, and I nod. When Keith says the name, I remember it from Lana's collection. "The pothead's guru," she calls him, but as far as I know she only smoked once last summer.

"You smoke?" I ask. That doesn't fit.

"Nah, but I like his mellowness." Keith tosses two Marley CDs onto the bed. "You should borrow them. Your parents have a CD player, right?"

"That's all they have. They're not into all the latest gadgets." I have always been a little embarrassed about my parents' aversion to all that wasn't necessary.

"Trust me. It's better that way. There's something about holding the case, having something you can touch as a reminder of the music. You can't get that from downloads." He turns off the lights and turns on the black light before lying down beside me.

We stare at the glow-in-the-dark posters on his walls—

fluorescent reds, greens, oranges, and yellows. Bob Marley sings about one love and one heart, and I feel the beats of my heart matching the beats in the song.

"He's good, right?" Keith asks, heat from his breath tickling my ear.

"Relaxing," I say, surprised at how easy it is to be in this moment.

"Do you want a massage?" he asks—guy speak for feeling you up, Lana always says.

"Yeah, thanks." Isn't this why we're here?

I turn over on my stomach and he massages my shoulders, shoulder blades, and back.

"You're really tense." He uses his elbow to take out a mid-back knot.

I guess Marley and Keith can't erase every trace of my house. He lifts my shirt and I focus on the feel of his hands on my skin. *Nice hands*, I remember writing at the retreat.

After five minutes, he whispers, "How was that?" and lies down beside me.

"Good, thanks." I feel his breath on my face, and his lips are inches from mine. I lick my lips with nervousness and anticipation.

"You have really nice lips," he says.

"Tha—" I begin, like an idiot. But he's already kissing me, and doesn't let me finish.

I match my tongue's rhythm to his and run my hands over his shirt and through his hair. I've got these moves down.

"You're so hot," he says, tugging at my sweater. He

undoes the first three buttons and pulls it over my head. Three seconds later his shirt is off too.

He rolls on top of me and starts a kissing trail from my neck to my belly button. He unhooks my bra.

"Is this okay?" he asks, his hands on my breasts.

"Yeah," I say, but I wish it was darker so it wouldn't be so obvious that he's staring at me.

I pull him down so his chest is on mine, and I kiss him. Our tongues link together like they're dancing. Then he shifts positions and somehow I'm on top.

I try to move us back so he'll be in the lead again, but I'm not strong enough. I roll off him and onto my stomach, super self-conscious.

"What's wrong?" he asks, rubbing my back.

I tense up again and feel stupid and immature.

"I don't know what I'm doing," I finally say. Big shock to his system, I'm sure.

"No, you're doing great," he says, pulling the blanket over us before he starts kissing me again.

In the covered darkness, I let him touch me and don't worry about how I look or sound as he kisses my body. It's easy to lose myself here, to just let things happen without wondering about the next steps and what everything means. Soon he's on top of me again, grinding, and this time he doesn't try to flip us.

"God, you're so pretty," he says.

I move my hands over his back and press my fingers into his flesh as I've seen the women do on a *Real Sex* episode

Lana and I watched once. He groans louder and his breath quickens, and then he's lying beside me again.

"You're so amazing," he says, kissing me lightly on the lips.

I rest my head on his shoulder and put my hand on his thigh. His jeans are wet. I guess I wasn't that bad, then.

Keith gives me another kiss, then gets up and takes a pair of jeans with him to the bathroom. They're faded, like the ones he wore at the start of our date, and I see they're not Tommy Hilfiger at all but from a thrift store.

"When do you need to get home?" he asks when he comes back. He's putting on his sneakers. I search for my shirt and bra and slip them on, using his sheets to block me, the confidence and otherworldliness I felt in the darkness now gone.

It's eleven, and my curfew is not until twelve, but Keith looks ready to go. I take the Marley CDs he loaned me. "Now's fine."

———

In the car, he opens the window and lets the chilly air in. We don't speak, but I flip through the stations trying to figure out which songs we would both agree on. He doesn't know I'm playing this game, but when I stop at "Friday I'm in Love"—sometimes I get lucky—he smiles, and I feel we've connected.

"Did you have a good time?" Keith asks when he pulls up to my house.

"Yeah," I say blushing.

"Good, me too." He kisses me. A good-bye kiss. Soft, quick.

I wait for him to say he'll call me later, but he doesn't.

"See you Monday," I say.

"Right." He opens the door for me from the inside.

As he does this, I see my mother open the screen door and step onto our porch. The light above the mailbox accentuates her pale face and the stains on her robe. I freeze and hold on tightly to the door handle to stop my fingers from shaking. *Twelve squared is 144.*

She stumbles down the first step and grabs the railing for balance before sitting on the second step. The tinkle of the ice cubes in her drink breaks the silence of the night. I grip the door handle harder and my breath comes in quick pulses. I see only her, and jump when I feel Keith's fingertips on my arm.

"Are you all right?" he asks.

Thirteen squared is 169. I can't even look at his face. What must he be thinking? *Guess this girl's mom is a partier too.* I untangle my hand from the door and step out of the car in a daze.

"I'll be fine."

"Are you sure?" He turns off the engine and begins to open his own door.

I wake up. "Yeah, it's cool." I keep my voice steady and this time I look at him.

He's tense. Everything from his face muscles to the way his fingers are white on the steering wheel from holding it

161

so hard. He's thinking he didn't sign up for this. A girl with hang-ups who claims she has allergies in October. A mother who stumbles outside with a drink at eleven at night.

He's still waiting, the car in park. I need him to go in case there's a struggle getting her inside. He's seen too much already.

"I'm fine. Really." I try to smile.

He hesitates, his eyes scanning mine, but I've learned to make these plastic too. I close the car door. Finally he gives me a small wave, says he'll call me later, and turns on his engine and drives away.

"Was that your runner boy?" my mother asks. She smells like vodka.

"Yes, that was him." I don't want to say his name because then she might use it. I don't want to hear how it sounds on her lips right now.

"He's handsome, but not much of a gentleman. He didn't even walk you to the door." She sips from her glass.

"Let's go inside," I say.

"I'm fine where I am," she slurs, gripping the railing and leaning her head on it.

Soft, multicolored television glows reflect from the houses around us, and I wonder what the families inside are watching. My mother groans and vomits into our bushes.

"We need to go inside," I say again, extending my hand to her.

Her voice rises. "I'll go when I'm good and ready."

In the house next door, someone closes a window and

turns off the lights. "Do you want our neighbors to come out here?" I ask.

This makes her move. She attempts to get up on her own, with only the railing for help, and almost falls. I take her arm, and this time she lets me lead her inside, the whole time talking about the boys back in her day. How they'd meet the parents and walk their dates to the door, how men these days are different.

I lead her to her bedroom, where she complains about my dad's snoring. I don't tell her that she'll pass out soon enough.

She asks me about my date as I sit beside her and hold her hand. I think about how a little over a week ago, while sipping tea at the kitchen table, I agreed we'd talk later.

"We saw a movie," I say, but luckily she's already asleep.

I stay there a little while longer, having a conversation with the mother in my head. The mother who once told me about her first kiss (atop a Ferris wheel) and couldn't wait to hear the details of mine. I tell her about how soft his lips are and the way my stomach jumps each time he touches me. She asks if he kissed me good night and when our next date will be. I tell her about the drunk stranger who makes my hands shake. I say I think the stranger scared Keith away.

TWENTY-SIX

Instead of focusing on lessons on Monday, I spend the day going over worst-case scenarios, imagining the real reason Keith hasn't called me yet. One: he didn't drive away after our date but stayed parked in the shadows, listening and watching as my drunken mother threw up in the bushes before I dragged her inside the house. Two: he did drive home, but after a good night's sleep decided that he doesn't need extra stress his senior year and is currently planning ways to let me down easy. Three: he realized what was going on with my mom and decided it was too much for him to handle, but, wanting to think of himself as a good guy, contacted the school's Peer Listeners program to help me and it's only a matter of time before some good Samaritan senior calls me down for a heart-to-heart with him and the school social worker. And four: Keith got home and found Holly waiting for him in only a trench coat. Keith gave my mom and me one last thought before being drawn under Holly's spell. In the end, he decided no-strings-attached sex was an easier way to spend senior year.

By the time the three o'clock bell rings, I've added four other depressing scenarios to my list.

"Oh God," says Lana when I meet her at her locker. "Just go talk to him. If he goes off the deep end again about partying—or whatever story he comes up with this time— kick his ass to the curb. Who needs that stress?"

"I guess," I say, hoisting my backpack off the floor and onto my shoulders. It's easy for Lana to be so logical. In the version I told her, my mom—slightly tipsy—had just come home from another party.

She smiles sympathetically. "Your mom is losing her touch, but it will be okay. *Everyone's* seen their parents have one too many." She gives me a quick hug. "Be strong, girl."

I flinch at her choice of words. Is there anything else a Bondar can be?

———

I am tough, I think as I come around the still empty track for lap two. *I can handle everything on my own*, I tell myself as my heart beats faster. Ahead of me the track curves and bends, and I sprint to finish the laps. No pacing, just run, run, run. I increase my speed so my legs no longer feel light and weightless. I pound my feet into the graveled lane, doing everything you're not supposed to do as a long-distance runner. Faster, faster, until I can barely catch my breath, until there is nothing in my head except the sound of sneakers on rocks. I push forward, telling my mind to erase my anger and anxiety, to just be one with the road. Four laps finished, one mile done, and I run faster to complete another lap, not caring that my legs will be shot by the time practice starts. I feel like I can run everything away, like each painful breath out takes with it all worries and each breath I take in brings with it a new calm.

By the time other team members get to the field, I've run two miles and I'm lying on the grass, arms and legs stretched out, staring at the shapes the clouds have made in the sky. I try to focus, to be in my happy zone, to not think about what I'll say to Keith. But now that practice is about to start, my sense of calm and the little wall I created around myself begin to disappear. Voices shout and laugh, and Coach blows his whistle three times.

I sit up in time to see Holly on the bleachers and Keith beside her. She laughs at something he says and touches his arm twice before gathering her books to leave. They hug each other good-bye, and she whispers something in his ear that makes him laugh. My mind flashes to the barn, his arm around her waist; to our conversation on Yom Kippur, where his face let me know he was leaving something out; and all my attempts at composure disappear. I take deep breaths and turn my back so that Keith can't see my face when he makes his way over to stretch.

"How's it going?" he asks, putting his hand on my shoulder.

"Fine." I shrug off his touch.

He sits on the grass so he's facing me, but doesn't

attempt to touch me again. "What's wrong?" he asks, but I get the feeling he doesn't really want to know. Probably because he already does.

I take another deep breath and push my chest to the ground. I feel the same way I did when we started talking on Yom Kippur, just wanting to get done with this conversation. "Busy weekend?"

"Kind of. My buddy Joe's girlfriend broke up with him so we spent all weekend burning shit she gave him and trying to soothe his crying ass." He shakes his head, pretending to look sad. "Poor bastard."

"Lucky for him you're such a good friend," I say sarcastically.

Keith laughs. "It's how guys are. We don't wallow with pints of ice cream or sit by the phone—" He stops. "Shit, I was supposed to call you, right?"

"So I thought." I look up at him. His face reveals nothing devious. He really looks like he was so wrapped up in other things, he just forgot. Am I the one who's acting crazy this time? Getting mad at him for nothing? Thinking he's the one freaking out about my mother when he probably never noticed anything to begin with?

"Let me make it up to you," he says, reaching for my hands and stretching them behind my back. He looks sincere, and I think the fear was all in my head.

I lean into his touch and I want to fix all our misunderstandings, get us back to how we were when our lips first touched and he told me I smelled like vanilla.

"Let's do something on Halloween," he says. His breath tickles my neck.

"Sure," I say, my voice sounding sickeningly light and sweet. "That would be great." I decide Lana was wrong. He wasn't making excuses. He *wants* to be with me.

Keith gives my lips a peck, a kiss so quick I would barely know it happened if I hadn't seen him lean in. Coach blows his whistle and waves his arms, motioning for everyone to meet on the track.

"C'mon," Keith says, already running ahead.

I watch him sprint toward the others, not looking back once to see how far behind him I am.

I drag my aching legs beside the other stragglers and pretend Coach's continued shrill whistles and yells to "move your asses" don't apply to me. In front of me, Keith waves, and I smile, happy that he's thinking of me after all. *You were just making drama where there wasn't any. This is a part of your life that's easy,* I tell myself. Keith waves again, and this time I look behind me and see Holly by the bleachers, waving away.

I make my way to the starting line and position myself as far away from Keith as I can. Coach fires his starter pistol and twenty pairs of legs set off. I'm ahead of them all.

"Pace yourselves, pace yourselves," I hear Coach yell, but I keep running.

"Yo, Alyssa, wait up," Keith yells, but I ignore him.

"Damn it, Bondar! You need to practice pacing. How can you expect to run three miles with a decent time if you sprint?" I can see Coach's red face, but I don't care.

I just keep running and running, pretending I'm alone on the track and that my legs can carry me. It's not that hard. I have gotten good at lying to myself.

TWENTY-SEVEN

Mr. Pinto is supposed to be Indiana Jones, but the whip he keeps snapping a little too happily totally screams S&M.

"Move along, move along, get to homeroom, people," the teachers take turns shouting, actually thinking school work will get accomplished today. Most of the faculty is dressed up for Halloween and hard to take seriously—the school nurse is wearing a sweatsuit and whistle and the gym teacher is wearing a nurse's uniform and a stethoscope. He'd look a lot better if he shaved his legs.

Lana runs up to me and even Mr. Pinto turns his head. She's wearing the leopard-print leotard we bought at the mall, a small black skirt that stops right below her crotch, and a black headband with cat ears. Her tail is black velvet. When she bends down to help me with my books, or so she says, her boobs almost spill out, practically kissing the floor.

"No shawl?" I say.

She giggles. "My parents had to leave for work early today. Nice, huh?"

I nod and suddenly don't feel so sexy in my sparkly flapper outfit and strappy pumps. I raise myself to full height so the dress, which is slightly above the knees, appears shorter.

"You look great," Lana says, and from the enthusiastic way she says it, I know she means it. "The heels are a nice touch. Like I said, if you've got the legs, show 'em."

I hear a sharp whistle and then Ryan's voice. "Lookin' good, Lana."

She laughs her sexy laugh, her Trish laugh. "Not so bad yourself, Ry." But her eyes meet Jake's as she says this. She may as well be talking to him, since both he and Ryan are dressed as rap stars.

They nod at me. "Hot shoes," says Ryan.

"Thanks," I say. I shift my feet as Ryan and Jake's eyes slowly sweep my legs.

I look down the hall for Keith but see only two guys dressed as sumo wrestlers and a girl in a Mrs. Butterworth costume. She's carrying a plate of pancakes and syrup. Jake tugs playfully on Lana's tail, and she shrieks.

"Hands off," she says in a throaty voice.

"That's not what you said last night," says Ryan, and he and Jake slap palms while Lana pretends to be insulted.

The second bell rings. We should be in homeroom by now, but no one is. The teachers yell, "Homeroom, people, homeroom," but no one moves. The teachers sigh. One collective sigh heard over the megaphones. It's Friday, so even if it wasn't Halloween, we wouldn't be feeling all that productive.

Lana's leaning against my locker after Jake and Ryan have gone, still looking starry-eyed.

"Isn't he cool?" she says, not specifying Jake or Ryan.

I don't think either of them are, but she looks so happy I agree with her. Then I think about what Ryan said. *Last night.* "Have you been hanging out with them a lot?"

Her eyes change, and she rubs her thumb over her fingernails. She bites her lip and pretends to get something from her backpack. She shrugs.

"Here and there. Trish and I went to a diner with them last night," she says, adding quickly, "I would have asked you to come, but you were with Keith."

"I was," I say. And what bothers me is not that she's hanging out with Jake, Ryan, and Trish, but that she doesn't really want me there.

"Where is he anyway?" she asks, relieved now that a possible confrontation has been averted.

"Right there," I say, pointing fifty feet away.

Holly is hanging on one arm, a blonde senior on his other. But the blonde is also connected to a guy in a hot-dog outfit, so she doesn't worry me. Keith is dressed as an old-time gangster in a black pinstriped suit and wide-brimmed hat. He's carrying a gun holster, minus the gun. Holly is wearing a business suit, but the top three buttons of her fitted jacket are open, showing cleavage that rivals Lana's. Her hair is in a bun, held together by a pencil, and she's wearing glasses. She's carrying a notepad too, and I don't know if she's supposed to be Keith's secretary (if gangsters even had secretaries, that is) or a naughty librarian.

Keith waves when he sees me and mouths, "Later."

"What was *that*?" Lana says.

"I guess he's busy." Not that it should surprise me.

Since the whole thing with my mom a week ago, he's been distant. He still stops by my locker, but not every day. We stretch together, but Holly's always there before practice. And we've continued to make out, but I can gauge when it will happen. On the days he throws out innuendos along with the stretches, like yesterday, or waits for me at lunch or stops his hackey-sack game long enough to jog toward me and kiss me in front of his friends, I know we're hooking up. And I know that on these days, I should find my backbone and say, "No, not unless you've finally figured out what you want. Am I your girlfriend, your friend with benefits, what?" But I don't do this, because all I want is for him to be kissing me so I can forget everything and everyone else. So I can feel for that hour that he really wants me and cares and that this part of my life is normal.

"That's just crap. I can't believe he's acting like such a dick. And the Bitch all over him." Lana is ranting. "I thought he didn't like party girls." More proof that he was just making excuses.

"Maybe she's turned over a new leaf. Let's just forget it and get to class."

Lana looks around, checking to see if Ryan or Jake has reappeared. When she sees they haven't, she links her arm through mine and struts to class.

Keith laces his fingers through mine across the pizzeria table, and I try not to think about Lana trick-or-treating with Ryan, Jake, and Trish—without me.

"You can totally come," she said to me when the dismissal bell rang.

"I have practice." Like I do every day after school.

"Oh, that's right, duh," she said and made a face like she wished I didn't. Maybe she meant it.

"Save me some candy," I said.

"Yeah, totally." And she ran off, her tail and boobs bouncing away.

Now, I focus on Keith, his fingers gently stroking my knuckles. It's good to have plans with him, even though he looked like he'd forgotten when I asked where he wanted to get dinner.

"I like your costume," he says, keeping one hand on mine and moving the other to my legs under the table.

It's hard to eat with him rubbing my knee. "Yours too." I pause and try to keep my voice casual. "What was Holly supposed to be?"

Keith shrugs. "Who knows? She just likes any excuse to show her tits."

I cringe at his choice of words. "I thought you guys were friends." I play with the cheese on my pizza and look up to see his reaction.

"Hey, it's not like I have a problem with what she wears." He laughs, and I'm no longer hungry.

I don't understand why he's been acting like this, so cool. Like he could take us or leave us. What happened to the boy who wanted to talk things out on Yom Kippur?

"What should we do tonight?" I ask, changing the subject.

"I don't like her that way, Alyssa." Keith leans closer to me across our booth. His hand squeezes my knee.

"You never kissed her?" The question is not one I meant to ask, but once it's out I know this is what's been nagging at me.

He looks uncomfortable and runs his hand through his hair. "Just once. It was a mistake."

I take my hand away and play with the sugar packets on the table, opening each one and letting it spill slowly into my water. "The night at the barn, right?" I already know the answer to this too.

"You were doing your thing, dancing with your friends, with that guy…" He lets the sentence trail away. "I'm sorry." His voice is genuine.

That night was full of mistakes. I give him a pass. "Does she know it was a one-time thing?" I can see her whispering in his ear, her hands touching him at every opportunity.

He shrugs. "I told her I just wanted to be friends."

I stir another packet into the water, hating that I care so much.

"Alyssa," he says taking my hand again, "I'm not seeing anyone else right now, okay?" This time his voice loses its bravado. It lets me know he cares.

I want to ask him if this means he's "seeing" me, but I just say, "Okay."

———

We drive around Glenfair and park beside my old elementary school—a great spot for star-gazing, but also a prime make-out area. We lie on a grassy hill, the same one I used to go sledding on years ago and that you can see from my house, far down below. In the summers, I'd stand on my porch listening to the sounds of laughter, moans, and clinking beer bottles coming from the high school kids. Even at ten, I knew what they were doing. Even though I wasn't ready for that world back then, each time my orange sled raced down the hill months later I still felt their energy sizzling in the cold, white sprays. Like touching the same spot they did would make me more grown up.

Looking down the hill, I can make out the trees that serve as a barrier between this world and the one beyond. The stars twinkle. An airplane flies by. For a moment it looks like a shooting star. I point out the Big Dipper. Keith shows me Pisces. I feel warm, like I did in his room. And I trick myself into believing we're a couple.

"Doesn't it bother you that we don't know much about each other?" Another roar of plane.

"We know things," he says. "I know you like it when I do this." He squeezes my knee. "And this." A kiss on the neck. "And this." A kiss on my lips, fingers tracing circles on my stomach.

He pulls me to him for more kisses, and I try to hold out because if I give in, I'll be too lost in him to bring this up again.

"That's not what I meant."

He sighs and pulls away. "I know what you meant, but why the questions? Is it the Holly thing? I told you I'm not into her. Mistakes happen."

I turn away from him. "It's just—I mean." I hesitate, but I need to say it because it's going to weigh on my mind if I don't. "Everything just seems different since our movie night." I don't mention my mother. That's implied. And I still don't know what exactly he saw of the situation. How much he's figured out.

The shadow of lamplight falls on his face and he sits up. "It was a good night. I had a good time. But it's my senior year, you know? I don't know if I want something serious right now. I told you that before."

He did. What made me think he suddenly knew what he wanted with his dating life? My eyes well up and I blink to the sky.

He takes my hand. "But I like you a lot and don't want to hurt you. I want to hang out with you. Who knows what will happen?" He kisses my cheek.

"I'm getting cold," I say, and Keith gets a blanket from the car and wraps it around us.

Far away I hear voices of trick-or-treaters. They get softer. No one is coming this way. Even the moms know to take a different route. Swings sway in the wind. They're by the playground, away from this hill. I remember Lana and me on the swings, pumping our legs faster and faster so we could see who could get higher.

I remember the night of my thirteenth birthday, my mother and I finishing our "girls' night out" with those swings. We spun ourselves, twisting the chains until they were tight. Then we raised our feet off the ground and let the chains unwind, squealing the whole time. In the silent night, my mother told me about her first date (a boy named Sasha who saved all his piggy bank money and bought her ice cream, all paid for in change). She said my time would come too. Before I went to bed that night, I stood on my porch—a teenager, a "grown-up"— and wistfully listened to the kids on the hills.

I picture my house now. There's probably a light on in the dining room, illuminating crumpled papers and rainbow-colored liquid in crystal glasses. My father is just finishing his ten o'clock news. Soon he'll go to bed, close his eyes, and dream of a world different from ours. I play with the grass, plucking it from the ground, making little piles by my toes.

I feel Keith's eyes on my face. There's an expression on his face I can't make out. Concern? Understanding? Recognition? But that look quickly fades away. He squeezes my knee, and I turn to him. His face has a longing. I let him kiss me and pull me down to the grass, like I imagined the older kids doing years ago.

But now his kisses are different, careful, like if he presses too hard, he'll break me. I don't want to be fragile, weak. I kiss him back hard, and we are back to doing what we do best. Only now, unlike the last few times we hooked up, he stops once my shirt is off. He doesn't try to pull at my pants. I don't have to move his hand. He covers us with the blanket and strokes my hair. I think back to what's beyond the trees and pretend the sky is Lana's canopy bed. I close my eyes and let myself dream, and put off thinking about what being grown-up really means.

TWENTY-EIGHT

I don't want to see any little girls out there, Glenfair. Get ready to beat their asses!" yells Coach Griffin.

It's the first Friday in November and our last meet at Dunkerhook Park before the county championships. We finish stretching as Coach begins his pep talk—as always, a variation of "don't screw up."

The other teams are huddled by their coaches for inspiration and, out of habit, I look around for fans. My father couldn't take off from work and my mother couldn't part with her bottle, so I shouldn't be surprised that I see no one.

"Okay, team," Coach is saying now, "let's show them what we're made of. Get them by their balls."

"What about the girls? Should we get them by their boobs?" I whisper to Keith, who's standing on the side with the other sprinters, only here for moral support.

He looks at my chest. "Only if I can get yours," he says, grinning.

I laugh and shove him. Since Halloween, we seem to

be back to normal. Keith is back at my locker at lunch, and he sometimes picks me up on the way to school. Maybe he's decided a girlfriend is not that bad, or maybe he's just more relaxed now that I know where he stands. He nudges me, and I have to postpone thinking for another time.

"Relax. You worry too much about everything," he says, and I hate that the expression on my face is so transparent.

As I wait for the race to begin, I map the route in my head and remember which trails have more trees to block out the unusually warm sun.

The pistol goes off and I stumble on my start. Clear your head, I tell myself.

I focus on the trees and markers ahead of me. One mile, smooth glide. It would be so easy to sprint, to feel that rush I get knowing everyone is behind me, but I pace myself. Two miles, and the sun is beating on my head. I block it out, and listen to the sound of my feet pounding the dirt. My adrenaline is pumping, but I'm not at the point yet where I forget everything else around me. Two and a half miles. A little more than half a mile to go.

Coach holds up his stopwatch and shouts my time. If I keep this up, I'll be running a six-and-a-half-minute mile. I push myself, but now I'm feeling the sun more, and my mind is racing even as I try to block out all non-running thoughts and breathe through the cramp in my side. I finish in twenty minutes, which is beyond respectable, but only good enough to place third. Coach is ecstatic. It's a great time for a sophomore and, if I get the same time in the championships, it qualifies me for state. But I'm mad at myself for losing focus.

Keith runs over and hugs me. "That was awesome!"

I see the rest of my fan base—Lana and Ryan—walking toward me. They're grinning. How did she get him to come? Why did she ask him to come? It doesn't matter; I'm just glad she's here. I pin my third-place ribbon to my shirt.

"We have to celebrate," says Keith, hugging me. Now that he's back on Lana's good side, she'll come too. Thankfully Ryan has plans, but he says, "Nice job, Bondar," before he leaves. I'm in the moment—happy for my ribbon, for Keith's hug, for Lana's cheer, for the sun beating down on me, which no longer feels too hot. I feel like I want to do an extra mile. I grab my water bottle and feel the cool drink in my throat. Then I hear the sound of my mom's slurred voice. Shouting my name.

It seems like everyone around me is standing still. No more cheers, no more hugs, just silence.

I see Mom through their eyes. A disheveled figure in baggy jeans and a too-snug T-shirt that's stained pink with cranberry and vodka. A blue rubber band, the kind that holds together stalks of broccoli, tying up her hair in a messy ponytail.

This woman runs toward me through the crowd, and I don't have to look to know they're all stepping back, trying to get away from this undesirable person. They're watching her, getting ready to call or text their neighbors about the crazy Russian woman only feet away. This is as exciting as

Glenfair gets. Right now, all they see is the kind of stranger only found on big-city streets, nowhere near their manicured lawns and hedges trimmed in pretty spiral patterns.

She's stumbling, and I race to her so she won't come closer, so no one will know for sure what's happening. So I can protect her from the thoughts already forming in their heads. They could speculate or spread rumors, but if I get there before they smell her, they won't know for sure. There will be no proof or stories that start with "Remember when Alyssa's mother got wasted and showed up at the cross-country meet?" People won't be able to use her as an example to illustrate that bad things happen in suburbia too.

"Kookalka!" she says a little too loudly, extending her arms to me.

"Mama, stop. Please," I say in Russian. And now I feel them staring at me.

"I finished my work early so I could come see you, and you're embarrassed?"

She's screaming in Russian, and people are watching, and the liquor on her breath is creating its own trails around us. I want to run through those trails to make the smell and her go away.

I need to calm her. "No, no. I'm glad you came. It means a lot to me that you came."

I hear myself crying and I don't want to be. Not here. I can imagine what people are saying, making up the conversation we're having because they can't understand it.

I see Keith walking toward me, and I put my hand out

to wave him away. Does he look relieved to not have to deal with the drama? *Cosmo*'s advice: *Guys want a relationship to be fun. Save your drama for your mama.*

Lana runs over and puts her arm on the other side of my mom. She helps me push her through the crowd, and I can see her looking around. I'm guessing she's searching for Ryan, hoping that he's already left. But in Glenfair, it doesn't matter that he's not witnessing this. Word will spread fast.

———————

"Ungrateful little girl," my mother mumbles as Lana and I lead her into my house.

A stronger stench of alcohol greets me at the door. My mother tries to push away from me, but I lead her to her bedroom and put a bucket near the bed.

Lana slinks back, and I can only imagine what she's thinking. She hasn't been to my house since that day we ate cinnamon buns in my room. She doesn't know that this is the norm, that my mom's drinking is not the same as hers or that my mother doesn't need a Russian restaurant as an excuse.

"Why don't you go?" I say. I don't want her to stay any more than she wants to be here.

"Are you sure?" She fidgets with her thumb. I know she's just asking to be polite.

"Yeah. Thanks. I'll call you later." I open the door and envision the alcohol smells making a break for it.

"No, wait." Lana pulls her shoulders back like she's found some new courage. "I want to help."

I'm about to ask her if she's sure, but I think she'll come to her senses and leave. A part of me really wants to have someone here, to not be alone, to be with someone who knows the old me—the me whose biggest worry was how to properly kiss my hand.

"Thanks," I say. We hug and then burst out laughing, because it feels like we're having a TV moment. The laughter feels good, even if it's kind of uncomfortable.

"Put me to work. What can I do to help?" she asks.

Dishes with crusty food are spilling out of the sink, and I think this will keep us busy. "I wash, you dry?" I suggest hopefully.

Lana looks disgustedly at the pile but attempts a smile and agrees. We get through half the stack with Lana telling me about how Ryan was waiting at her locker after school today, and how she hopes he realizes she's not into him "that way" but figures she won't bring anything up unless he officially makes a move because it's getting her closer to Jake. I nod and say, "That's awesome" when she says that Trish liked her shoes. I'm glad she's getting what she wants and no longer leaving me behind. Hearing Lana plot her next moves is a good distraction from the mess that awaits me upstairs.

"But what about you and Keith? Here I am blabbing about a guy I don't even have and you have someone real to deal with. At least he hasn't been acting like a shit lately, so that's good." She dries a dish, still thinking. "I hope he doesn't freak out about your mom now." She doesn't look at me when she says this, and I get the feeling she's worrying about more than just Keith freaking out.

"I didn't let him come near us, so he probably didn't know she was drunk. Do you think I should have let him help?" I mean, that's what boyfriends, or potential boyfriends, are supposed to do, right? Protect their girls?

Lana stops drying and looks at me like I'm out of my mind. "Are you serious? Of course not! Not if you want him to still date you, which you seem to want. I mean, you didn't even want to tell *me* about your mom. If Keith thinks he'll have to deal with all this now, he'll run. Plus, if you put it together with the time he saw your mom plastered after your date and his anti-partying soapbox…" Her face looks like she's concentrating hard on something.

Finally she smiles, relieved. "Don't worry, I'm sure he didn't know what was wrong. I bet no one did. Even if they suspected something, we can fix that." She has color back in her face now and starts drying the dishes again.

I'm about to ask her what she means, but a glass slips from my hands and breaks on the floor. I start picking up the pieces and cut myself on one of the jagged edges, drawing blood. I focus on the pain in my hand because that's easier than dealing with all the thoughts in my head.

"Oh my God! Are you all right?" Lana runs to the bathroom for bandages without waiting for an answer.

I run my hand under the cold water and watch the blood make its own path in the sink. My body starts to shake and today's events come flooding back.

"Put pressure on it to stop the bleeding," Lana says, coming back into the kitchen with a bandage. There's a butterfly design on her nails, and the wings seem to flutter as her shaking hands help me with the bandage.

I don't know how she knows this, but I do what she says. It seems to be working. She tells me to sit down and finishes drying the dishes on the counter. We say nothing, but I see Lana's lip quiver. I'm thinking that knowing the old me isn't enough for her anymore. I wonder if this is what's on her mind too—that this is not the house she remembers, that hanging out with her best friend didn't include washing dishes and cleaning up blood. I feel sorry for both of us.

"I'm going to go," she says when she finishes the drying.

There's no need for me to ask if she's sure. This place isn't for her. Pretty things die here, get caught in a net and are pounced on and crushed before they can be released. I open the door. This time she only gives me a quick hug, one of those flimsy kinds where your fingertips barely touch the other person, like you don't want to catch whatever it is they have.

"Call you later," she says, already out the door, happy to escape.

When she leaves, I wash up the blood remnants on the floor. For a minute I think of leaving them there for my father, to see if he'll spin this as another "inconvenience." "This is what she made me do!" I picture myself yelling. "You can't hide behind the news anymore." But he'll only see what he wants to see.

I think of what else I can do to keep my brain from reliving all the moments of this day. There are more dishes in the sink, but I can't finish them without soaking my bandage. The smell of alcohol leads me to the dining room. A glass of red liquid is overturned on the table, drenching the assignment my mother was working on. Underneath the smudged title of *Bonding with Your Teen* is one completed paragraph. The header says *Be an Athletic Supporter* and the passage talks about going to your teens' sporting events.

I laugh at the title. At the irony. At her idea of support. I laugh because I'm afraid if I start to cry again, I won't be able to stop.

———

At six o'clock, I check on my mother and watch as she moans, throws up in the bucket, and then wordlessly extends her hand for the Tylenol on her night table.

As seven o'clock nears, I set the kitchen table. The meal I prepared—pasta with canned spaghetti sauce—is no stuffed cabbage or blintzes, but I don't have the time or desire to cook elaborate meals like my mom once did. A refrigerator inventory revealed we did not have any food from the Russian store either.

"Hi, honey, sorry I'm late. There was a pile-up in the tunnel," my dad says when he walks through the door. He places his briefcase on the floor, loosens his tie, and falls into the living room recliner, as if these tasks zap him of any energy he has left.

I hover in the doorway as he changes channels. Once again, bombs explode on screen and people's houses are destroyed by storms, but my dad is content. Like my math answers, world tragedy is comforting to him because it's something he can depend on. Tuning in to the tube, he can shout at the anchors and feel like he's doing his part to change the status quo—even if he's not making a difference where he actually could.

"*Papachka*—Daddy—" I begin at the commercial. I don't usually call him this, so maybe if I do now, he'll think whatever I have to say is important.

He lowers the volume on the television, checks his watch, and looks at me expectantly.

I try to say what I want to in the two minutes I have. Once the commercials end, he'll ask me to wait for the next break, and I can't hold the day in any longer. He needs to know so that it can fester inside him, like it has been inside of me, growing, filling with pus, getting ready to explode. It's time for him to take care of everything, to deal with the tragedy in his own world.

"She came to my meet drunk," I say, and wait for the pain to lighten. He clenches the remote in his hand until his knuckles turn white, but he doesn't turn off the TV. My insides are still raw, and the image of her running to me shouting "*kookalka*" has carved out a hole in my brain.

"Are you sure she was drunk?" I can tell he's trying to keep himself from shouting, and I assume a stupid question like this is meant to buy him time.

I clench my own fist to stop it from shaking. It hurts to squeeze my maimed hand, so I lean against the wall, hoping the hard surface will support it. "She was stumbling and smelled like she'd bathed in vodka. She was shouting in Russian to anyone who would listen." I try to keep my voice level too. If I become nasty, he'll say, "Watch yourself, Alyssa. Who's the parent here?" And if he says that, I'd have to tell him the truth and say I have no clue.

He nods and his face looks pained, like the time he slammed his finger in our old Buick when I was seven.

"Are you all right?" he asks, getting up from the couch and walking over to me. He places his arms around me, and I lean into them.

"I could be better," I say, my hands shaking less.

This is how it should have been months ago. My daddy protecting me like I'm still a small child. I don't remember much about Russia except for the fruit cup—the kind with the little red cherries they served on the plane coming to America—and holding my dad's hand tightly in the terminal. "*Eta moy papachka*. That's my daddy," I told everyone around us as I gripped his arm. I know I'm much older now, but I miss the feeling that he can make everything good again.

"I should have just taken off from work and come to see you. Then this would not have happened. I can only imagine what it must have looked like to everyone," he says. "Did your friends see? What was she thinking, going out in public like that? All we need is for the local paper to write about this under Public Disturbances."

He's still hugging me, but I pull away. "Don't worry. I got to her before anyone smelled her," I say, my voice flat.

He relaxes. "Thank you." He strokes my hair, and I want to let him, but it isn't right. He isn't getting what the real problem is.

"Everyone seeing her isn't the only issue," I say. "She was plastered. Again. I had to clean her up. Again. What about me, leaving a meet I placed third in, to deal with this crap?" My voice is raised and I don't care.

He steps back like I slapped him. "Alyssa, you need to calm down. You think everyone seeing her is no big deal? Wait until people start talking, asking questions. It will be a big deal. We didn't move here to have you stand out."

"Get her some help, then." I'm crying and shaking again, and move away from him when he tries to wipe my tears.

"I'll talk to her. She won't do this again."

I hope he means the drinking in general, but it doesn't seem like he knows how to handle that. So they'll talk, and now she'll stay home when she's drunk. What progress.

I walk past him to the stairs and avoid his eyes.

"Wait. What happened to your hand?"

He finally sees it and looks anxious, but it's nothing he can fix. Not with the way he plans on going about things. "Don't worry about it. None of the neighbors saw it happen. We're safe."

"Alyssa." His tone is warning.

I run up the stairs and slam the door to my room. A few seconds later, I hear footsteps. They pause at the top of the stairs, deciding if they should go to my room or my parents'. They choose the latter. I hear my mother's voice. She's awake. I tiptoe to my door and slowly turn the knob so I can listen to their conversation. Their door is slightly ajar and I strain my ears.

"What did you think you were doing today?" I hear my dad say, the volume rising in his voice. It's not in control like when he was talking to me.

"I had a long day and three deadlines. I deserved a little break." Her voice is whiny. I hate when she gets like that.

There's rustling, and I imagine my dad changing out of his work clothes and laying his slacks, perfectly creased, in the pants press machine near their bed. In control, even though his voice is not.

"You want a break? Run yourself a bath or take a nap. Don't show up drunk at your daughter's event." A drawer slams shut.

My mom whimpers. "You're right, Marty. I'm so sorry. It was so stupid of me." This softens my dad, and I picture him walking over to my mom, her with a wet towel on her head, all pale and sickly looking. I hear nothing except mumbling, and then my mom's voice, stronger this time. "It was in front of everyone, Marty. I can't believe I walked across the field like that in front of everyone."

Again with the *in-front-of-everyone* crap. That's why she's sorry about today, not because of how she might have made me feel. Well, if other people's reactions will stop her from doing something stupid like this again, fine.

I hear my father open their bedroom door and I run to my bed so he won't know I was listening, but he doesn't come to my room. The living room TV is shut off and there is a clanking of silverware in the kitchen. Down the hall, my mother starts snoring, and downstairs my dad turns on the kitchen television. I hear him cursing at the set. My phone rings, and I hope it's Keith even though I don't know what I would say to him. Caller ID tells me it's Lana. I'm glad she's thinking of me, but I don't pick up. It's only eight o'clock, but I am exhausted and done talking for tonight.

I get into bed and put in the *Songs to Play When Life Sucks* CD Lana made me last summer when I moped about her leaving for the Catskills. Outside, it starts raining and claps of thunder, like the bombs on the television, drown out Lana's CD. I fall asleep and dream of explosions, one after another after another, blowing our house to bits and leaving only a pile of rubble and scorching flames.

TWENTY-NINE

Y ou can't make the towel too hot or else it burns instead of soothes.

This is what I've learned from the last few months with my mother. Today, I'd like to be the one lying in bed with the wet towel spread across my forehead. But I have to go to school, be responsible, and even without the too hot towel the burning will come—the humiliation from my mother's scene on Friday.

The sweet, cinnamony smell of doughy *ponchiki* wafts upstairs as I dress for school. This is my mother's own way of lessening the pain, her surefire plan to get me to accept the apology that was so obvious on her face all weekend, but which her lips were too scared to offer.

"*Kookalka*, I'm so sorry," she says, tears in her eyes, when I get downstairs. There is a cup of coffee and the "Dear Abby" column on the table in front of her. She stretches her arms out to me like she wants to hug me.

I remember how she stretched out her hands to me at

the meet, and my stomach tightens. And that word again—I never thought the word "doll" could make me feel love and hate at the same time.

Her arms are hanging in the air, waiting. It's awkward, and the uncertainty in her face leaves a lump in my throat. Her hands look out of place, like they're on their own, out of her control. It makes me sad, and I get ready to forgive her, but then she says, "I shouldn't have done that in front of your friends."

I know that's what she told my dad, but her tears made me think she got it, got that it was about more than that. I mean, aren't writers supposed to be more sensitive than other people? Aren't they supposed to have some kind of extra awareness gene that the rest of us don't?

"You shouldn't have done that at all!" I snap at her. The sugary cinnamon rolls in front of me are now making my stomach turn, and my mother looks sad again. She finally puts down her arms and folds them on her lap. They look out of place there too.

She sips her coffee and looks at the paper as if Dear Abby has some wisdom for her. I think she's going to cry, but she pulls herself together. "You're right. I'm sorry. This is no excuse, Alyssa, but I've been so stressed out. You don't know. Your father and I, and this job ... things aren't very good."

"Can you go to counseling?" I know this is something my parents would never do, the epitome of airing out our dirty laundry, but I throw it out there for lack of something better to say and because a part of me thinks maybe that's all she needs to stop the drinking.

My mother laughs. "Seriously, Alyssa, that's very cute."

I think about old television shows, like *The Cosby Show*, that are replayed on Nick at Night. If the parents raised their voices, the kids would set up an intervention, and one of them would say, "Are you getting divorced?" Then, the parents would shoot back some snappy comment and everyone would laugh, crisis averted. But no one yells here. No one acts like they care about anything. My dad has the news, my mom has her vodka, and that seems to be enough.

I feel sorry for the hands on my mom's lap, the ones that got tired of waiting for a hug. I want to stroke her hair and tell her everything will be fine. Maybe then she'll do the same for me.

"You can't keep doing what you're doing." I sit on her lap and am afraid she's going to tell me I'm too old for this. Instead, she hugs me close to her and kisses my forehead.

"We're trying. But it's not like your father is around that much." She takes a sip of her coffee and stares into the muddy liquid, like a fortune-teller trying to see the future.

"That's because you're always drinking."

She looks at me and says, "Would it be any different if I stopped? The news is on all the time. We don't talk. We don't go on trips anymore. And in bed—"

I put up my hand to stop her. The closest I ever came to knowing anything about my parents' sex life was when I was looking for a pair of knee highs in my mom's dresser but found a vibrator and edible body cream instead. Up until now, I've been pretty successful at blocking out that whole incident.

"I'm sorry. So sorry," she mumbles. "You're my daughter. I'm supposed to be helping you, not the other way around." Her voice breaks, and I let her lean her head on my shoulder.

She sees my bandaged hand and takes it in hers. "I'm sorry," she says again.

I nod. Just thinking about the other night makes my skin sting.

Tears fall down her cheeks, and I stroke her hair.

We sit like this, my mom, Dear Abby, and me, until I have to go to school. I think of that phrase my parents always say, *yaitsa kuritsu uchat*, "the eggs are teaching the chickens," and wonder when it will be the other way around again.

———

I go to my locker through the rear entrance. The only people gathered back there are the potheads, and they have better things to worry about than my mom. Even if they did hear about her, they'd think she rocked.

Lana and I played IM tag all weekend, talking to each other's away messages. If I had normal parents, I'd have a cell like everyone else. But apparently it isn't a "necessity." Thank God for Internet homework or I wouldn't even have email. I checked my messages one last time before bed last night and had a new one from Lana, written in bright pink letters: *Hope you're okay. Worked things out for us. Tell you tomorrow.* I don't know what that means. If it weren't for the words "for us," I'd think it was about Ryan or Jake.

As I walk through the crowded hallway, my stomach feels queasy because I'm expecting a press conference at my locker. And I'm getting the feeling that Keith, the one person I'd really like to be there, won't be attending. He emailed me Saturday to say he'd be out all weekend and would explain later, but if someone really liked you, wouldn't they call to hear your voice? Maybe when I told him to stay away at the meet, he got the idea that I didn't want him around at all. Or maybe he freaked out again. For a minute I actually think about disguising my voice and calling in sick, but with my luck I'd get caught. I stare straight ahead as I walk, pretending that the people I see are the only ones who can see me.

Lana runs up to me as soon as I get to my locker. "Where were you? I was waiting out front for like ten minutes!"

"You're too hyper for Monday morning," I say when I see the big smile on her face. "I came in through the back."

"I've got good news." She's practically jumping up and down, her boobs bouncing inside her tight, pink, fuzzy sweater. I wonder if she's hoping Jake or Ryan will walk by.

"Don't leave me hanging then. Out with it," I say.

"Okay, so after Friday's disaster, I called Ryan just to feel him out. See if he heard anything, you know?"

I nod.

"Of course he did, so I played dumb and let him talk. Whoever he got his info from was pretty accurate, so I needed to do damage control." She's getting more excited and tries to drop her voice so people can't hear us.

My stomach drops. Just what, exactly, does Lana consider *damage control*? "Is this the good part?" I ask dryly.

"Uh huh." She smiles slyly. "I told him your mom had her tooth pulled and was on meds, and the dosage was a little high. I swore up and down, and he totally bought it because, get this, the same thing happened to his dad!" She finishes and looks at me expectantly, like she's waiting for applause.

"And he's going to pass this on to everyone else?" It seems too easy.

"Already done. I saw Ryan and Trish while I was waiting for you, and they were both really cool about it and asked how you and your mom were. I'm sure at least half the sophomore class knows by now. So, catastrophe averted." She throws her arm around my shoulder, smiling wider than ever.

I move away from her and throw my books into the locker with a thud, pretending Lana is lying below them. I tell myself that this is Lana's way of handling the situation, and she thinks that she did what was best. It shouldn't matter that it was all about her quest for greatness. All about what others would think. Just like with my parents. Not about protecting me. I throw another book into my locker and it hurts my hand.

"Whoa. Why are you mad? I told you it's all taken care of."

"Yeah, thanks again for that," I say bitterly. "The thing

is, you didn't talk to Ryan to help *me*. You just don't want my life to interfere with yours."

"Look, I know you had a bad weekend, but don't take it out on me. What I did was for both of us."

I gather more of my books, this time less fiercely so I don't bang my hand again. Am I expecting too much? Life isn't a geometry problem where full credit is only given if a proof is solved by the teacher's methods. She helped things, didn't she? Does it matter if it wasn't really about me? *It does*, a voice screams in my head, but I push it away. I've been feeling lonely too long.

"I'm sorry," Lana says finally. "I didn't think you'd be mad." Only she doesn't really sound sorry, and the way her voice goes up an octave on the word "mad" lets me know that she knew exactly how I'd feel.

I stare at my books and don't answer her because I'm afraid whatever I say next will cause a fight. She shifts her feet and kneels on the floor beside me.

"How's your hand?" This time her voice is concerned and genuine.

"It's all right. Getting better. No big catastrophe," I say, feeling better when I see her wince.

I decide to give her partial credit for her efforts.

———

My fifth period health class is an easy A. This year's teacher, Mrs. Krane, is more concerned about us liking her than really learning something. Right now, she's going over homework and high-fiving everyone with the right answer. I look down at my paper and frown, hoping she'll think I have the wrong answer and pass me by. She does, and I doodle little hearts in the margins of my notebook and think about Keith.

Mrs. Krane stops talking and writes the word *Objective* on the board. She puts a colon after it and adds *Start of Alcohol Unit*. It seems like Lana's plan worked; no one even glances in my direction, but I feel as if the room is spinning. I close my eyes and put my head down on my desk, hoping this will steady everything. My hands feel like they will start shaking, and I place them on my lap so no one will see them.

It's then that I hear Mrs. Krane's voice by my desk, asking if I want to go to the nurse. I nod, and a hand helps me up. I know it's Lana's because I recognize the multicolored wings on her nails. Now everyone's looking at me and whispering. Are they wondering if I took my mom's meds? Outside the door, my legs still feel rubbery, and not in that good, first-kiss way.

"You look like you're going to pass out," Lana says as we walk down the hall, me leaning on her arm. I used to want crutches because you get to leave class early, everyone wants to carry your books, and you're a minor celebrity until your leg gets better. People stare at me as we walk, but it's not the admiring *hey-what-did-you-do-to-your-leg-can-I-sign-your-cast?* kind of look. It's more like the *what's-wrong-with-her-I-hope-she-throws-up-in-the-hallway-so-something-cool-can-happen-around-here* look.

I focus on stepping forward and blocking out the noise

around me, and Lana opens her mouth a few times but says nothing until we reach the nurse's office.

"Do you want me to stay with you?" she asks.

I can't tell if she means it or not, so I shake my head no.

She doesn't leave, and concentrates on pulling the beads of fuzz off her sweater.

I move away from her and lean on the doorframe so she doesn't feel like she has to support me. She continues to play with the beads of fuzz.

"What?" I ask.

"I'm sorry about before." This time she really does sound apologetic.

"Forget it." I can't talk about anything deep right now, and even if I could, I filed this topic away already.

"It's just, I—" she stutters.

"Really, Lana. It's done." I don't want her to say anything else because I have a feeling it will only explain why she did it, and I already know.

She nods and leaves, and I give the nurse my pass and lie down on her brown pleather couch. There are pencil holes in it with pieces of foam sticking out and people's initials scratched on the surface. No one pays attention to me, and that's how I like it. The nurse brings me a Dixie cup filled with water, but she can't give me Tylenol because my mom forgot to fill out the consent form we got at the beginning of the year. On the wall in front of me are dusty pamphlets about sex, drugs, and alcohol. Two guys who don't really look sick flip through the one about safe sex while nudging each other. They must be freshmen because the novelty of those brochures is gone for the rest of us. I'm embarrassed for them because everyone knows that reading those things in public and giggling while reading them is like shouting you're a virgin. Most of us would rather not broadcast it to the whole world.

The nurse tells the gigglers to leave, and I notice a bright orange brochure behind where they were sitting. *Alcoholism: The Merry-Go-Round Called Denial* is written in white bubble letters on the cover. I think about stealing one of these while no one is looking, but the nurse seems to be staring at me.

"How are you feeling?" she asks. I'm positive now that she's watching my eyes roam the pamphlets. Does she think I'm the one with the alcohol problem?

"Tired." I close my eyes, ending any opportunity for further conversation. The bell rings, but she doesn't make me leave. I think of the carousel at the mall and the old couple holding on to the golden harnesses of the horses, smiling and laughing as the ride went round and round.

When I fall asleep, I dream of my family on a carousel. My dad and I are on horses and my mom is on a skinny brown beer bottle. She doesn't like the bottle because the brown is not as pretty as the red, blue, and gold of our horses. She asks if we can switch or change the bottle's color, but my dad only laughs in response. I want to help her, but the ride attendant doesn't let me. The horses and bottles move faster and faster and people fly off one by one. When the ride is over, my mother, clinging to her bottle, is the only one left.

———

I manage to sleep two hours and miss the rest of the school day, but there's a note from Lana on my locker telling me she'll call me after her chem detention. With practice cancelled due to another faculty meeting, I decide there's no reason to stay. I pack my books carefully to avoid hitting my hand again.

"Let me get that." Keith crouches down beside me and brushes his hand across my good arm. I stand up and let him help, but say nothing because I'm not sure if my voice will convey happiness at his touch or bitterness for his weekend desertion.

"Where were you this morning?" he says, unfazed by my silence.

I have no choice but to answer. "At my locker," I say, like it should be obvious. Looks like Bitter Alyssa won out.

"I passed it but didn't see you," he says, and I remember Lana and I went to homeroom early.

He takes my good hand, and butterflies are in my stomach again. I will them to stop fluttering or morph backwards into moths, because I want to stay mad.

He reaches up to put his hand on my knee. In my mind, I move away. In my mind, he looks hurt and guilty and knows exactly why I don't want to talk to him. In my mind, he says, *Alyssa, I'm so sorry. I should have called you. Are you all right?* But there, at the foot of my gray locker, next to walls the color of Pepto-Bismol, or pink birthday cake frosting depending how you'd rather see it, I bend down to kiss him because it feels so good. Because his mouth on mine and his arms around me make me feel like he wants me and doesn't care what anyone else around us thinks.

"Was your weekend okay?" he asks, taking a break from my lips. He's back to my books again, not looking at my face.

I lean against my cold metal locker and think about the question. I feel his eyes on me now, but what can I say? Does he really want to know? Is he asking about what happened after the meet? I don't think Lana's version of events reached the senior class. His hand is on my knee again, squeezing it, like he cares. *How much?*

"It could have been better," I say. I meet his gaze and hold it. He looks away first.

"Your mom," he says, playing with the zipper on my backpack as if he needs to adjust it to get all the books in. There are only three. "She'll be fine, right?"

This is what I wanted. For him to be concerned.

"I don't know," I say, and this time he jerks his head up and looks at me. Not through me, not at a point in my face just below my eyes. This time, his eyes actually meet mine, and he holds my stare.

He may have expected me to lie. To say everything was fine. But this is me, and it's too hard to play so many different games. Something today has to be about me.

He nods slowly and goes back to fiddling with my backpack. A part of me wants him to persist and ask what was wrong with her. That same part imagines me telling him and crying on his shoulder while he tells me he'll always be there for me. But this is not how the conversation would go. How can he say he'll be there for me when he has yet to call me his girlfriend and can't even call during a weekend?

He stands up with both our bags and notices my bad hand. "What happened?" he asks, and the concern in his voice is comforting—like the pillows stuffed with real goose feathers my parents brought over from Russia, which I still sleep on.

I want to hold on to my anger, to ask which friend was dumped this time, but he takes my hand in his and traces the lines of the bandage.

"Friday," I say and feel a lump in my throat. All of a sudden I'm tired again, like the nap in the nurse's office never happened. Maybe I've just been using too much energy to keep the truth in. I feel like I'm back in my health class, and *Alcohol Unit* flashes before my eyes like it's on one of those neon signs blinking outside strip clubs to lure in horny men.

Keith takes my hand and kisses it and puts his arms around me. "I should have called," he says. And in that sentence I hear his *I'm sorry* and *I care about you*.

I bury my face in the coarse fibers of his wool sweater and breathe. He hugs me to him tightly. He doesn't try to usher me out of the school or tell me someone might see. He might not call me after this, because who wants a girl with so much baggage? But he's not showing it. He just strokes my hair. Just like in my fantasy. Unlike in my daydream, he doesn't say everything will be fine. But that's just as well because then he'd be a liar, and it's about time people started telling the truth.

———

At the car, Keith opens the door for me and makes sure I'm in before heading to the driver's seat.

"Better?" he asks, squeezing my good hand.

"I will be." I put my hand on his knee.

He opens his mouth like he's going to say something, but puts in The Cure CD instead. He skips tracks until he gets to the one he wants. "'Round and Round and Round'," he says as the song starts. "It's about keeping it real."

I close my eyes, lean back on the seat, and smile. Maybe he gets me after all.

"What?" he asks, and I can hear the smile in his voice too.

"Nothing. Just thinking that you have good taste in songs."

———

We drive around in circles, listening to music. He brings my mother up three times, but I don't want to talk about her. He parks in front of my house and kisses me. His touch is more tender than it's ever been.

"I'll call you later," he says, and I know this time he will.

I'm halfway up my front walk when Keith yells my

name. "Alyssa, wait." He runs up to me and gives me the CD we were listening to in his car. "Remember to keep it real."

"And if people can't handle that?"

"Screw them." He kisses me again, then jogs back to his car and speeds off.

I hold the CD tightly and open the door. "Just screw everyone," I think. Not a bad mantra to have.

———

I drop my backpack in the hallway and think *screw it*. I fall down on the couch, and the cushions swish *to hell with everyone*. Outside, a car with a bad muffler speeds down the street, following a badass tune of its own. I follow its rumble in my head, letting it shake me up, distance me from the girl who cares. "Just screw everyone!" I yell, and it feels good.

Until I feel the eyes. I know she's standing beside me even before I open my own eyes. What I don't know until I look at her is that the weepy, fragile figure I left this morning is gone.

Mom is wearing jeans that flare out at the bottom and a silk blouse—one of her I'm-going-to-be-sober-now outfits. Her slippers have been replaced with heels and her hair is pulled back in a rhinestone clip.

"What's the occasion?" I ask, gesturing to her ensemble, attempting to keep the care out of my voice.

"I did a lot of thinking after you left this morning."

She motions for me to join her in the kitchen. "Tea?" She puts the kettle on the stove before I have a chance to say yes. "And what struck me is that our relationship shouldn't be like this. You taking care of me, me the mess I've been." She pauses and places a small tin of cookies on the table. "I made these," she says proudly.

I grip the CD case and push the cookies away. "Maybe the tenth time's the charm," I say and get up from my chair, escaping the all-too-familiar scene.

"Wait for the tea. Chamomile is a great soother," she says before I have a chance to leave the kitchen.

Screw soothing. "I'm good."

"Alyssa," my mother calls when I'm already on the stairs. "I joined AA."

I stop, foot in midair, already poised to get away. This is different. This could be progress. I feel the ridges of the CD case in my hand and try to hold on to my new mantra, but hope squirms in.

I slowly make my way back into the kitchen where my mother is sipping her tea. She places a cup before me and continues talking like I never left. "I went to my first AA meeting this afternoon and got a sponsor."

Big changes.

"What about the whole town knowing?"

She frowns. "Well, that's still a concern, but my sponsor is making me see that this is something I shouldn't worry about."

Big big changes.

I swallow the warm tea and think of past chances to

talk that were lost. I don't want that to happen again. I tell her about my life in bits and pieces, careful not to reveal all my feelings. She strokes my hair when I talk about Lana.

"It will work out," she says. "This is a hard time, though. I bet she's just finding herself like we all are. In the end, she won't forget what a good friend you've been to her."

I nod, feeling lighter, because she said what I've been wanting to believe.

"I'm so sorry I haven't been there for you," she says.

In the living room, the angry girl is staring outside, waiting for me. I want to be her, to live by her motto, but it's already too warm inside me.

THIRTY

Scented candles cleanse your aura. Salts de-stress and rejuvenate. Say "oohhmm" enough times and you are transported to a world of calm.

Since starting AA a week ago, this has become my mother's new world. She's even convinced a magazine to let her write a piece on outside forces controlling our health. I am not sure what this means, but the idea has planted a permanent smile on Mom's face and lets her experiment with massages and skin gels free of charge.

With school closed due to a teaching convention, I had envisioned myself in my mother's world today. My body soaking in fragrant bubbles, vanilla candles surrounding the tub like a halo, my head resting on a bath pillow, and soft music erasing tension from my mind. My parents had other plans.

Dad seems to think that me staying home will somehow invade my mother's writing space and "spirituality haven" and he doesn't want any chance of a relapse. So as my mother lies on our living room couch with music resonating from the television's New Age channel, a water-filled eye mask over her eyes, her hands covered in a home-made seaweed cream, I am on a New Jersey Transit bus with my father headed to his job.

As a kid, I loved going to work with him. There was something exciting about the way he crinkled his brow and stuck out his tongue so just the tip was visible whenever he was deep into a project. I liked that everything else around him fell away when he was concentrating, that he had such commitment to something that only that thing mattered. Like he used to be with my mother and me.

Once we are in the city, it's only a ten-minute walk from Port Authority to Dad's office. This New York office is similar to the one I remember. Rows of drafting tables with crisp white paper, colored pencils, geometry tools like protractors and compasses, computers beside the tables, a water cooler in the hallway, a transistor radio on his desk. There's an empty table next to his, and he has it set up with graph paper and colored and mechanical pencils, just like when I was little. In those days, I'd pass the time drawing and pretending I was just like him, only my houses had chimneys and cobblestone walks and looked like houses rather than the nests of lines in his blueprint.

"I know you're too old to draw all day," my dad says, embarrassed, redness creeping into his cheeks. "But maybe you can use the graph paper for a geometry activity. I bought you a book with logic problems and geometry figures you can graph." He sounds hopeful and looks pleased with himself, and I love him for the effort. The book—written by a math whiz I had to research last year—is actually cool.

"Thanks. It's perfect." I give him a hug.

He gives me a toothy smile and I notice how white his teeth are. Too white, like when he used one of those teeth whitener sets to impress my mom for their anniversary three years ago. I wonder if he's trying to impress her now.

People wander to their desks and wave as if they know me. I guess it's the excitement of a distraction, someone to break up their usual routine. "It's about time you brought some help here, Marty," says a guy in a blue suit. "We need fresh blood."

"You gonna follow in your dad's footsteps?" asks a woman with a pink face and gray-tinged beehive.

"I haven't decided what I want to do yet. Something with math." I know they don't *really* care what I want to do and are just being friendly.

"Oh, Lynette, she has time. She's still a kid," says Blue Suit. He winks at me, like we're in on something together, and I get a feeling he doesn't like Lynette too much.

"A kid? No, she's what? Sixteen, seventeen?" She leans close to me, trying to find my age on my face. She smells like onions. My dad must know this already because he steps back as soon as Lynette inches toward our table. I stifle a laugh.

"Don't make my baby grow up too fast. She's only fifteen and has plenty of time to decide what she wants to do," he says, stepping in between Lynette and me. I think he's holding his breath.

"You've got a good dad there," says Blue Suit as he and Lynette go to their desks.

I nod and smile, and Dad looks relieved. Did he think I'd disagree or say something like, "No, my dad's an ass, and here are all our problems…"?

"I'm so glad you came to work with me today," he says, and I can tell it feels like old times to him too.

As he starts to work, I notice the photographs on his desk. There's this year's school picture of me, taken the third week of classes. I like my smile in that picture. It's not super toothy or tight-lipped. It looks real.

I see my father look at the picture too. His face is nostalgic and sad, and I realize he's not staring at my picture but at the one next to it, of him and Mom. They both look about twenty. There's a daisy in her hair and she's wearing green sandals and a green paisley dress that goes down to her knees. My dad's in faded blue jeans and a white T-shirt that shows off his muscular arms. He's leaning against a fence, a cigarette in one hand, the other arm around my mom. She's laughing one of those deep, open-mouthed laughs and he's trying to appear cool and serious, but the crinkles around his eyes and mouth give him away. I never knew my dad smoked. I turn over the picture so I can see when it was taken. There's no year, but my mother has written "Minsk, perfect third date" in Russian.

"That's a nice picture," I say, putting my arm around him. "Old, though." When I was little, he had recent pictures of all of us.

"I don't have any good current ones. Not real ones."
He rubs his temples.

He means the ones without fake smiles, the ones where the eyes don't reveal what really happened that day, the ones that don't remind you just by looking at them that you'll never wear that favorite dress or pants or shirt again because it's the same outfit you wore the day you cleaned up vomit, or cut your hand, or came home to find your wife moaning on your bed reeking of alcohol, a washcloth on her forehead.

"Maybe you'll be able to put up a new picture soon," I say, in Russian so that no one will understand us.

He smiles and continues to rub his temples. I look at his face. There are no laugh crinkles like in the picture, and his eyes don't look happy. He seems old, and not just because it's been more than twenty years since the picture was taken. One of his hands shakes a little as he picks up his pencil to do a sketch, and he slumps his shoulders while outlining a plumbing fixture. He finishes and puts his arm around me.

"How did she get better before?" I ask, thinking there will never be a perfect time for this question.

He looks surprised. "When?"

"In our first apartment. I've been remembering things. The two of you drinking in the kitchen while you killed mice." The toe of my sneaker makes patterns on the floor.

He looks at me thoughtfully, maybe trying to figure out how much to tell me, how many gaps to fill. "It wasn't like this then," he says finally. "She had some bad weekends, a few bad nights, like all of us who came to a new country did, just trying to cope. But then we picked ourselves up and moved on. We had to find jobs. One of us working would not feed you. Your mom took whatever task came her way, working her way up. She just snapped out of it."

At first I think he's editing the memory for me, but his voice and face tell me that's how he remembers it. Maybe that's how it happened. Maybe the difference now is that there aren't enough dreams out there for her to chase.

He looks at his pictures again. "I hope I can add a different photo here, but that may not be possible."

I lean my head on his shoulder and think about the days he worked late. I understand better why he avoided us, why he didn't want to say my mom had a problem. It's hard to accept, to believe, that she's the same woman he laughed with years ago. I don't like that he left me alone to clean up the mess, but I can forgive him because I know we're in this together now.

I pull away so as not to make a scene in his office, but everyone is too busy drafting to pay attention. The one or two people who do see us, the Lynettes of the office, smile and put their hands to their hearts, like this father-daughter bonding moment gives them hope for their own teens.

"I'll bring this picture home tonight," he says. "I think your mom would like to see it."

I go back to my desk after my father hugs me tightly once more. I see him take the photo of him and my mom in his hand and absently stroke her face. Then, he puts on headphones and turns on his radio, letting the news transport him to his own safe and happy place.

THIRTY-ONE

My mother has found God.

And not the version of God where you only go to services on the High Holy Days. This is the real thing—the every-weekend-in-synagogue kind of religion. She says it helps her stay sober and the Program recommends it. That's what she calls it—the Program. Not AA; no one who goes there calls it AA. The Program—*It Works If You Work It, So Work It, You're Worth It.* She says this every morning while looking in the mirror. Her articles focus only on the spiritual too. This week she's working on a piece called "Feeling Down? Lift Yourself Up By Your Soul." It's about new ways to treat depression, like walking through labyrinths.

Going on two weeks of sobriety—the longest she's ever been alcohol free—and I have a new mom. It's weird, but in a good way. Let her find as many higher powers as she needs as long as it stops her from praying to the porcelain god. She's trying to make this a family affair, too, by leaving new pamphlets on the kitchen table each day for my dad and me. "So You Love an Alcoholic" was the latest one. She says we have to learn about the disease so we can understand what she's going through. I understand this, but it feels a little too-much-too-soon for me. I mean, I'll completely support her, but I'm not ready to go to Al-Anon meetings—the AA equivalent for friends and family of alcoholics. Why make all the effort, I wonder, if there's a chance this new version of her will go to pot just like in the past?

My father spits three times and knocks on wood when I talk like this, saying it's just inviting the demons to come back. I ask him why he's not going to meetings if he feels this way. I know the real reason is that he's thinking the same thing I am, but he just says, "Support your mother, Alyssa," and knocks on wood. I guess to counteract the thoughts in his head.

After synagogue tomorrow, he and Mom are going on a picnic and a hike. She bought new sneakers for the occasion and her cheeks get flushed whenever she talks about it. Last night, they went for a walk and when I looked at them through the window, they were holding hands. It's like they're on a reality relationship show and the TV counselor is giving them daily assignments to revitalize their love life. The only thing with those shows, of course, is that half the time the couples go back to their dysfunctional selves once the therapist leaves them to their own devices. Then, instead of an update of a happy couple walking side by side on a beach at sunset, you see a caption like, *One month after the taping, Louise admitted to having another affair. Jeffrey moved into his parents' garage.*

———————

"Good, you're awake!" says Mom when I open my eyes and see her sitting on my bed Saturday morning. She's wearing a burgundy suit and her hair is pulled back with a burgundy clip.

"Unfortunately," I say, still groggy. It's only eight, and waking up before noon on weekends should be against the law. "Where are you going?"

"I thought *we* could go together," she says, a little too perky.

Something the two of us could do in the morning, which involves formal attire. This means the synagogue. Crap.

"Can't you talk to God without leaving the house? I'm sure he'll hear you," I groan. Saturday morning services are three hours long, and I understand the need for spirituality, but wouldn't God prefer you to be awake when talking with him?

"It will mean a lot to me if you come. I need the encouragement, Alyssa." She looks me in the eyes and squeezes my hand.

This must be what my dad meant when he said to support her. But he gets to do something fun like prepare food for their hike. I force a smile. "I'll be ready in half an hour."

"Thank you." She kisses me on the forehead. Then, just as she's almost out my door, she adds, "I thought we'd try the new Russian synagogue that just opened. It will mean so much more if I can understand the prayers."

Fantastic. Three hours of Hebrew I don't understand combined with written Russian translation I can read at the level of a four-year-old.

———————

Only three rows have people in them when we arrive. Smart people wait until ten thirty or eleven to show up. The really dedicated worshippers, apparently us, arrive for the entire service. We sit down and my mom hands me a prayer book. I sing along to the familiar tunes and focus on the melodies, not the fact that I don't know what I'm singing about. Hebrew school only teaches you the blessings, and how to read Hebrew so you can pray.

The really ambitious teachers also teach you important phrases like *Ani rotza lelechet l'shirutim*, meaning "I have to go to the bathroom." This is not in the pages before me.

I look at the rest of the congregation. They're all really into it. Must be the Russian translation. I sound out the words in my head and get through a quarter of the page before the rabbi moves on to a new prayer. My mother's face is calm, and she sways back and forth like the rabbi and the other patrons. This is not the Yom Kippur sway of a month back. It doesn't look like she's trying to find the strength to go on; it looks like she's already found it. The

Program must be a powerful thing. I see her lips move as she forms the words.

Another hour passes and the rabbi gives a speech about the Torah chapter of the week. It's called *Chayei Sarah*, or "The Life of Sarah." The rabbi discusses what our lives mean and the legacy we leave behind. "What does being alive truly mean? Why do you live?" My mother beams like her life is being renewed and squeezes my hand. I'm glad I came with her.

When the service ends, we shake hands with the rabbi and proceed to the adjacent room where all the food is. My mom stops to talk to a woman I've never seen before, and I wonder how she knows her. Both of them look uncomfortable having me nearby, so I excuse myself and get a cup of diet soda and a bagel.

"Sorry about that," my mother says as she sits beside me, whitefish salad and tomatoes on her plate.

"Who was that?" I ask through a mouthful of cream cheese.

She hesitates, and I nod, understanding. Someone from the Program. Another Russian alcoholic. This is comforting. Another Russkie who stopped hiding behind trash cans of recyclables.

I watch the woman out of the corner of my eye. There's no one at her table. I wonder if she has kids. "She can sit with us, you know," I say.

My mother shakes her head. She doesn't have to explain why this would be a bad idea. It would be obvious then how my mom knows her, and it would embarrass the woman.

When everyone finishes eating, the rabbi asks us to form a circle as we sing the post-meal blessing. Most people know it by heart. My mother belts out the notes and her AA friend is doing the same. It's as if the words are coming from deep inside them and jumping into the air around us. They look happy, centered, strong. Gaining strength from each other, becoming one with this new world before them, finally finding themselves.

THIRTY-TWO

Mr. Pinto looks up from the magazine he's reading, turns up the volume on the television, and checks the clock on the wall.

It's three days before Thanksgiving and classes have been shortened to thirty minutes to make room for the annual pep rally. Everyone is dressed in their school spirit shirts, and no one wants to be here.

The flick playing is an eighties film called *Mr. Mom*, about a guy who has to take care of his kids while his wife works outside the house. It has funny moments like the baby throwing flour on the dad and him slipping on food, but it's predictable. Lesson learned: man realizes how hard his wife works and no longer takes her for granted.

It makes me think of my house. Almost three weeks of sobriety, and my father has only worked late twice. My mother has signed up for yoga and a women's drumming circle; she's writing articles about them and gets to take classes for free. Her daily attire screams serenity—flowing ankle-length skirts over leggings, a leotard beneath a loose hemp shirt. She ties her hair back with ribbons made out of recycled material. And she's begun writing poetry in both Russian and English. She keeps trying to get me to go to her spoken word and drumming sessions, but I've seen her practice her beats and lyrics at home and there's something really naked and raw about the experience. I'm afraid I'll learn something about her that I shouldn't know.

Mr. Mom and his wife are arguing about household duties while he tries to cook a batch of pancakes. That's also something my mom has gone back to doing. Even with her classes and work, she's managed to serve a home-made dinner every night. Maybe this was part of the deal she made with my dad. She seems to enjoy the cooking lately, so it might just be something she decided to do on her own. Last night, she made *blinchiki* again. The Russian pancakes are one of Lana's favorite foods, and my mom has been after me to ask her over. I don't want to know how Lana will react to the invitation. Or, even if she's psyched to come over, what if the smell of *blinchiki* is replaced by liquor by the time we get to my house?

Lana writes something in her notebook, crunches it up, fits it in her pen cap, and drops it by my feet. I look at her, surprised, and she motions for me to pick it up. I know she's been hanging out with Trish more, but she must really be in with them to do the pen thing.

She had a dentist appointment this morning, so this is the first I'm seeing her today, and she looks ready to jump out of her seat. She watches my face as I read the note. *Jake kissed me last night!!!!*

I want to grab her hands and do the girly thing where we squeal and jump up and down. *Oh my God! Where? How? Tell me everything!*

Ten minutes of class left, and the note passing is not going to do justice to Lana's kiss.

"May I go to the bathroom?" I ask, not waiting for Mr. P to call on me.

He glances at his watch and nods. "Better take your books, just in case."

"I need to go too, Mr. P," Lana purrs.

He looks like he's going to object, but then shrugs and waves us both out. He doesn't want to be here either.

Lana checks the bathroom stalls and makes a production of kicking each one open even though she doesn't see feet.

"Enough already. Tell me," I say, my voice reaching whining level.

"All right," she says, leaning in as if the bathrooms are bugged, "we were at a little get-together at Trish's—"

"Trish had a party?"

"No, not a real party, a get-together. Just Ryan, Jake, me, and her cousin. If it was something big, I totally would've invited you." Her voice has the same syrupy quality I've heard her use on teachers when she's trying to get out of doing assignments.

"Yeah, sure." I start to apply lipstick to give myself something to do until the awkwardness goes away.

"Anyyywaaay," Lana says. "So we were at Trish's, and we were drinking some beer and Boone's, nothing hard-core. Jake and I weren't really drinking, just one beer each, but Ryan had like five even though he drove me. He's sloshed and stumbling all over the place, knocking into stuff. Trish gets pissed because she thinks he's going to wake her parents, so she says everyone has to go home."

"You didn't let Ryan drive you home, did you?" I ask, wide-eyed.

Lana rolls her eyes and looks annoyed. "No, Mom, but that's all part of the story."

She pauses and looks into the mirror, smiling. She takes out her strawberry-flavored lip-gloss, runs it over her lips, and does an exaggerated smack. She glances at me, like she wants me to press her for more details, and all I'm thinking about is whether she didn't tell me about the party because of the drinking.

"Don't you want to know what happened next?" she asks.

"Totally. I was just waiting for you." I hope my smile doesn't reveal my thoughts.

"Okay. So Jake says he'll drive both Ryan and me home, and after we drop Ryan off, Jake takes the long route to my house, past that recycling center on River Drive."

I nod. The recycling center is the other hot make-out spot. Not 'cause there's anything romantic about it, but the entrance is hidden away between these huge trees, so it's easy to park there without being seen. And when someone says, "I helped my parents with the recycling last night," everyone knows what it means. Well, if I said it, it might have a different meaning.

"So, he parks, right? And then leans over and goes, 'Hi,' like how guys do when they want to make out. But I've had lots of guys say this, and Jake's 'Hi' was way sexier. And I said 'Hi' back, and he just leaned in and kissed me. It was so amazing. He used just a little tongue and gave me a small bite on my lip. Then he slowly ran his tongue over my lips." She sighs and leans on the sink like she'll fall over.

"That's so awesome." I hug her. "Are you going on a date?" I regret the words the minute they're out of my mouth.

Lana's face falls, but she quickly regroups. "It just happened last night, Alyssa. We're just chilling, seeing how it goes. No rush."

"Of course." I put my hand on her arm as an apology, but she recoils.

"Why are you always thinking ahead? It was really cool last night. Don't act like something's wrong because he didn't make plans for our wedding."

"You know I'm hopeless when it comes to dating. Obviously, I'm really happy for you." I put my arm on hers again.

She doesn't say anything, but doesn't push my hand away either. Instead, she puts on more lip-gloss and blows the mirror a kiss.

"It's all good," she says, her voice syrupy again.

At the pep rally in the gym later, Keith is sitting with the rest of the seniors on the bleachers across from our class. I look for Holly and finally see her by the band. Apparently she's a majorette—which is a step below cheerleader, but the short skirt she wears makes up for the lack of coolness. It shows her butt every time she bends down to pick up her baton. She bends down a lot and looks at Keith. I watch Holly watching him. He's too absorbed in his conversation to notice either of us.

Lana manages to find Ryan, Jake, and Trish, and rushes ahead to sit with them. I hang back, unsure if she wants me to follow.

Trish nudges Lana and nods in my direction.

"Yo, Alyssa," Lana calls from her spot. "You need some special invite or something?"

Then she and Trish crack up and I make my way over to them, also laughing, as if I totally understand why they're hysterical. They start talking about how tailgating should be allowed at the upcoming homecoming game. They're wearing their hair the same way, in a half ponytail. Both take out their compacts at the same time and reapply copper lipstick and strawberry gloss. Ryan grabs the tube of lip-gloss out of Lana's hand and makes slashes under his eyes in football-player style.

"Oh, so mature, Ry," Lana says, and Trish rolls her eyes.

"I wanna be like you, Trish," Jake says in a high-pitched

voice, grabbing Trish's lipstick to draw slashes under his eyes too.

Trish and Lana giggle like it's the funniest thing in the world, but Lana's eyes look mad. Like this is some flirting ritual and Jake went for something of Trish's rather than hers. Ryan pretends to be insulted that no one laughed when he grabbed the lip-gloss, only I don't think he's pretending.

The band starts playing, a sea of red and gray polyester and poo-bah hats bouncing up and down to "Louie Louie," then "Hot, Hot, Hot." They throw in Bon Jovi to spice it up and then do a "Go, Fight, Win" cheer with the cheerleaders. The noise in the gym is deafening. Everyone is stomping their feet and clapping their hands. The football team runs out. The cheerleaders do cartwheels and a pyramid and the majorettes twirl around them. Holly does a cartwheel and flashes a big smile at Keith when she's done. *Screw her.*

The football coach gives a speech about how this will be the year the Glenfair Pirates beat their rivals, the Fighting Dragons, even though Glenfair hasn't won a Thanksgiving weekend game in ten years. And everyone knows, dragons can kill any pirate with a burst of flame. The cheers grow louder. No one except the football players cares who wins or loses. For the rest of the school, this rally is an excuse to miss class. Beside me, Ryan is looking at Lana, and Lana is trying to inch closer to Jake and oh-so-casually touch her knee to his. Trish grabs Lana's hand as each class jumps up in their seats and screams to prove who's the loudest. Ryan leaves to go to the bathroom, Trish gets up to get a drink, the noise reaches concert level proportions, and out of the corner of my eye, I see Jake squeeze Lana's knee. They hold hands out of others' view and drop them when Ryan and Trish return.

Across the gym, Holly makes her way to Keith. She puts her hand on his arm and he lets it sit. She moves her other hand to his knee, and he removes it—finally—and gets up. He walks toward me and winks, motioning for me to go out in the hallway.

We walk around the corner to the lockers farthest from the gym doors. There are beads of sweat on Keith's forehead and his hair is wet from the heat of the gym.

"Hi, track star," he says.

"Hi," I say, and he pushes me against the locker. We kiss, and our sweaty fingers lace together at our sides.

The band breaks into "Livin' on a Prayer," and all I can think of is Keith's hands on me. And the Bitch. I tell myself to focus on the kissing. After all, he did get up when she got too close. But why, when we finally seem to be getting closer, does he still tolerate her flirting?

I pull away but still hold his hands. "You looked like you were having a good time in there," I say.

"Much better time out here." He presses against me, mouth on mine again.

I focus on the feel of his body on mine as I'm pressed against the locker, his mouth on my ear lobe, his hand on my waist and creeping under my shirt. This is how it's done in Lana's and Trish's world. But I keep seeing Holly.

"Does Holly like you or something?" I ask, in between kisses.

"Who cares?" Keith mumbles, mouth on my neck.

I pull away, and he looks annoyed when he gets a taste of locker.

"Well, that night at the barn may have been just a mistake to *you*, but if she still wants you ..." I feel my insides getting hot.

"Didn't we already have this conversation? I like *you*, remember?" He wraps his arms around me.

Then why not show it more? "Fine."

"Good." He kisses me again.

I wonder which part of him is keeping it real—the side that kisses me or the side that lets Holly get close.

"Pep rally is not over, guys," says some teacher stationed over by the gym door. "Move it back." He's not enthused, and if he could let everyone leave right now, he would.

"What are you doing this weekend?" Keith asks, squeezing my shoulder.

I shrug. "Nothing huge. Family and stuff."

"I'll call you and we'll make plans, 'K?"

I nod, and we go in just as the majorettes and cheerleaders begin another dance set.

I sit beside Lana again. Her knee is now superglued to Jake's. They bend their heads close together and whisper, and Ryan and Trish join in. They seem to move farther away from me. Trish and Lana join hands again as they jump out of their seats and mimic the cheerleaders' dance.

Ryan and Jake slap palms when the pom-pom girls do their cartwheels, revealing their briefs. The four of them continue with their conversation, and Lana casually moves her books off the floor and places them on the bench beside her. Between us. Now there is a small tower separating us.

I become part of the background, just another girl in a Glenfair school spirit shirt. I imagine Lana and Trish blending into that world as well, just two sophomore students. On the gym floor, Holly throws her baton in the air and flashes Keith a toothy smile. Then she twirls and sees me. Her eyes narrow, and her smile becomes small and tight-lipped. I close my eyes and try to push her into the background as well. Everyone blends now. No one is special. No one can hurt.

THIRTY-THREE

I t's fine that your mother is into all this religious shit now, but why does she have to tell my mom about it?" Lana gripes as she sets up orange cones.

I ignore her and focus on my own booth: beanbag clowns. Knock them down and win a prize. True, helping the Russian synagogue run a fundraising carnival is not my first choice for how I'd like to spend a school-free day, but it sure beats the days when I had to clean up vomit and play nursemaid. Plus, both my parents are here and they seem to be having a good time. Lana's parents made a donation instead of volunteering but sent Lana to help with the grunt work, which is probably why she's still muttering.

"Hey," she says, squirting a water gun at me, "you're not listening to me." She's in a better mood now because a new mom just asked for her babysitting contact info. Lana has managed to turn this into a networking opportunity.

"Sorry, I wasn't sure if you were done whining." I

squirt water back at her. Good thing it's not too cold out today.

She holds her hands up in surrender. "Truce, okay? I need to look my best, you know."

"I thought Jake and the gang were on vacation." This was the only reason Lana agreed to do this. If they were in town, there's no way she would risk being seen in public helping out at a Russian event. Especially only blocks from Jake's house.

"They are, smartass. And don't start with that again, please."

I sigh. "He likes you now. They all do. I just don't get what the big deal is."

Lana scowls and focuses all her attention on setting up the two last cones of her mini obstacle course. When she finally speaks, her voice is low and tense. "You're right. You don't understand. You think everything is so simple. A fucking math problem or something."

I blink back tears and watch her walk away to schmooze with another mom. All my beanbag clowns appear to be laughing. At me? At her? At the idea that my life is simple? If they only knew.

The carnival is underway, the speakers blasting a combo of Russian and Jewish songs, and Lana has returned to her booth all smiles. Four more new clients. We make small talk, neither of us mentioning our last conversation. A little girl of about six comes to my booth and knocks down the clowns. She chooses a *mahtryoshka* as a prize. I would have chosen the same thing, even though all Russian homes are already full of these brightly painted wooden dolls. Each one opens up to a smaller red, orange, and yellow woman in Russian garb until you're down to the last one, the size of a pinkie nail. There's just something about having your very own set to play with. I wonder if the girl will make up stories for this doll-within-a-doll-within-a-doll.

When Lana and I were younger, we used to have contests to see who could take them apart and put them back together the fastest. I see Lana watching the little girl. Then she looks at me and smiles. The old Lana, the old smile.

"I used to always beat you," she says.

———

The speakers blast a Russian song about birthday wishes, and we take a fifteen-minute break while someone else mans our booths. Lana uses the time to chat up more people and I find my parents.

"Marty, Thanksgiving is in two days and we'll have a house full of people, or have you forgotten?" my mother hisses.

My parents are off in a corner, my mother's earlier serene expression replaced by one of agitation. My father is trying to look calm, but the throbbing vein in his neck betrays him.

"Julia, relax. You will have time to get everything ready. You always do." That may be true, but we all know she wasn't struggling with sobriety at past Thanksgivings.

My mother takes a break from her freak-out to notice me. "Why aren't you at your booth, Alyssa?"

"Break time," I say. And because I can't help myself, I add, "Why aren't you at yours?"

Both my parents glare at me and my father gives me a warning look. The birthday song gets to a stanza about a magician arriving in a hot-air balloon with gifts and special powers. I look up at the sky, but there's only a plane passing.

"You're planning on staying and helping, right, honey?" asks my mom. She doesn't wait for my answer. "Because if you stay until the end and help clean up, that will make it easier for your dad and me to leave now."

I grit my teeth and work on keeping my mouth shut. The plan was to volunteer for half a day. Staying until the end and cleaning up was never part of the deal. Now I have to make up for them. "Fine," I finally say.

My mom rushes over to the rabbi to tell him the arrangement, a smile on her face like she's perfectly normal. She's really trying to be, but I can't imagine that it will last.

"We'll see you later," says my dad as he squeezes my shoulder.

I watch them walk to the car, their shoulders tense. The women at my booth are glancing at their watches, and I move to relieve them. The birthday song winds down, and another kid knocks over all the beanbag clowns. I wish

I could borrow the clowns' faces. To just laugh, laugh, laugh as life punches you down.

———————

When there's only an hour of the carnival left, Lana and I get another break. This time, we pass the minutes eating *zephyr*—pastel-colored, sugary marshmallow snacks. In the booth next to us are shish kebabs and meat-filled pastry, and the men and women cooking them are dressed in old Russian garb—kerchiefs, long multi-colored dresses, fuzzy boots.

"This ended up being fun," Lana says, licking the sugar off her lips.

I laugh. "Can you repeat that?"

She crosses her eyes and shoves me. "Yeah, yeah, I know I was bitchy."

"It's your personality," I say sweetly. "What can you do?"

I run back to our booths before she can hit me. The lines to all the events have gotten much shorter, which is good because almost all our prizes are gone. Lana manages to squirt me with the water gun again, but it's late in the day now and the water feels colder.

She picks up the gun again, then freezes. "Jesus Christ," she mumbles.

"Lana! We're at a synagogue, and the rabbi is, like, right there," I say.

Lana just stares, and I follow her gaze. "I thought they were skiing," I say, as Trish, Ryan, and Jake walk toward us.

"They were *supposed* to be. Maybe I got the days confused?" Lana bites her lip and starts wringing her hands.

"Relax. What are they going to do?"

The song playing now is one my mother sang to me when I was little, "Arlequin the Clown." It's like a Russian version of Dumbo, only it's about a clown who nobody likes. No matter what he does, he can't get people to laugh.

"Yo, yo, what's going *on*, ladies?" asks Ryan when he, Jake, and Trish get to our table.

They take everything in—the booths, the clowns, the smell of foreign food, music in a language they don't understand. Trish fixes her headband. "Why didn't you tell us about this, um, gig?" she asks.

"It just came up. Besides, I thought you were going away," says Lana, a hurt look in her eyes.

"We are, girl," Trish says. "Tomorrow."

Then Jake walks over to Lana, whispers something in her ear that makes her blush, and rubs her shoulder.

I see the rabbi watching us and think about how I have to do double the work to make up for my parents' ditching. "Um, you guys wanna play something?"

Lana tenses up again, but I refuse to meet her eyes.

"Yeah, sure. We'll play. I can do this clown thing with my eyes closed," Ryan says.

"Maybe it would help if you wore one of those kerchief things," says Trish, laughing.

"How come *you're* not wearing one, Lana?" asks Jake.

"Shut up," Lana says, and giggles like Jake said something so amusing.

"Enough talk. I need to concentrate." Ryan gears up for a swing. He knocks all the clowns down with one shot.

"Nice job." I give him a *mahtryoshka*.

He starts taking it apart as Trish looks on. She actually seems interested. Maybe it's a girl thing.

"When are you done here?" Jake asks Lana.

"I have to stay and clean up. So maybe an hour?" She runs her finger down his jacket.

"You can't cut out earlier?" Jake asks, licking his lips. I think I'm going to be sick.

Lana rolls her eyes. "It blows, I know. I'm only here because my mom made me come. Total torture all day."

Trish and Ryan have managed to get two of the dolls open and are now working on a third.

"Later, then," says Jake.

"Yeah, later," says Ryan, still working on the doll.

"Good work, girls. But I still think you'd look better with the kerchiefs," Trish says, and they burst out laughing. "Or maybe you can do one of those Russian dances to get more people," she calls back as they walk away.

I watch them head down the street and see that the *mahtryoshka* has fallen out of Ryan's hands. He doesn't bother to pick it up.

The speakers play Arlequin's chorus—visions of a sad clown sitting in the center of the circus ring, his own tears forming a river around him. Lana starts putting away the pieces of her booth, and I see her hastily wipe her eyes with the back of her hand.

"They're just jerks," I say.

She swallows and turns away from me. "No," she says, her voice shaking, "they're not."

I work on cleaning up my booth. I know whatever the four of them do tonight won't include me. One of the clowns falls to the floor, and I pick him up and put him in a bag. The song on the speakers winds down with Arlequin finding a friend. The clowns around me laugh and laugh.

THIRTY-FOUR

It's three o'clock, an hour before everyone arrives from Brooklyn for the big feast. My father and I are setting the table, and my mother is keeping an eye on the turkey and roasts in the oven while mashing potatoes. There's a CD playing, masking the tension. The song is one of my favorites. It's called "On the Ship, the Music Keeps Playing," and it's about a woman whose boyfriend left her to pursue his dreams. She's watching from the shore as the ship embarks on its journey, but her heart is breaking because there's nothing she can do to stop her guy or the ship from leaving.

When they play it in Russian restaurants, everyone puts their hands in the air as if waving good-bye to the ship, then over their hearts to show the woman's sorrow. It's a sad song but the beat's peppy, and with everyone's arm movements you'd think the woman was having the time of her life. Lana says it's an "I Will Survive" for the Russian crowd.

My father brings up crates of alcohol from the basement

and the clinking of glass halts us. I stop setting the table. My mother stops mashing. My father puts the bottles on the table and stares at them. My mother leaves the kitchen and sets the wine and shot glasses beside each place setting. The music is not loud enough to cover our anxious breathing, which sounds louder to me than the vocals and saxophone of the music.

I make a production of folding the napkins into triangles. My hands shake. My father walks behind my mother and puts his arms around her. She's too tense to respond. *"And on the ship, the music plays,"* the woman on the CD sings in Russian.

"I won't drink tonight," he says.

My mom grips a chair and her knuckles turn white. "I have to learn to be around it. Anyway, you have to drink if I'm not."

And this is true, because for the spotlight to be off her, for no one to ask why she's not partying, my dad has to act normal.

"But I am standing on the shore."

"It's too soon," I whisper, smoothing out a napkin because the triangle wasn't completely even. I unfold and refold it. There are creases in it that are making it difficult to create symmetry. I tuck the end under a plate to keep the fold in place.

"And though my heart is breaking."

"It will always be too soon," my mother says.

"I can do nothing more."

In the kitchen, she resumes potato mashing and oven

watching. My father finishes unpacking the booze, kisses the top of my head, and goes into the living room to watch football.

I continue folding napkins and make up a game. The more perfect triangles I get, the better the chances my mom will stay sober. It's a stupid game, but it reminds me of something my mom and I used to do when I was little. Whenever I was anxious before a test or about going back to school after a long vacation, we'd walk around Glenfair looking for snowmen or blooming flowers or leaves of a certain shade. Then my mom would say, "If we find five" (the perfect score in Russian schools) "roses" (or leaves, or snowmen with red scarves, or whatever), "everything will be fine." We always found what we were looking for. By the end of the game, I'd feel calm. So far, I've folded four perfect napkins, but being that there are twelve place settings, I aim for seven—to get more than 50 percent. I get to six before my mom asks for help in the kitchen.

"Just a minute," I say. "I'm almost done."

"Alyssa," she says, an edge to her voice, "I need help with a salad now."

I leave the napkins as they are on the table, my quota not met. When I go back to the dining room, they're already folded—my father finished for me—but they're not perfect, and I don't have time to fix them. The guests will be here in twenty minutes and I still need to get in the shower. I head upstairs, hearing the CD stuck on the last verse of the chorus.

"I can do nothing more. Nothing more. Nothing more."

"How's school, Alyssa?" asks Uncle Vlad, one of my dad's brothers, slapping me on the back. "Hope you're not studying too hard. A young girl's gotta have fun too."

"Oh, I'm having fun. We had a pep rally the other day." I go into the kitchen to help my mom carry the salads into the dining room. I hear my other uncle talking to my dad about not working too hard. Everyone in my family works too hard, but when they get together they all talk about having fun because it's a reason to drink more and unwind.

With the salads, bread, caviar, and smoked fish served, my mother and I join everyone at the table.

"What took so long?" asks Uncle Vlad. "We have to drink more to make up for lost time. Everyone but you, Alyssa." He winks at me.

Vlad's new wife, twenty years his junior, is pregnant and Vlad is filling her glass with beer. She drinks it. The doctor told her she needed to gain more weight, and my relatives have been saying that beer is a good way to fatten her up. I tell them to read the label on the bottle—the one that advises pregnant woman to refrain from drinking—and they laugh at me.

"We've been doing it this way in Russia for years. You turned out fine," my dad's cousin says.

My mother stiffens and picks at her chopped liver. Vlad scoffs at her empty shot glass and fills it with cognac. "What's with the water, Jules? You'll fill up before you can drink the real stuff."

Everyone laughs, and my father diverts the attention from my mom by doing a shot of scotch.

"Vlad," I say, "tell us about the famous people you drove today." He works for a big limo company in New York and loves talking about the celebs he picks up. Get enough liquor in him and he'll tell you who snorted cocaine in the back seat.

Vlad gets excited and forgets all about my mom's untouched shot glass, and so does everyone else. I glance sideways at her while listening and laughing at the right spots—like when he tells my dad to cover my ears because the next part, about what a certain couple did to each other with whipped cream in the back of the limo, is too raunchy for the kids. Only there are no other kids here, because my cousins are all older than me and spend Thanksgiving with their spouses' families.

More wine is poured, but my mother fills her glass with juice. Uncle Vlad's eyes linger on her, but my dad makes a toast "to this great meal" before he can comment. Everyone drinks, and my mother uses that as an excuse to start clearing the table so she can bring out the yams, grilled vegetables, and meat-filled *piroshki*. The turkey, roast, stuffing, cranberry sauce, and mashed potatoes are yet another course. It's no wonder everyone drinks so much when they sit at a table for over five hours.

"Help your mother," says my dad. He really means, *check up on her*.

I bring everyone's dirty plates to the sink and get nervous when I don't see my mom in the kitchen. She probably went to the bathroom, I tell myself, but after I put the hot dishes on the table and she still doesn't show up, I search the house.

I see her sitting on her bed, phone in one hand, wine glass in the other. "It's too hard," I hear her say.

Then she's quiet, except for an occasional "uh-huh."

"No, there is no other way. That's how our holidays are. I need to learn to deal with it," she says.

Then more "uh-huhs" and "that's rights," and then she gets annoyed and shakes her head.

"I can't just leave here right now and go to a meeting. I'll try tomorrow."

She grips the phone and I know she's getting angry. I see her drink the wine. One sip and then she spits it back out and slams the glass on the night table like it's hot and has scarred her hand. Wine spills on the bed.

"I said I'll try. It's not easy. Well, I'm calling you, aren't I?"

I feel guilty for listening, but I need to know how this ends.

"Yes, yes, I understand. I did call you for a reason. You're right. I'll go to a meeting tomorrow."

She hangs up the phone and I hear her talking to the bathroom mirror. Then she returns to the bedroom, takes the wine glass, and pours it into the bathroom sink. I've stayed long enough.

Downstairs, my father raises his eyebrows at me and I smile, as if to say she's all right. But she doesn't come down for another twenty minutes, just in time for the turkey and another set of toasts. She's pale, and Vlad would normally comment on something like that, but he's had one shot too many to notice. I give her a kiss on the cheek, and she responds with a weak smile. My father's wine glass hasn't been touched, but at this point no one would know if he was downing shots of water or gin. One of my aunts hollers for another toast, and my dad pours sparkling cider for my mom and me. We raise our glasses, laugh, and hope no one can see that we don't belong in this picture.

———————

I offer to clean up once everyone has gone. This is as much to be alone with my thoughts as it is to help my parents. When they gratefully head up to bed, I pour lots of soap and water into the sink and cover my hands in suds. I concentrate on the water bathing the dishes and imagine it's a small waterfall. It relaxes me, but I keep thinking about the conversation I overheard. It's a good thing she called her sponsor, I tell myself. Better than if she gave in to her urge to drink. This shows she's really trying. Still, it doesn't sit easily in my stomach. I picture her pale face, white knuckles, strained voice. I'm proud of her, but I wonder if she'll call next time. When both my father and I aren't home. When she has a looming deadline. When another article is rejected. When life gets to be too much. My hands start to shake, and I stop washing and sit down. I don't want a repeat performance of the broken glass.

The ringing of the phone startles me. I have a feeling

it's Keith before I even look at the Caller ID, since no one else would call me after eleven. Maybe Lana, but I bet she's out with Jake, working off those extra holiday calories with a recycling center make-out session.

"Hey," I say. I'm still annoyed about Holly, but I can't help being happy at the sound of his voice.

"How was your Thanksgiving?" he asks, concerned, as if he knew that today would be hard. I picture him on his bed, lying on his back, staring at the posters that glow in his black light.

"Long. You know how it is when family gets together." I try to keep my voice light.

"Yeah, I know." His voice sounds tired. Not just late-time-of-night tired, more like too-much-to-deal-with tired.

There's silence, and I want to be on my bed too so we can both be doing the same thing, but there's still a large pile of dishes waiting.

"Do you want me to come over?" he asks.

It's so tempting, but would he be willing to just sit and talk? *No boy comes over this late just to talk*, I picture Lana saying. Besides, what would my parents say if they woke up and found me with a boy? Still, it would be nice to rest my head on his shoulder and escape, even if he can't fix everything.

"This late?" I ask.

"We don't need to do anything," he says, reading my mind. And it hits me—maybe from the sound of his voice—that he's the one who needs someone.

"There are lots of dishes to wash."

He laughs. "I'm good at that."

"All right. Come over."

I change into jeans and a sweater and brush my hair, but leave my face makeup free. Dirty dishes stay in the sink, and I wait.

———

As soon as he walks in, Keith wraps me in a hug and kisses me on the forehead. His hair is tousled, his cheeks are red, and his breathing is quick like he's just completed a run, but I heard his car pull up so I know he drove here. (Plus, he's wearing slip-on sandals with socks—another sign he didn't run.) He takes off his red, hooded Glenfair sweatshirt to reveal a tan T-shirt with a small bird in the corner, then takes my hands in his and stares at me as if he's taking me in. His breathing slows, as if the touch of my skin is calming. His eyes don't leave mine, and I wonder what he can see in them. I feel more naked than I've ever felt with him and let go of his hands. His breathing is still a little quick.

"Why so out of breath?" I ask, turning my back to him and starting the water.

"Sprinted around the block twice before coming in. Just had lots of energy to burn off." He adds more soap to the sink.

He's behind me now, and I feel his breath on my neck.

"Wash or dry?" I ask. I can feel his eyes on my back but I don't want to turn around, afraid he'll stare again.

"I'll wash," he says, looking at my dishpan hands.

I move aside to give him space, and he turns me to him and kisses me. He pulls my body close to his, and his arms around me make me feel safe. But his kiss is starting to feel urgent, like he needs the kiss, like he needs me, and I know what that's like. It scares me to have someone want me, need me, as much as I need them.

I gently push him away, and he looks apologetic and embarrassed, like he gave too much away. We wash dishes in silence for ten minutes, and then ... maybe because I want to change the mood, maybe because it seems like the relationship is getting intense even though that's exactly what I wanted, maybe because I want to have an argument that pushes Keith away before he realizes what I already know, that two needy people can't save each other ... whatever the reason, I bring up Holly.

"Have you seen *her* since the pep rally?" The question is a little stupid, because where would he have seen her?

"Who?" Keith asks, pouring clean water over a dish and handing it to me.

"Holly." I glance at him sideways to gauge his reaction. He pauses and turns off the water.

"Joe and I went to Applebee's last night, and she was there."

I suck in air through my teeth. I wanted a fight, but I really didn't expect him to say he'd seen her.

"How convenient," I mutter.

"I didn't tell her we were going. Everyone goes there when there's nothing to do. If I ran into her at CVS, would that be my fault too?" He has an edge to his voice now and his eyes look tired and sad, and I feel bad that I started this argument. But I don't stop.

"It's just that she hangs all over you and you don't seem to care."

"What do you want me to do? I push her away, I tell her I'm with you. Yesterday Joe and I ended up leaving 'cause she was trashed and tried to kiss me."

"She did WHAT?"

I'm not even mad at him now. I'm mad at her, that skank of a girl who gives the rest of my gender a bad name. And I'm glad he walked away. Doesn't it say something about him that he's even telling me this? But I know a part of me is scared about the next time. Just like with my mom, it seems. What if he doesn't push her away next time?

"I really can't do this right now. It's been a long night," he says, turning on the water again.

I watch as the sink fills up with white soap and all the food crust is hidden, just like when it snows outside and covers all the litter, and for that moment you think everything is perfect and beautiful.

With Keith refusing to fight back, there's nothing that's moving me to keep going. I think he'll leave because of the Holly thing, but he finishes washing the dishes and heads out to the backyard. I follow.

Keith leans on the deck rail and unwraps a peppermint candy, offering a piece to me. The taste reminds me of our many kisses. He puts his arm around me, and I let him.

"I'm sorry about bringing her up," I say.

"No, you're right. I'd be pissed too. But we're cool now?" He squeezes my shoulder.

I nod and let the candy rest on my tongue.

"Why did you say you had a long night?" I ask quietly.

"Why did *you*?" he asks.

He turns to face me and stares, his eyes penetrating mine. And I know he knows.

I look away.

He sighs. "I saw your mom leaving the church. She was there for the Program, right?"

My heart drops and I stare into the darkness. The only thing I hear is that he saw her, and he knows. The lingo doesn't hit me right away.

Keith takes my hand and makes me look at him. "My dad's in AA too, and I saw her walk out with him and some other people. And I remembered the night of our movie and the cross-country meet, so I was already thinking about it. No one else knows," he says, seeing the worried look on my face. "If you haven't lived it, 'wrong meds' seem as good an explanation as any." He smiles.

I laugh. So he'd heard Lana's story but didn't say anything, and he's suspected all along and let me be. His earlier pulling away makes sense now. I realize that he didn't know if he could deal with that scene again, didn't know if he was needy too, or strong enough to save us both.

"How long has your dad been sober?" And it must have been his dad—not an ex—who he was talking about on Yom Kippur. Of course he wouldn't want to be with a party girl.

"Eight months tomorrow—the longest he's ever been dry—but he's tried many times, and you never know with the holidays. All my family in one room can suck on a normal day. With the booze flowing, it's even worse."

We walk down the deck steps, the scent of peppermint marking our path, and lie down on the damp grass. I rest my head on his chest and he strokes my hair.

"And your mom, when did she stop drinking?" he asks.

"Three weeks ago, but she was a mess today." I place my hand on his knee, and realize that I'm talking about my mom but my hands are not shaking.

"She made it, though. That's what's important."

"Yeah, but for how long?" I look up at a twinkling star, which turns out to be a plane.

"You can't think that way." Keith stares at the sky too.

My watch tells me it's almost two a.m., so we help each other up. I walk him to his car and give him a soft kiss before he gets in.

"I'll see you Saturday," he says. "Will you be all right?"

"Yes," I say, but my mind is asking *for how long*?

"I'm here for you," he says. "Unless Holly calls, that is." He grins.

I punch him on his arm. "Funny man."

"Seriously, anything you need, I'm your guy." He tilts my head up so I'm looking at him, and this time I don't turn away from his stare.

THIRTY-FIVE

We have a Christmas tree. In Russia, it's a New Year's tree, but to American Jews it's all the same.

It bothered me when I was younger because it's even decorated like a Christmas tree—with ornaments and tinsel—and has presents under it. Some people in school had Chanukah bushes, but they were short little shrubs decorated with blue and white ribbons, the colors of the Israeli flag, and there was a Jewish star on top. Our tree has a regular star.

In Brooklyn, it wasn't a big deal because most Russians had trees, but in Glenfair all the kids thought it was weird—except for Lana, whose parents decorate the outside of their house in blue and white lights. And I'd complain every year, until finally we began decorating with the ornaments my parents had brought over from Russia. The lights cast rainbow colors on the walls, making the orange bulbs of our menorah appear even brighter, and my thoughts now only go to the beauty of it all.

This year it's even more important to stick with our tradition, but with the Thanksgiving preparations, I'd forgotten we'd be tree shopping the next day.

"Are you ready for the smell of fresh pine?" my dad asks at the breakfast table on Friday morning, looking up from his paper.

I'm relieved that things are still going according to plan. I boil water for instant coffee, which I don't normally drink, but I'm exhausted after last night. Then I think of Keith and me, our worlds finally coming together, and I feel lighter and more alert.

My mother is taking deep, yoga-style breaths and pauses to smile at me before resuming her exercises. Her hair is pulled back into a tight ponytail with a navy blue ribbon, and she's wearing a blue velour warm-up suit and blue sneakers. I can tell she tried to hide the circles under her eyes with coverup, but she didn't do a very good job. Still, she looks more put-together than yesterday. A cup of black tea and orange slices, arranged in a semicircle on her plate, rest beside her on the kitchen table. She takes three more breaths and eats two pieces of orange. My father squeezes her hand and then goes back to the paper, feeling around for his fork and then stuffing eggs into his mouth.

There are random snow flurries outside, but not the kind that will stick or even fall for long. Just some flakes making a brief appearance, like they'll wear out their welcome if they linger. All that's missing from this picture is a crackling fire in the next room.

The tea kettle's whistle pierces the silence. I drop my

butter knife, and my mother jumps at the clanking sound it makes. My father misses the fork-mouth connection and pokes himself in the cheek. As I go under the table to pick up my knife, I notice my mother wringing her hands, squeezing her knees together to stop her shaking legs.

———

We drive to Western Jersey, an hour and a half away, to pick out our tree. We've always used the day as an excuse to get away and "see how the quieter half lives," as my father says. The half that doesn't even have a CVS for miles. The half that lives in a house in the woods, in a Hansel-and-Gretel forest away from everything else. The calm is comforting, especially since we're all on edge.

On the drive, my mom has her eyes closed and takes deep breaths. My dad has the radio station turned to classical music, hoping it will ease my mom's nerves even though it's frazzling his. I spend the drive doing Sudoku puzzles. Soon my breaths are as even as my mother's, only I'm not trying hard like she is.

My mother opens her eyes as we pull into the lumberyard, and I watch her take everything in. The log cabin office, tied-up trees, chopped-down trees, local men and women in flannels and fleece-lined hats, city folk in leather jackets and designer jeans, breathing on their hands to keep them warm—their idea of roughing it—and people's breaths, white and billowy, floating into the sky.

"This will be good. It's good we're here," my mother mutters as my dad helps her out of the car.

"Of course it is, Jules," he says. She looks up, startled, as if she's surprised that someone joined her private conversation.

Frank, the owner of the yard, runs up to us and pats my dad on the back. This place is a mom-and-pop chop shop and he knows all his clients.

"How've you been, Marty?" Frank asks, adjusting his hunting cap so that it covers his ears. "Could use some brewskies, huh? Will warm all of us right up!" He gives a booming laugh and elbows my dad in his side.

In the past, Frank and my dad knocked back brandy while talking about my family's roots and how alcohol was a staple in the Russian army. My mom, the designated driver, would only have a few sips, mixed with her tea, and I'd be given hot apple cider.

Today, my parents tense up, but Frank doesn't notice. I rub my sneaker in the dirt, making checkered boxes and imagining what numbers would fit inside each to create the perfect puzzle. My mother says something about seeing a tree she likes and walks far ahead toward a cluster of tied-up pines. My dad tells Frank that after last night's meal, his stomach can't take anything foreign, and good ol' hot cider—dry—would be the perfect prescription. Frank looks disappointed, but then shrugs and goes into his cabin for three mugs.

"Crisis averted," my dad says with a forced smile, and

I know he's trying to convince me of this as much as he is himself.

———

"This one's a beauty," says Frank as we look at a tree with all-green needles.

"That it is," says my dad, "but we'd have to raise the roof to make it fit."

"That's why you have to move out here to the country. You can build what you want and don't have to deal with all those zoning regulations you city folk have," says Frank.

I laugh out loud. Only here can Glenfair be considered a city.

"How's this one?" asks my mom. She's motioning to a tree about six feet tall. We've had bigger trees in the past, but this is a year where less hassle is better.

"Looks good," says my dad, letting out a large sigh of relief like he's been holding it in for hours, afraid to release it too soon. A gust of white travels up from his mouth, over our heads like an umbrella, and high into the sky.

Frank just shakes his head and drinks his brandy/cider mix. "City folk," he says again with a laugh, and goes inside for the chain saw.

———

Three Sudoku puzzles and two hours later, we're in our warm living room breathing in fresh pine. I run my fingers over the needles and like how they're still sharp enough to hurt if you press them into your skin. Mom is usually the one who gets the tree decorations out, but she's sitting Indian-style on the wooden floor, her eyes closed, her nose almost touching the needles as she breathes in and out for silent counts of one, two, three.

She manages to do ten sets before my dad returns from the basement with the *New Year's Stuff* box. He kisses my mom on the top of her head and helps her up, but she seems to be doing everything in slow motion, like she's not fully there with us, like to do anything at normal speed will take energy she doesn't have no matter how many breathing exercises she does. My dad looks at her, concerned. It's the same look—alert but tired eyes, weary smile—that he's been giving her since she became sober. And the way he kisses and holds her is so gentle, like he's worried she'll fracture at any moment. This I understand.

Normally, we throw tinsel at each other or make fun of decorations from years past, like the Jewish star I made out of macaroni when everyone else in my kindergarten class was gluing sparkly angels, or the New Jersey Devils bumper sticker my dad converted into an ornament using a clasp from one of my mom's earrings. But today, with a few nervous smiles, we decorate in silence. It's not a quiet calm that descends—it's more like a cloud of smoke you have to find your way out of so you don't suffocate from inhaling poisonous fumes. Only there are no firemen to help you and no axe you can break down doors with to escape. The smoke just keeps building, building, building until it takes away all your air, making you forget you once used to breathe easily and even longed for days when you laughed so hard your breath got away from you.

My mother takes a glass doll out of the box. It's from Russia and was a gift from my dad on their first New Year's together. She strokes it lovingly, and carefully hangs it on the tree. The sun shines through the blinds and the doll sparkles. My parents smile and squeeze each other's hands. My mother closes her eyes, like she's trying to freeze the moment. I do the same and take a picture of this scene in my mind. For two minutes, there are no breathing exercises or tension or smothering smoke, just the three of us, eyes closed, arms around each other, holding onto something that we hope will keep us all from breaking.

THIRTY-SIX

When I awake Saturday morning, snow has painted my window white.

I run to the living room bay window and watch as it piles up. No one is out yet, and today I don't mind being up at seven in the morning on a weekend. There's still a good hour before some dog will yellow the surroundings. I hear the town plow in the distance, but it hasn't reached our street yet, so there's no gray slush marring the perfect road by my house either.

I pick up the phone to call Lana. I know she loves walking in the first snow, creating footprints before anyone else, but I change my mind. That was a Lana who didn't mind spending time with me. She doesn't exist anymore. Or, even if she does, I'm not sure how much of her is allowed to come out before New Lana punches her and tells her she's not cool enough.

The light in the basement tells me Dad is back to work,

and the clicking of computer keys says the same about Mom.

I pour a new twig-and-berry cereal into a bowl and park myself in the recliner by the living room window. The plow makes its way to our street, but the sidewalk is still untouched. Some kids are outside now building snowmen and snowwomen. Until we reached seventh grade, Lana and I always made snowgirls.

"There's not enough girl power out here," Lana would say. "We need to fix that."

So we'd bring out skirts and flowered headbands and button-down sweaters that no longer fit us, and get to work. We used wax lips for the mouth, blue gobstoppers for the eyes, black licorice for the eyebrows. The last time we did this, the local paper was on the prowl for first-snow stories and saw our girl. The photo made it onto the front page. Lana and I didn't, but our misspelled names were in the caption. We felt we'd done our part for women's rights.

If our snowgirl were around now, she would wonder how Lana went from promoting feminism to using her boobs to get out of assignments and into Jake's back seat.

I put my cereal bowl in the sink and walk to the dining room window to check out the hills behind our house. They're not packed with sledders yet, but a lot of people are already there. I wait until eight, then call Keith, who picks up on the first ring. First snows wake everyone up early.

"Heeey," he says lazily, and I wonder if he's lying in bed, looking at the snow, with only boxers on. I think about how warm I'd feel lying next to him, my head in the crook of his elbow, covers around us.

"What are you doing?" I say.

"Not much. I was about to take a walk before some dog ruins the scene."

"You want company?" I ask, smiling.

"Sure. My street's still unplowed. Meet halfway?"

I picture him putting on his boots and making his way to the door.

When we get off the phone, I throw on jeans and a purple V-neck sweater and stop by Mom's office. She has her face in her hands and is shaking her head.

"How could I have missed it? These damn holidays." She doesn't see me in the doorway.

"What's the matter?"

She doesn't turn around to look at me, just takes her head out of her hands to search frantically for files. "Are you spying on me, Alyssa? Why are you always watching me? I'm a big girl."

"I—I wasn't. I came in to tell you I was going out." I feel a lump rising in my throat, and the smoke that left us yesterday is starting to rise again into my lungs.

"Nice of you to *tell* me. You don't *ask* if you can go out these days?"

She looks at me now, and her eyes are mean. They're her drunken eyes, only I don't smell alcohol.

"No, I'm sorry. I didn't mean it like that, I—" I have forgotten how to talk to this version of Mom.

"Forget it. You can go. It's fine. I don't need you lurking

around with that judgmental face of yours." She waves her hand dismissively.

I stand there, waiting for her to apologize for her shortness or to even ask me where I'm going, and with whom, but she just resumes her grumbling.

I make my way down to the basement and knock on my dad's office door. I hear CNN in the background.

"You're up early," he says.

His eyes have that perpetually weary look and he seems distracted.

"First snow, you know how it is."

"Yep." He's outlining something on his drafting table. "You heading out?"

"With Keith. Is that okay?" I don't want to make the same mistake I did with my mom.

"Sure, just check in so I know when you'll be home. With both Mom and me working today, I doubt there's going to be a big dinner thing, so you may want to go out." He hands me some bills and then uses his compass and ruler to create room dimensions.

"Okay. Thanks." I give him a kiss good-bye.

He smiles and raises the volume on the television set when he thinks I've left. From the foot of the stairs, I watch him measure the patterns on his paper, adding more lines and shapes to his drawing. He doesn't look at the TV, but seems more relaxed just having its presence in the room. He pauses and then rolls his head from side to side. I don't want to add to his stress, but I'm afraid if I don't say something, we'll all shatter into little pieces.

I step back into his office. "I just saw Mom, and she doesn't seem good."

He moves his eyes to the television screen before answering. "She's having a hard day because she got her deadlines confused. Two projects due this week instead of next, and she's worried she didn't talk to enough sources. She'll be fine. Don't worry."

He looks away from the TV and gives me what he intends to be a reassuring smile. Then he turns back to the screen, but not before I see him grimace and rub a shoulder blade.

"You'll check on her?" I ask.

"Of course. Have a good time." The smile is still on his face, and I know he's waiting for me to leave so he can return to his work and his television and take off this mask.

Once I'm outside, I let the cold penetrate my jacket, and I feel my insides shiver. Mrs. Stein's dog pees on our snow-covered grass, and I break into a brisk walk toward Keith's.

———

I'm two streets away from Keith's house when his car pulls up next to me.

"They started plowing, so I got my car just in case you needed a break from the cold," he explains. "But we can still walk if you want," he adds quickly, not wanting to disappoint me.

The twenty-minute walk was enough for me. "I'm good," I say, getting into the car.

His cheeks are red, and I realize he must have gotten his fill of the cold while shoveling out his car. He pulls me in for a kiss and squeezes my knee, and this makes the thawing out so much easier.

"How were the tree festivities?" he asks.

He'd mentioned he wanted to help decorate because he's never had any kind of tree.

"Things were tense yesterday, but they seemed to end well. I'm sorry we trimmed it without you." I put my hand on his arm.

"Totally cool. I figured it was something you guys wanted to do on your own." He kisses my gloved fingers.

I think of telling him how quickly things have spiraled downwards, but I'm finally calm and I don't want to release the bad energy into the car, especially when the closed windows will keep it around us and not let it escape.

He looks at me, like he's checking up on me, but only squeezes my hand and doesn't ask any more questions.

"And how was your day yesterday?" I ask.

He plays with the radio to find a channel that hasn't started their annoying twenty-four-hour Christmas medley.

"It was an after-holiday day. My mom went to the gym, my dad to AA, I went for a run, and then Joe came over to watch football." He shrugs. "Nothing eventful. One day of drama is enough."

AA. I had forgotten that there was a meeting yesterday. A meeting my mom didn't go to.

"Yeah," I say softly, but my mind is already racing.

Keith pulls over. He takes my hands in his.

"What happened?" he asks, rubbing his thumb over my knuckles and then on the inside of my palm, as if massaging my hands.

"Nothing." I take a deep breath, but it catches in my throat. "Yet."

I wait for him to say everything will be fine and that I shouldn't worry, but he doesn't.

"You'll be okay even if she's not," he says.

I stare at him. How is that possible? He pulls me to him so my head rests on his chest, and strokes my hair.

"You think you won't be, but you will," he whispers in my ear.

Maybe this will be my new mantra. Think it enough and it will be true.

———

At the mall, Keith and I walk hand in hand and make up our own truths about the people we see, like my mom and I once did.

"What do you think of them?" Keith asks, pointing to a mismatched couple. The woman is model-pretty and wearing tan knee-length boots over her jeans with a tan cashmere sweater. The guy's unshaven, in a sweatshirt that says COLLEGE, and his belly is hanging over his jeans.

"Maybe he's the only one who understands her, and she was choosing between him and some hottie, but the hottie couldn't see into her soul like truck driver there," I say.

Keith rolls his eyes. "I was thinking arranged marriage."

"Cynic." I poke him in his ribs. "I have one for you. What's your take on skateboard dude?"

Keith takes the guy in. He's sitting on a bench, skateboard in one hand, the other hand slapping his knee to a beat from his iPod. He's wearing a suit and tie.

"He's home from college and is supposed to go to an interview his dad set up for him, on a Saturday no less, but he's blowing it off to hang out with his buddies. He figures the 'real world' can wait. Or maybe he tells everyone he works on Wall Street but is actually an up-and-coming Tony Hawk. Of course, he has to keep that on the DL because he's not good enough to show off yet."

"Look at you being all creative," I laugh.

"There's more to me than my hot bod, girl."

"That's too bad, because I like my boys dumb so I can have my way with them." I giggle and jump out of the way as he tries to slap my butt.

He chases me, making sure we don't run into any of the people giving us pissed-off looks. I feel like we're in middle school, and when he grabs my arm and kisses me, I have that familiar weightless feeling I hope I'll always feel when he touches me.

"Get a room," someone says, bumping into us. I turn around to find a grinning Lana, Jake by her side.

"Hey," I say, suddenly feeling shy.

"Check out what I bought," she says, steering us to the walls so we're out of everyone's way.

"It's bad enough you dragged me with you. Now I have to listen to a replay?" Jake says.

"You'll get yours," Lana says flirtatiously, running her fingers through Jake's hair.

"And *we* need to get a room," I say, as Keith and Jake launch into talk about Thursday's football games. I guess even if boys aren't friends, they can always find common ground.

Lana pulls me away from them and shows me two pairs of spike-heeled shoes, a teddy—which she says she picked out while Jake looked at video games—two pairs of jeans, and three low-cut sweaters. Babysitting must have been good this month.

"Did you sleep with him?" I ask, thinking of the new teddy. I don't think it's for any future games of runway modeling.

Lana blushes and wrings the little handles of the lingerie bag. "Last week," she whispers. "I was going to tell you the next time we hung out. It's not something I can just IM, you know?" She's looking at the floor as she's talking.

Her keeping this a secret from me shouldn't be a surprise, especially with the way things have been lately, but I feel an ache just the same.

"What did Trish say?" I know that she made the time to tell *her*.

Lana bites her lip and sighs. "I told her before, because she'd have tips for me. I didn't want to go into this blind." She knows what I'm really asking. "And, no offense, but I needed more help than your hand could give me." She laughs like she did at the pep rally, like it's a joke we'd both find funny, like I'm not the one left out.

I don't laugh. "I have to go."

"No, wait." Lana's voice softens and she puts her hand on my arm. "I'm sorry. I shouldn't have said that."

"Whatever." I take her hand off my arm.

"Alyssa, please?" She grabs my hand so I can't go. "You know you're my best friend." Her eyes beg me to stay. The handles of her lingerie bag are shredded.

"So you tell me," I say, but I smile and let myself get pulled in once again.

"I was telling Jake about our snowgirl today," she says, more relaxed.

"I was thinking about that too. Seems so long ago."

"It's like forever since we hung out." She puts her arm around me as we walk back to the guys. "We need to do a girl thing soon. Catch up."

I think again of Lana having sex, of all the talks in our rooms over the years, how she coached me on kissing and told me about her summer boys, what we imagined our first times to be like. Things she no longer wants to talk to me about.

"Soon," I agree, because what else is there to say?

———

Keith and I spend the rest of the afternoon lying on his bed, making out and watching movies. His parents knock around dinnertime to tell him they're going out, but his mom only slightly opens the door and speaks from the hall-way. We've been in his room when his parents were home before, but I still get embarrassed each time. Today, for example, my bra was somewhere in his bed, sandwiched between a pillow and a blanket, when his mom turned the knob.

"She must think I'm such a whore," I say when she's gone, covering my face with his pillow.

"Oh, yeah, she does," he says with a straight face. "But I told her you only do it with your eyes closed, so she felt better."

"What?" I stare at him, horrified, but then he bursts out laughing. He thinks it's cute that I worry so much about his parents.

"Relax. My mom's a teacher, remember? She knows what's out there. Trust me; she doesn't think you're a whore." He rubs my back under my shirt and kisses me. "But, if you ever feel like you want that inner wild Alyssa to come out, wear those low rise pants with the thong again, I won't judge."

I throw my pillow at him and he throws one back at me. Soon we're wrestling each other, him pinning me to the bed. I like his weight on top of me, protecting me, each kiss taking away my breath and all of the day's bad thoughts. With his parents gone, I feel freer, like the Alyssa who once swam in a sea of glitter with her best friend. We pull off our shirts, and they get lost in the tangles of his sheets. He moves his mouth down my body, stopping to kiss my breasts before sliding his tongue down my stomach and then pulling at my jeans. I unbuckle his and throw them into a pile with the rest of our clothes. He gets on top of me, and it's just the thin fabric of his boxers and my flowered cotton underwear separating us. I pull him toward me and kiss his neck and chest as his hands fumble inside my underwear.

"Do you ... want to?" he breathes in my ear, and even though a part of me does, I still don't feel completely ready. *Sweet, inexperienced*, Lana thinks.

I shake my head no, and he rolls over onto his stomach, breathing hard, and pulls me next to him.

"I'm sorry ..." My voice trails off.

"Stop." He kisses me on the nose. "Whenever you're ready."

I kiss his neck and he puts his arm around me so my head rests inside his elbow, like that spot was created for me alone.

"I love you," he whispers, and I don't say anything back right away because I don't know if I just imagined the words. But then he looks into my eyes, and I know I didn't.

"I love you too." I close my eyes to remember this moment and take pictures in my head. His hair, sweaty, across his right temple. *Click.* His fingers, drawing circles on my thigh. *Click.* His arm, tightly around me. *Click.* His words, falling across my body. *Click.*

When I let myself in at ten o'clock that night, my house is quiet except for the sound of my dad's snoring.

"How was your day?" My mother's voice suddenly echoes in the dark.

Startled, I follow the sound. She's sitting in the kitchen with the lights off, a half-filled wine glass in front of her.

"What's that?" I ask, shivers running up my spine.

"Sparkling cider," she says sarcastically, and I know it's not. "Don't worry, warden. I didn't drink it."

"Then why do you have it?" I walk into the kitchen slowly, as if approaching a scared animal. One false move and the drink goes down her throat.

"I've had a rough two days, and if I can look at this and not drink it, then I know I can make it." She swirls the wine in the glass, lifts it to her nose and inhales.

"Maybe you should just call your sponsor." I gingerly sit in the seat beside her.

"Why? So she'll tell me to go to another meeting? That's not realistic. There's alcohol everywhere. You have to face it to learn to beat it."

She smells the wine again.

"But meetings are supposed to teach you how." I want to tell her that if she had gone yesterday, she might not be in this situation right now. But I don't know how to bring up the subject without her knowing I heard her on the phone.

She sighs. "I'm trying this today. I'll go to the meeting tomorrow."

"Holidays are a hard time for people," I say, thinking of Keith's family. "You'd think they'd have extra meetings or something."

"You'd think." She looks me in the eyes. "Why don't you go to bed? I'll be fine." Her voice is tired.

"I can stay up. I don't mind." I put my hand on hers.

"Don't play cop, Alyssa. I told you, I'm not drinking," she says, irritated.

I know arguing with her will only make things worse, so I lean in to kiss her.

"Good night," she says and quickly moves her head—but not before I catch a whiff of wine on her breath. I stare at her back, and this time she doesn't turn around and look me in the eyes.

THIRTY-SEVEN

My mother's office is silent this morning. The breakfast table has no special foods waiting as an apology. There are still twenty minutes before I normally head out for school, but anything is better than sitting in the quiet house, not knowing what's to come. I step out into the chilly air, for once not checking on my mother.

Across the street, a snowwoman is half-melted, face blending with neck blending with waist. The sun shines on her and she drips. But it's not really warm, not with the wind biting through my scarf, the cold seeping in through my gloves and hurting my fingers. I walk quickly, clearing my brain, focusing only on getting to school as quickly as possible and falling into Keith's warm arms.

A car pulls up. Not Keith's. A window rolls down. "Hop in, it's a bitch out there," says Lana from the passenger's side, quickly rolling her window up.

I can no longer feel my fingers. "Thanks, Clara, you're

a lifesaver," I say to Lana's mom as I climb into the back seat.

"Not a problem. It's nice to feel appreciated," she says, looking at Lana.

"Thank you, *Mother*." Lana rolls her eyes. Then, sweeter, "Can Alyssa come over tonight?"

"As long as you finish all your homework, I don't see why not. Alyssa is always welcome."

"Thank you, Mama." This time Lana sounds like she means it. She turns to me. "You'll come, right?"

I laugh. So like Lana to make plans with me without asking me first. "Right."

"Great! We'll have so much fun!" she squeals, grabbing my hand. Her cell phone chimes and she flips it open to check her text. "Oh duh," she says, slapping her forehead. "I forgot about movie night at Ryan's tonight."

I take my hand from hers and put it in my lap. "We'll do something another night," I mumble.

"Lana," Clara warns.

"You two think so little of me," Lana says quickly. "I was going to ask Alyssa to come with. Obviously."

The car is warm, but I'm getting chills again. "Nah. You should go yourself."

"Alyssa, please? I've really missed you." She tugs at my jacket like a little kid.

"I doubt they want me there."

"Of course they do! They love you. You just have to get to know them better." She keeps tugging.

"It might be fun," says Clara. She looks hopeful and

I get the feeling she thinks my going will keep Lana in check.

I sigh. "Fine. I'll go."

"Yay!" says Lana, finally letting go of my jacket.

It's not until we reach school that it hits me there was never going to be a girls' night, that Ryan's house was the plan all along.

———

"Over here," Lana's voice calls from inside the trees surrounding Ryan's heated pool.

The four of them are sitting on recliners around the pool. Lana, eyes glassy, is watching Jake roll a joint. Her hat is pulled low over her ears.

Trish is staring past the trees at the neighbors' Christmas lights, which peek through the tall hedges and create rainbow reflections in the pool. "Pop a squat, Al," she says, then starts laughing, repeating the phrase.

"Don't mind her. She becomes a total idiot when she smokes," says Jake. He blows on his hands to warm them up, then licks a side of the paper and seals it shut, trapping the weed inside.

I sit down in an empty recliner while Jake searches for a lighter.

"Put on something trippy," says Lana. "Oooh, I know." She rummages through her backpack and pulls out her iPod. "Tracks five through ten are all Bob Marley."

I put the iPod on the docking station but I'm having trouble finding the right songs.

"C'mon, Alyssa, change it. Change it. Chaaange it," Lana whines.

"Fuck. Just pick a song already," Jake snaps. Then, softer to Lana, "I'm sorry, baby, but you know how that voice gets on my nerves."

Lana giggles and says something in Jake's ear, and he gives her the lit joint. They pass it around amongst themselves, bypassing Ryan, who appears to be sleeping or passed out. Then, remembering that I'm here too, Lana offers it to me.

"I'm fine for now. Thanks." I recall the last time I partied with all of them, my hair covered in vomit, my knees caked in dirt. I want to leave, but Lana, in her warped way, is trying to include me. I need to try too.

Trish stares past the hedges again, suddenly laughing, and Ryan stirs.

"Were you going to finish my stash without me?" he asks, stretching his hand for the happy cigarette.

He inhales deeply and holds it in longer than the rest of them, finally letting the smoke out slowly. "Niiice," he says in a low moan and slides off the recliner to lie down on the illuminated cement and stare at the sky. He's smiling and looking content, and it's a refreshing change from the Ryan who tries so hard to please everyone.

Trish is still laughing, and Lana throws a recliner cushion at her. "Jeez, shut up," she says, passing the joint back to Jake and burrowing her hands under his shirt for warmth.

He inhales quickly and then lets the smoke out, blowing it into Lana's face. Bob Marley's songs, not as calming as when I listened to them at Keith's, flow in the air around us. I watch everyone through the haze. New Lana, New Trish, New Ryan, and Jerkier Jake.

"Alyyyssaaa," Lana says in a singsong voice, "come here. Why are you so far away?"

"She said 'come,'" says Trish and laughs again.

I move my recliner closer to Lana and she puts her head on my shoulder. It's weird, lying there next to her and Jake. Jake takes beer, vodka, and shot glasses out of his backpack. He tosses a beer to each of us, and then lies back down next to Lana. I feel his eyes move over my sweater and I roll onto my stomach.

"This is like that time at the barn," Trish says, hysterics done. "Let's make a toast to something."

"Alyssa and I like to make toasts. Remember? At the party?" says Lana, stroking my hair, too high to care that she brought up her parents' Russian party.

"That's what Russians do," says Ryan, coming to from his staring contest with the stars.

"To living single, seeing double, and sleeping triple," says Jake, raising his beer.

"I second that." Ryan raises his beer too.

"Pigs." Lana laughs and clinks her bottle to mine and Trish's.

The four of them chug their beers, but I only take a sip of mine.

Trish grabs shot glasses and fills them with vodka, spilling a quarter of the bottle into the pool.

"Dude, come on," Ryan whines, and this sets Trish off into another laughing fit.

"What should this toast be to?" Lana looks at me.

"The lights," says Trish, grabbing my arm. "Let's toast the Christmas lights."

Jake snorts. "That's gay."

Trish pouts and she looks like she's going to cry.

"No, I like it. The lights it is," I say.

Jake sneers at me but pours everyone another shot.

"I wish I had a tree," Trish says, ignoring the shot in front of her, images of the lights dancing in her eyes.

"You can always see mine," I say, feeling sorry for her.

She smiles. "Thanks," she says, then looks confused. "You have a tree? I thought you were Jewish too."

"A New Year's tree. It's a Russian thing," I say, poking Lana.

I wait for Lana to agree or add something like, "Yeah, it's a Russian thing, you wouldn't get it." Instead, she turns away from us.

"Do you have a tree too, Lana?" asks Jake, grinning.

"Yeah, like with menorah ornaments or something?" Ryan laughs.

Lana turns back to us, smiling, but her eyes are vacant of all niceties. "I don't know what she's talking about. Alyssa's family is way shadier than mine."

Jake smirks. "Tell us more, Alyssa. Is there a Jewish star on top or a dreidel?"

Lana laughs like this is the funniest thing she's ever heard. Trish and Ryan join in. I stare at them, frozen, like I am watching from the sidelines as some other girl's best friend pretends she never knew her.

I should never have come. "I'm going to go."

Trish stops laughing first. "Wait, does this mean we can't see your tree?" She looks longingly at the lights again.

"Trish, you are such an idiot," says Jake.

"What? What did I say?"

Ryan shakes his head and Lana turns away again.

Trish takes my hand, and her nails dig into my palm. "I'm sorry," she says. Then to Jake and Ryan, "Maybe she's just confused, you know? Had too many, like her mother?"

I snatch my hand away and Jake and Ryan laugh.

"It that it, Alyssa?" asks Jake. "Is that why you don't want to drink with us? Did you already throw back a few with your mom?"

Lana turns back around slowly, like she hasn't decided if that is in fact what she's doing. "I told you guys that in secret," she slurs.

"Whatever, Lana," says Ryan. "It's a compliment. I wish I could function on alcohol like you Russians."

"Shut up," says Lana. "You're being stupid."

"No, I agree with Ryan. It's a compliment." Jake laughs. "C'mon, Alyssa, are you afraid you'll become a lush like your mom?"

I take a deep breath. I will not cry here in front of

them. I look at Lana to see if she'll say anything to Jake. She looks at me and then back at him. *Stand up for me. I dare you.*

"Shut up." She says it very quietly, eyes lowered.

"I'm going to go," I say again.

"I'll talk to you later, Al," Lana mumbles, looking at a spot at the other end of the pool. I think about how, not that long ago, at another pool, she stared wistfully at Jake, Ryan, and Trish—Lana and I on one side, the three of them on the other.

"Yeah, later," Jake smirks.

At the gate, I hear Trish laugh again and scream about making another toast. "To good times," she says.

I turn and see Lana's smile shift in and out of the moonlight.

"To good times," they all say.

Lana's voice is the loudest. Her face disappears into the smoky air.

THIRTY-EIGHT

My head is fuzzy when I wake up the next morning, a result of little sleep, of a night spent crying to Keith while he comforted me over the phone.

I drag myself out of bed, ignoring the frostiness that has made a home of my window pane. In the bathroom, I turn on the shower and move the dial to hot. I get in, letting the water erase all cold, staying there until the bathroom is completely coated in steam, the water starting to turn cool. By the time I'm out and dressed, I feel lighter. Maybe it's because of all the tears I lost last night or maybe it's a load being lifted, a relief that comes with no longer having to try.

———

The next night, the weightiness comes back. When the sounds of the seven o'clock news instead of my mom's voice announce dinnertime, I know for sure that everything has turned to crap once again. It seemed my parents had a deal the last three weeks: no booze, no news. Tonight there is no clanking of silverware or pots and pans, and I feel my stomach clench at what awaits. I give it thirty minutes—hopefully enough time for my dad to unwind from work—and go downstairs.

He's leaning back into the couch pillows, eyes fixed on the television like it's the most important thing in the house. Despite his position, he looks tense—back erect, shoulders stiff; feet planted firmly on the ground, not crossed; hands clenched into fists on either side of his knees.

"No dinner tonight?" I ask quietly from the doorway.

His head snaps around. He's surprised to hear my voice.

"Your mom left a message on my cell saying she wasn't feeling well and to grab something on the way home." He gestures to the crumpled-up sandwich wrapper before him.

"Have you checked on her since you've been home?" I already know the answer. And I'm sure he's telling himself that he didn't because he's gotten used to the new routine too.

He looks down at his hands. "Damn it. I should have known. Thanksgiving, the deadlines, we had a fight last night." He mutes the TV.

"She didn't go to the meeting yesterday, did she?" I sit on the couch across from him as my legs turn rubbery.

"Hence the fight," he says.

The glare of the TV reflects on the tree and bounces

off the silver tinsel. The glass doll shines brighter than ever. I see my dad watching it too.

"So you haven't eaten?" He's suddenly energized, like something inside him has awakened.

"I was waiting for you. I didn't know the new plan." My voice shakes and I think I'm going to cry. It feels like everything is collapsing once again.

"Your dad has everything under control," he says, turning off the news and crossing into the kitchen. "I'm no Chef Emeril, but I can make my special Sunday omelet."

"I can help." I try to get up despite the cloudiness in my head.

"No. You've done that enough."

I lean my head back against the couch and close my eyes. Sounds of my mother's snoring make their way downstairs and mingle with the sizzling noises in the kitchen. *You've done that enough.* My dad's words play themselves over and over in my head like a bad recording in slow motion. The sizzling subsides and I hear clinking of silverware and plates on the table. Setting the table and taking care of dinner—jobs that were mine. It takes everything inside me not to go upstairs and check for empty bottles.

It's not the family's job to take care of the alcoholic, said one of my mom's pamphlets. Tears fall down my cheeks because finally, after all this time, my dad understands and is taking care of me. I cry harder because I no longer have a role. I didn't think it was possible, but I feel even more helpless than before.

"Want a ride, hot stuff?" Keith asks in the morning, his car suddenly beside me as I walk to school.

"My king," I say as I get into the car.

"I do what I can." He mock bows—or as much as you can bow while at the steering wheel. "Any listening preferences?"

I flip through his CDs and put in The Smiths' "Asleep." The singer's voice is slow and haunting, almost hypnotizing.

"Not this song, Alyssa," Keith says. "Do we really need to make going to school more depressing?" He tries to turn off the CD, but I move his hand away. The music is soft and calming, like a morbid lullaby.

Keith takes advantage of my lethargic state and pops the CD out, flooding the car with bubblegum music.

"See what you made me do?" he asks. "Now I'll have Britney freaking Spears in my head all day." He makes a face and I know he's trying to make me laugh.

I manage a weak smile.

"She's drinking again, isn't she?" he asks when I say nothing.

"Britney? Could be."

"Cute. You know what I mean," he says.

"I guess some things were too good to last, huh?"

"You can't save her," he says, quoting the pamphlets Mom used to leave out.

"Maybe it's not as bad as before." She was doing so well, and I want to believe that the empty bottles I found in the trash last night, the little broken pieces of glass in the sink this morning, the sleeping in, are just a small glitch in her sobriety, that she'll be back on the wagon tomorrow.

"Yeah, maybe, but you know what? It doesn't matter." He pulls into a parking spot.

I stare at him. "Of course it matters." He, of all people, should understand this.

He shakes his head and gets out of the car. "Wait here."

The first bell rings and then the second, and I turn off the engine just as he opens the door.

"What the hell? We're going to be late."

"We're not going," he says starting the car again and putting it in reverse.

"I don't need another detention, Keith."

"Relax. I talked to Coach. He'll take care of it." He turns the radio up loud, drowning out my unspoken words and thoughts.

———————

He stops at Dunkerhook Park. It looks different in the winter. The path where Keith and I ran is covered in slush and footprints, and the falls are almost frozen.

He rummages in the back seat, grabs a blanket, then hands me a sweatshirt and insulated gloves. I raise my eyebrows at him.

He shrugs and shoves something in his jacket pocket. "I used to be a cub scout. We had to have spares of everything. Let's go."

By the falls, he clears a spot on the ground with his sneaker and puts the blanket down.

The gloves and sweatshirt make a big difference, but I still would rather not be out here. "Is this a romantic thing? Because we can just as easily hook up in the car."

"I come here sometimes to get my head straight," he says. "It's better in the warm weather, but it does the job either way."

"Something bothering you?" I put my hand on his arm.

"You are."

I glare at him and remove my hand. "Sorry for not being a chipper majorette."

He rolls his eyes. "Oh please. Not her again."

Does everything have to be a game or puzzle? "What are you talking about?"

"The conversation we were having in the car."

I run through it in my head, not sure which part annoyed him. It's too cold for deep thinking.

His face is exasperated. "Okay, forget that conversation. Let me tell you why else I come here." He takes a miniature bottle of Jack Daniels out of his pocket.

I think about our parents and have no words.

"I don't get drunk, Alyssa," he says. "I have one swig. That's it."

"Because … ?"

"Because I can. I don't drink at parties or anything like that. Just a shot, two or three times a year. I never want more. I don't even get a buzz."

I think of that night at Lana's house after our fashion show, champagne in my hand, staring at the sky and floating away. "Then what's the point?"

He opens the bottle. "That *is* the point. I get nothing out of alcohol. I don't crave it. When I doubt who I am, when I wonder what will happen if he slips again, the shot reminds me that I am not him. Will never be him. That he has his life, and I have mine, and I can only control mine."

He takes a sip, like this is another part of the test, and then closes his eyes and takes a large swallow. He looks straight ahead, past the falls, reminding me of when we sat here during the retreat.

I stare too, redefining what it means to be strong. This is not my father's and mother's way of thinking—which is to keep taking hits until you collapse and lose yourself. Being strong is walking away from it all, even when staying is what you wish you could do.

Keith gives me a small nod, like he can see that I'm getting it. He passes the bottle to me. I shake my head no. Just because I understand doesn't mean I'm there.

———————

At 11:00 p.m., I wake up to a crack of thunder and rain pelting on my windows. I lie awake and stare at my ceiling as my eyes get adjusted to the dark. A bolt of lightning illuminates my walls, the same moment I hear a crash from downstairs. Muffled voices yelling. Another crash. I get out of bed and creep to the top of the stairs.

"Go watch your news and leave me the hell alone," my mother slurs loudly.

"I would, but we have a daughter, or have you forgotten?" My father's voice is raised, but he's not shouting. In fact, his tone is eerily even.

I walk quietly down the stairs and stand just outside the kitchen so I can see them, but they can't see me. My mother is in a blue flannel nightgown that goes down to her knees and is ripped at the hem. Her hair is pulled back in a ponytail, but there are stray hairs sticking out all around her head. She's holding a glass of honey-colored liquid, and droplets spill onto the white kitchen tiles.

"This has nothing to do with her. I'm just unwinding. You should hear the stories of others in the Program. Then you'd see how lucky you are." She turns away from my father and stumbles into the living room.

He follows her, neither of them noticing me. My father clenches his fists, and I can see him mentally counting to ten.

"Lucky?" He laughs hollowly. "When exactly have we been lucky? The time Alyssa hurt her hand or when she spent mornings cleaning our bathroom? I'm just an idiot for ignoring everything for this long, thinking you were just having bad days, hoping all of this would just fix itself."

"Shut up!" she screams. "Just shut the hell up!"

She starts to walk away, but trips on the power cord for the tree lights and falls. The tree comes down with her. There are crashes all around me—thunder, her glass, the ornaments, the glass doll. The tree itself just misses her, but there are shards of ornaments and broken glass everywhere.

She gropes for the doll as my dad pulls her away. She pushes away from him and crawls back to the shiny pieces, cradling them in her hands, not caring that they're cutting her and making her bleed.

"Stop it," my father says, his voice low. He picks her up and carries her to the couch, leaving trails of blood behind.

I remain frozen in the hall while he gets peroxide and bandages and cleans my whimpering mother. He sweeps up the living room mess and puts the tree back up. It doesn't sparkle anymore. I finally go back to my room, crawl into bed, and pull my blankets around my shaking body. I hear my father open the garage door and drag the recycling can to the curb. It's no longer thundering outside but the rain is pounding harder, trying to break down the walls of my room. I close my eyes and think of the first snow. How pretty and white it was. How the sunlight reflected off it and made the glass doll glisten. But when I finally fall asleep, the white is covered with black slush and red streaks.

———————

My alarm doesn't go off the next morning, and it's ten o'clock by the time I wake up. I put on a gray sweatshirt and black leggings and head to the kitchen, thinking of the secretary's smirk as she informs me I'll have to serve yet another detention.

"Hey, honey," says my dad. He's sitting on the couch watching CNN on low, but turns off the television when he sees me. "Put on your slippers before you come in here. Some glass broke, and I don't know if I got it all."

I follow the scents of vomit and cleaning product into the living room, stopping to inspect the tree and the damaged ornaments—animals and people missing arms or legs or half their bodies.

"They fell last night," my dad says, watching for my reaction.

"I saw."

He looks relieved. Now he won't have to lie.

"I'm sorry you had to see that," he says. "I'm sorry for everything."

If I speak I'll cry again, and it seems like that's all I've been doing lately.

"I can't live like this anymore," he says. "And neither can you. She's just not getting better on her own." His voice is soft and his hands are resting on his lap. I wonder if he spent all night thinking, formulating a plan, rehearsing what to say to me.

I sit next to him, and he pulls me to him and kisses me on the forehead.

"I called school and told them that we have some family things going on and you'll be out today and next week."

I stare at him, open-mouthed. I can't believe he told someone outside our family anything.

"They're gathering work for you and we can pick it up later today," he continues.

I still don't understand what's happening. Will I be staying home and caring for my mother? "Why won't I be in school?"

He takes a deep breath and gets up from the couch. I hear glass crunch under his feet as he moves to the tree. He faces it silently, looking at the ornaments and gently fingering the pine needles. He walks back to the couch and sits beside me again.

"You and I are going to move out, Alyssa. I've been looking at the paper all morning and found a few furnished apartments in town we can stay in until we find something better. I talked to your mother about other options, but she doesn't want to go to rehab."

My head is spinning and I feel my breath catch in my throat. I try yoga breathing, but it doesn't work and I gasp. My dad hugs me and rubs my back.

"It will be okay, Alyssa. It will. I promise." He repeats this over and over until my breathing returns to normal. *You'll be okay even if she's not.*

I'm suddenly very tired again, and he carries me to my bedroom and lays me on the bed, placing a quilt around me. He sits beside me and strokes my hair, and I fall back asleep. When I open my eyes he's still there, stroking my hair.

THIRTY-NINE

The Caller ID flashes my old house's phone number, and I have to sit on my hands to stop myself from lunging for the phone. The truth is that if my father wasn't here, I would have already been cradling the phone to my ear, trying to feel my mother through the lines that separate us.

The phone rings again and again, stopping when the machine comes on. My father looks up from the Sunday paper and we both hold our breaths, waiting for the message, but this time there is only a click. Dad lets out air, and in that release I hear relief, like silence from my mother is a good sign, like this unanswered phone call is what will finally lead her to sobriety. But I think the opposite is true.

We've been in this new apartment—which is one hundred times better than our rodent-infested first place in Brooklyn, and twenty times worse than our house where my mother now lives alone—for two weeks now, and my mother has yet to get better. I stare at the phone, willing it to ring again. This time, I'll sprint past my father and grab the receiver. My father must sense this, because he moves closer to the phone.

"You talking to her will not make things better," he says, not looking up from the World News section. He wants to give me the illusion that he's calm about all this, just catching up on current events. If he looked at me, his eyes would show worry, exhaustion, and defeat, and he's trying very hard to be the strong, protective father he hasn't been until now.

"I know, I know. *The only one who can help the alcoholic is herself.*" I mimic the Al-Anon speech we recite at every meeting. This life we're living is the world I once wanted—conversation during dinner alongside the news, Al-Anon meetings twice a week, a hotbed of support. The only difference between it and the fantasy life I'd created in my head is that my mother isn't part of it.

"That's right. And until she helps herself, we can't be in her life." He looks up from the paper and I see his misty eyes. "I miss her too, Alyssa."

I could say that we should move back, that this would give her the incentive to go to AA again, but I know from the secret conversations I've had with her—the ones where I promise I'll move back if she'll only stop drinking—that that's not how it would work. She's never sober when she calls, never agrees to my conditions, says I don't understand, that I'm purposely trying to hurt her. It is then that I tell her I love her and hang up before she can say, "If you really loved me, you would be here with me." Sometimes I wait to hear the words, tears running down my cheeks, just to see if I can handle them, just to see how strong I am.

I walk home from school thinking about the ways I test myself, thinking about what Keith said—how I'm not my mother, how I can control only myself—and thinking about that time on the porch swing when she called me her best supporter. In the distance, I see a blue Honda and I hold my breath, not daring to hope. Then it pulls up beside me, and I feel that my mother and I are connected after all, that she must have read my thoughts, that Keith is wrong.

It's not like the last time she picked me up from school, that day when we went to the mall. She looks sober, but she's in a pink velour jogging outfit, her smile too wide, too plastic, dark circles under her eyes that even concealer doesn't completely hide. I tell myself this is all because it's been hard on her without us—hard to sleep, hard to do the sobriety thing alone.

"Ride?" she asks, cocking her head to one side. This gesture somehow makes her smile seem more real.

"Why not?" I get into the car.

This time the music doesn't blast, and the wind doesn't blow our hair. I don't recognize the songs, but they sound slow and sad, and by the time I've put my seat belt on, my mother has turned off the radio. The silence is sad too.

She turns up the heat, but I'm warm enough in my hat, scarf, and gloves. I look at her as we drive; I want to read her while her eyes are focused on the road and she doesn't have the chance to transform her face into a new

296

mask. Her face looks thinner, as do her arms, and the big dirty jacket she's wearing makes her look fragile and lost. I search her face, but then we stop at a light and whatever thoughts she had in her head are gone, replaced by the plastic smile from earlier.

"So how have you been, *kookalka*?" Her eyes take me in.

"Fine, busy."

"Setting up your new room?" Each of these words is clipped, like she snapped them in two.

"I…" I'm not sure what the rest of the sentence will be.

She holds up her hand. "No, don't answer that. That was unfair of me. I'm sorry." She puts her hand on my head, but the gesture seems forced, like she's following some script she wrote for herself. "I know things must be very hard for you right now."

The light changes to green and she removes her hand from my hair and puts it back on the steering wheel. She says nothing more, but eases the car onto the highway and heads in the direction of the mall.

————

It's cold outside and already getting dark. This doesn't stop the pre-holiday crowds. Mom parks in an outside space, not seeing the slush by my door, and I soak my sneakers and socks getting out of the car.

"Crap," I mumble. My mother looks at me and her face falls.

"I'm sorry," she says.

Again, I feel like things are not going according to her plan, like she wants to recreate our last trip here. My toes are freezing, but I'm the one who feels bad.

"I'm not that wet. Don't worry about it."

She gives me a watery smile as we head inside.

The mall speakers are set to a loop of Christmas music, and there's a decorated tree and workers dressed as Santa and Mrs. Claus by the carousel. Mom's eyes linger on the tree, and she reaches over and lightly touches a glass angel ornament. Beside us, two middle school girls from Lana's street giggle as they wait in line to sit on Santa's lap and tell him what they want. They shove each other, daring one another to go first, their BFF necklaces dangling outside their sweaters. I pull my mother to the pretzel stand for free samples.

Today's distributor is the same angry girl from October, only now her outfit is spiced up with red and green striped stockings and a red apron. She hands everyone their pretzels without saying a word or looking up, and I can almost see a puddle of embarrassment at her feet.

"She must need this job badly," I say, smiling at my mother, prodding her to come up with a reason why Bitchy Girl works here as opposed to a store like Hot Topic or something.

My mother nods and walks over to the benches by the carousel. She sits down and follows the merry-go-round with her eyes, a smile on her lips.

"Who are you looking at?" I ask, sitting beside her. "Those teenage boys? I bet this is part of some fraternity pledging ritual."

"Yeah, maybe." She's distracted, and I wonder why we bothered coming here.

I give the game one more try. "What about punk chick?"

My mother looks at a girl dressed in purple and black. Her hair is spiked and spray-painted purple, and she has five piercings in each ear and one in her nose. She's sitting alone in a carriage on the carousel, waiting. And just as the ride is about to start, an older woman sits beside her. They both laugh and the ride begins.

"It's her mother," says Mom. "And this is their thing, this carousel. None of the girl's friends know she does this, and when they come over, the mom knows never to mention it. And they bond, even with all that."

I just nod. I have nothing to add, nothing that can take the sadness out of my mom's voice. I think of my dream about the carousel made out of alcohol bottles and squeeze Mom's hand. I don't want our lives to spin, spin, spin, leaving my mother alone to finish the ride.

We watch the carousel in silence for a few minutes, and my mother is careful to keep her face expressionless. I think back to a time when I knew my mother's thoughts just by the kind of smile she wore that day—before all of us learned to hide our eyes and true feelings, before we became strangers.

None of this feels right anymore. "I have homework to do," I say. "We should go."

She looks at the mother and daughter one last time and we head to the exit. We find our car quickly, and my mother pulls it around so I won't have to step in the slush to get inside. Then she puts the car in park, in the middle of the lot.

I envision a line of cars waiting for her to go, honking away, but when I look behind us, I see that she's not holding anybody up. She drums her fingers on the steering wheel and plays with the volume dial on the radio even though it's off. And in these few seconds I see the mask on her face fall away a bit. Only it's been too long, and I no longer recognize the look on her face.

"I'm trying, Alyssa," she finally says. "I really am."

"I know." But I don't know what "trying" means. Does it mean succeeding, or just trying and failing?

"It's just…" She pauses and takes a deep breath. "It's just not easy on my own."

I know she means without my father and me, but there's only one way my father would let us come home. "You mean you're not going to AA or looking into rehab?"

She sighs impatiently. "AA hasn't helped before and rehab is for people with real problems. I just need support." Something rolls out from under the driver's seat and she kicks at it. When she sees my eyes following the movement, she acts like she's stretching her legs.

But Old Alyssa sees the mini vodka bottles the same time I do, and she opens her eyes wide. She's too angry to speak, too mad at herself for almost believing again.

"I guess you're going to say those were always there?" I ask.

"What's the point?" my mother says, as if to herself. "Why really try when there is no one to try for?"

She wants me to say I'll talk to my father, that I'll lie as I've done before, that she'll get better once we come home, but I've played by those rules for too long. I'm stronger than that now.

"How about trying for yourself? Why don't you start there?" I ask.

"I won't ask again, *solnushka*. I promise." She turns to me, her plastic smile in place like she hasn't heard what I said. Soon this mask will fall away and another face will take its place—the face with the angry eyes. Old Alyssa turns away. She will not be there for that face.

"I'm sorry. No."

She hears me this time, and her fingers clench the steering wheel. Someone pulls up behind us and my mother puts the car in drive. Once we're on the highway I open the window, letting in all the noise and cold, willing them to enter her thoughts and wake her up. Instead, she passes my new apartment and keeps on driving.

"Stop—you just missed my street," I say, but she keeps driving until we pull into the driveway of our house.

"Why should I make an extra effort for *you*?" she says, tossing her cell phone at me. "Call someone to come get you, and give your father my best." The false smile is gone and the way she looks at me screams *traitor*. Without another word, she gets out of the car. Goes up the stone steps she once teetered on while I tried to get her inside, past the bushes where she vomited while leaning on me for support, into the house we once shared. She never looks back.

Old Alyssa turns away and taps her foot. Now that she's finally broken through my skin, she's done waiting, done trying. I pick up one of the little vodka bottles, take a sip, and swish the vodka inside my mouth, feeling the burn before swallowing. Because I can. I put the bottle back under the seat.

I pick up the cell and think of calling Keith. Then I change my mind. I'll tell him about everything tomorrow. Today, it's just me.

Just us, I think, as Old Alyssa stretches out her hand. I take it. We get out of the car, and we run. Through the wind whipping our faces, the numbness creeping into our toes, the darkness heavy and sparkling. We don't look back.

Acknowledgments

There are so many people to thank for the publication of this book—and for keeping me sane throughout the whole process (from conception of idea to final product).

Huge thanks goes to my current agent, Jennifer Laughran, who shared my vision for *Inconvenient*, for finding a publisher who felt the same way, and for always being supportive, responsive to my many questions, and for calming me down when my brain goes into overtime.

To my editor, Brian Farrey, for loving Alyssa, Keith, and the rest of the *Inconvenient* gang and having the faith to make their story become a real novel, not just pages on my computer. And for saying I'm a good writer and calling a passage "brilliant." A girl never tires of hearing that. To my first agent, Michelle Andelman, for believing in me and my book, bringing me into the ABLA circle, and giving fantastic revision advice that helped make *Inconvenient* the novel it is today. And to the whole Flux team— from Adrienne Zimiga, for creating a cover that went way beyond anything I ever envisioned, to my publicist and publicity manager, Courtney Colton and Steven M. Pomije, for sharing their great ideas and answering all my questions, and to my production editor, Sandy Sullivan, for finally helping me fix the exasperating timeline.

To Kristen Kemp, someone I consider a friend and mentor. Taking her novel-writing class was how *Inconvenient* came to be. Back then, it had a different name and a fugly story; she helped me see what the heart of it really was and told me, "You can do much better than this." There would be no *Inconvenient* without that class and Kristen's advice.

To all my readers—my sister Diana Finkel, who always found time to read this book in its various stages, who'd call me with new quotes and ideas for the characters, and who didn't give me too hard a time about Alyssa not having a sister. Love you! To Vinessa Anthony, who probably knows this novel and its characters as well as I do and who never tired of reading draft after draft after draft and giving revision ideas that were always spot-on. You're just awesome on every single level. Leos rule! To the Bokat Group, whose meetings pushed me to finish the first draft. To the Tenners, for helping me see I'm not the only neurotic one, and especially to Shaun Hutchinson, for the many many talks, emails, creativity, and fabulous support. A truly heartfelt *You rock!* to you.

To my grandparents—even though you are no longer with me, I felt your support the whole time I was writing this. Grandpa, you and me are the writers! To my parents, for bringing me to this country where anything is possible and never letting me forget that I have the opportunity to achieve all my dreams. And to my amazing husband, Stu. You didn't bat an eye (well, maybe you blinked a little) when I told you I wanted to leave teaching to see if I could make a go of this writing thing. You allowed me to take my time to make this dream a reality, and continue to support me in this writing journey. I love you.

Resources

It's important for teens with a loved one who is an alcoholic (be it parent, friend, etc.) to know they are not alone. Below is a list of resources I found helpful while writing this book.

1. *Al-Anon/Alateen:* This organization offers help to friends and families of problem drinkers. Alateen focuses on the teens affected by alcoholics.
   http://www.al-anon.alateen.org

2. *Miracles in Progress Family Teens Support Group:* This is an online group (message boards, chat rooms, online meetings) for teens affected by a family member's substance abuse.
   http://www.12stepforums.net/teens.html

3. *JACS (Jewish Alcoholics, Chemically Dependent Persons, and Significant Others):* This organization has a Teen Network that helps Jewish teens who are affected by a loved one's drug or alcohol abuse, or who wish to be educated about substance abuse in the Jewish community.
   http://www.jacsweb.org/teens

About the Author

Margie Gelbwasser was born in Minsk, Belarus. She emigrated to Brooklyn, New York, in 1979 and then moved to suburban New Jersey (to a town very much like Alyssa's Glenfair) in 1984. She is a freelance writer who has written for *Self*, *Ladies' Home Journal*, *Girls' Life*, and *New Jersey Monthly*. Her essays on growing up Russian and Jewish have appeared in *SMITH* magazine, *Lilith* magazine, and the anthology *Waking Up American: Coming of Age Biculturally*. *Inconvenient* is her debut novel. Visit her online at www.margiewrites.com.